How many lives has Scuffo?

I0546182

As the opening lines say, "becoming a cat was a surprise to the Reverend Harold Scuffington." From the moment we meet Harold, we see the immense complications to a man's life that becoming a cat can bring… especially if it is a cat like Scuffo… If he isn't under a bed, he is in it and what he sees, hears and experiences will change Harold's life forever!

Mac Black has returned to writing for adults with this fantastical and imaginative story of a Vicar, a cat and the consequences of rhubarb tarts…

Also by
Mac Black

For Young (and old) Adults

Please… Call me Derek
Derek's in Trouble
Derek's Revenge
Derek's Good Relations
Derek Takes Action

**For Younger Readers
(Illustrated)**

Sweaty and Pals
Sweaty and Pals, Again
Sweaty and Pals Smile

The Tale Of Maximillian The Mouse

All Rights Reserved

A CIP Catalogue record of this book is available from the British Library
ISBN 978-1-912777-22-8
FIRST EDITION

Also published as an e-book by U P Publications
ISBN 978-1-912777-23-5

4 7 9 0 1 6 8 5 2 3

Published in Great Britain, 2019, by
U P Publications, St George's House, George Street, Huntingdon,
Cambridgeshire, PE29 3GH. UK

www.macblack.info
www.uppbooks.com

How many lives has Scuffo?

mac black

ЧP

2019

1 AN ANNUAL EVENT

To say the least, becoming a cat was a surprise to the Reverend Harold Scuffington.

He was enjoying the vicarage Christmas get-together, an annual affair he'd first organised five years ago when he arrived in Woldenham, and which would have been an enormous disappointment to the local residents had it not been held. There he'd been, so happy, the life and soul of the party ...and then he wasn't!

It had been going so well too...

Woldenham is a large village and, as had become the custom, almost every resident contributed in some manner to the big day. Having been marked by a red circle on all the calendars in the village, the gathering in the Church Hall could not possibly be missed, and, of course, preparations began long before the defined date. Yes, Saturday, 20th December 1958, was to be a very special day.

Everyone would be in attendance – except old Mister Thomson, who was down with a severe dose of 'the runs'. The fact that old Missus Thomson, a village stalwart, was one of those who had baked, and cooked, much of the food that now sat on the table in readiness to be consumed by the hungry horde, had earlier caused a little panicky doubt in the Reverend Harold's head. *That woman, Missus Thomson. She'd been caring all week for her husband – the stricken person! What if she turned out to be a carrier...? What if her food...? Goodness! That could lead to the whole village going down with 'the runs'*

He dismissed the thought. *Anyway, if it did happen, it would make the day even more memorable!* He grinned smugly at his own naughtiness.

"Vicar! Have you organised a 'surprise' again?" shouted Monica Winter. She was at the top of a long folding ladder, attaching decorations to the hall beams, something he could never do as he had no head for heights. "Are you going to tell us what it will be, this year?"

The Vicar was looking smugly at young Freddy Fulton, standing on the floor and doing a grand job of holding the tall, rickety ladder steady – someone had to. *I really must talk seriously to the committee,* the Vicar thought to himself – *that ladder is dangerous and should be replaced, but they'll be reluctant to use funds for that.*

"Oh, I couldn't tell you that, Monica. It wouldn't be a surprise!" He was relieved for the young lad that this year Monica was wearing trousers. Last year he'd had to hold the ladder himself – and look the other way...

The Reverend Harold Scuffington took personal

responsibility for each year's 'surprise'. He hoped the magician that he'd booked, at the last minute, would be better than last year's female singer. Admittedly, she'd been at a disadvantage, having to sing accompanied by the out-of-tune piano played by Elsa Middleton. Elsa, having had to borrow her sister's specs to sight-read the singer's music, hadn't helped, and that drop of alcohol, '...to steady my nerves,' might also have contributed.

This year's star, a magician, had promised to do something rather spectacular. When the man said it, Harold had smiled and thought, doubtingly, 'I'll believe that when I see it...' The magician had also stated that he would be bringing his own taped music. The Reverend Harold's comment to that was, "Very wise..."

There was eager anticipation from all those assisting in the hall, and particular curiosity about today's special attraction because, at the far end of the church hall was the little stage. There, the curtains were closed and the whole area marked 'Out of bounds'. That space had become a closely guarded secret because on the previous evening, 'Marvello the Magnificent' had been to prepare his illusions. No-one was allowed to peep! Although access to the hall had been arranged between the Vicar and the Magician, the Vicar knew no more than anyone else. Although tempted, he'd been good and hadn't peeped, but he was more curious than anybody. *What had the magician been up to?*

"The food looks delicious!" the Reverend called to the

team of women who were loading the goodies onto the table at the other end of the hall. They were all doing a sterling job, but an involuntary *"Oh!"* came from him as Missus Thomson passed ...the farting noises and the smell. He hoped sincerely that ignoring the danger signs, and letting her be involved, would not come back to haunt him.

He so wanted this day to go really well. It might encourage some of the villagers to remember that the church was open on Sundays, and maybe even to appear and fill the pews. Now that would be an achievement!

"Careful with that light!" he called out to Monica, as she caused the dangling lamp to swing. There was a crackling, and a spark came from the wire near the ceiling. "Oh dear! We don't want any accidents!" he shouted to her.

Monica was lovely. *Maybe one day I'll tell her how much I like her*, he told himself. Yes... that had been a secret thought for a long time.

He stopped and stood there, in a daydream, gazing up at her. Deep down he wanted something exciting to happen, a calamity, though certainly not for her to be hurt. Just something that would permit him to show her what he really thought. As he stood, he imagined the ladder toppling, in slow motion, and him striding manfully towards the falling figure, in slow motion too, then catching her safely and securely in his arms. *She'd be so grateful. "You are my hero," she would say, and then, "Please whisk me away from here so that we can make mad passionate love," and he would, immediately...*

"That's all the chairs we have, Vicar!" shouted Tommy. "Will I get the benches in as usual?" Sweat poured down the face of Tommy Sinclair. No-one was sure what age he really was, but he'd been 'getting on a bit' five years ago when Harold had arrived as a young vicar in the village. There was no stopping Tommy. A willing helper right from the very beginning, and today he'd moved all the chairs on his own.

"Yes, but get some help with them, Tommy. Or you'll not be fit for the party."

Tommy was the local joiner. Everyone knew him. He'd been an inhabitant of Woldenham all his life, as had his father, and his grandfather. They'd been joiners too. Everyone believed the story that Tommy had never travelled farther than Codgestone – ever, even though Codgestone was barely three miles away. The reason, rumour had it, was that he was scared another joiner could sneak in, while he was away, and steal his business. "He's in with the woodwork, but that's better than woodworm!" was the local saying. Yes, Tommy was definitely the village's joiner!

The party would be getting under way very soon. The first arrivals were starting to file through the door. As the host, the Reverend Harold Scuffington went over to welcome them and all was going very well until, at the side of the hall, Archie Mitchell plugged in the little portable electric oven – and the fuses blew!

"Bloody hell!" came from Archie. "Every bloody year it does this! You'll have to get this bloody-well fixed, Vicar, or we'll all bloody-well go up in smoke!"

"Archie, will you curse and swear a little quieter, please..." was the hissed request as the Vicar rushed over, but he was talking to Archie's back. Archie was already on the move. He knew where the fuse box was and would fix it quickly. He was an expert at the repair – he'd had plenty practice.

And in they had come. Harold noticed that the same faces appeared first, every year. Almost as if they would miss out on something if they came later, but it was also because they were able to choose where to sit, thus avoiding the annoyance of having to be beside someone they disliked. Probably a good thing the Vicar had decided, after the embarrassment of the fight that threatened on that first year. As long as the Russell and MacGregor families were kept apart it could promise to be a peaceful, happily noisy, time.

The afternoon's activities had followed what was now a recognised pattern. The Reverend's welcoming speech opened the ceremony, full of jokes that usually had everyone giggling away merrily. He'd heard from the local teacher that these lily-white, but funny, tales became somewhat cruder when, in later weeks, they were retold in the Primary School playground.

In the stack of joke books, he'd acquired over time, he'd taken the trouble to mark carefully those he'd used in previous years. No repetition! He always added some local colour to them, names and places, and he'd built a reputation of being an excellent raconteur. If only he could have used some of the good ones in his sermons it might have meant a bigger congregation. He'd even considered finding out more about the juicier versions, and using these to pull in the crowds on Sundays – but decided that there could be a negative reaction from head office...

A little Christmas play came next in the programme, written and introduced by him and performed by reluctant members of the School Primary classes. Though Monica spent a lot of time coaching and encouraging the youngsters, when performed, it looked as if there had been no rehearsal whatsoever. It usually turned out to be amusing, but more from what went wrong, than right.

Children's party games followed. Strict control of these was required to avoid absolute chaos and that was where Monica did a good job. Her secret was that every child became a winner and left the floor with a little prize.

Food came next. It was every man, woman, and child, for themselves at that. There was never supposed to be any strong drink taken at the party, and there was always a plentiful supply of non-alcoholic fruit juices available, but the Reverend knew well that certain gentlemen couldn't enjoy themselves without having a drop of the stronger stuff. That was a problem at the first gathering. Fortunately, heated arguments, which could have become serious, had been avoided in following years, at least until now. Alcohol was still consumed – he'd accepted that, but a word by him to the wives had ensured that husbands took turns nipping outside, to have a swig of whatever was available. It wasn't a total ban, but they must not set a bad example for the youngsters. That was the rule. That also applied to the sneaky smoking that occurred outside the back of the hall.

After food, it was always Billy Mathieson. His accordion was a favourite. He knew what the crowd liked. Current popular songs had the younger ones singing along, and then some traditional tunes encouraged many of the older folk to do their bit and get up and dance. Billy had been well behaved in previous years, but it was known that he liked strong drink as much as the other males, so, the Vicar made him promise that he would remain teetotal until after he'd performed. Each year he'd managed to restrain himself and be good until after he'd done his bit – for which the Vicar was eternally grateful. However, he eventually had to be assisted home and helped to bed, because although a late starter, he made sure he caught up with the others, and kept going!

Then there was the opportunity for more food – or sneaky drinks and smokes, as the chairs were rearranged to form rows in front of the stage. Assistance was always in abundance at that juncture, and that's what helped prevent Tommy Sinclair's anticipated heart attack.

"So, if you would now like to stop eating..." shouted the Reverend, "...and take a seat," and as everyone knew the routine, the scramble then took place to get choice positions. A clap of his hands quietened them down and drew the required attention. This was the big one!

"Ladies and Gentlemen. The moment we have all been waiting for. It's time for this year's surprise item!" The Reverend Harold Scuffington was now in firm control, looking down on the audience from a position of authority at the front of the stage. The curtains were still closed.

"Hope it's better than last year," someone shouted from the floor. Everyone laughed, and the Reverend, crossing his fingers, hoped so too!

"Are you ready at the back?" His whispered question, through the curtain, was answered rapidly as a drum roll sounded.

"I'm starting the tape..."

That's promising, thought the Reverend, and raised his voice, "Ladies and Gentlemen, a warm round of applause for... Marvello the Magnificent!"

The curtains opened, and, as everyone clapped

enthusiastically, striding forward, wearing a top hat and a crimson-lined cape over his shoulders, was Marvello.

The magician's various glittery props were spread about the stage. He must have worked really hard last night, thought the Vicar. As well as preparing his props for the act, he'd fitted overhead lights of his own. It made the stage much brighter than the Reverend could ever remember – but also made him wonder why the fuse box hadn't reacted! *Hope he doesn't want extra money for that lighting...* mused the Vicar, *because – tough, there isn't any!*

He sat back and tried to relax, but it wasn't easy, while feeling so many in the hall were ready to criticise his choice – but Marvello was good! The Reverend Harold Scuffington could smile. This year was going to be so much better.

In no time at all, Marvello had his audience eating out of his hands, or at least being amazed at what he could do with them. A few card tricks brought applause, then "Ooooh...", as a rabbit was pulled from the hat and made to vanish in a cloud of silvery dust. Then coin after coin was removed from young Samuel Grey's ear. That brought cheers and laughter from his pals. However, things began to go a little bit astray for the magician when Samuel, trying to show off, claimed that these coins were his because they came from his ears. He even started arguing with the magician. Marvello quietened him though, when he produced an uncooked, link sausage from the other ear, and handed him that!

The headmaster of the village school always looked smart. He was the next victim. Each day, he showed, in his jacket pocket, a coloured handkerchief to match his tie, and this afternoon he was dressed smartly, as usual, sitting in the front row. His embarrassment was there for all to witness when Marvello, apparently, whisked out that hankie – and displayed it to be a pair of ladies' silk panties!

He might struggle to live that down, smiled the Reverend and shrank down in his seat, hoping the magician would avoid humiliating him. The act continued, light-hearted, funny and successful for the magician, and the vicar was pleased he'd been ignored, until it came to the grand finale...

"I will need someone to help me with my final illusion," announced Marvello, "and I think it should be the gentleman who has made this day such a success for you all. Do you agree?"

The loud cheer was followed by a chant begun by Monica Winter...

"Scuff-o! ...Scuff-o! ...SCUFF-O! ...SCUFF-O!"

The Reverend Harold Scuffington stood reluctantly, to a cheer. This was the first time that he'd heard his nickname being used deliberately for him to hear.

"Scuffo... indeed!" he said as he stood, and that got a giggle from Monica. "I didn't know that's what you called me... Right. What do I do?"

"Step this way." Marvello led him onto the stage, towards the curtained cabinet standing in the middle.

"Oh-oh! What's going to happen?" the Reverend asked, with trepidation in his voice. This hadn't been discussed beforehand...

"You will soon find out," said Marvello, opening the cabinet curtain. "Step inside, dear sir."

The Reverend Harold Scuffington entered and the curtain was closed.

"Will you help me," said Marvello to the audience.

"YESSSSSSS!" came back loud and clear, and feet began stamping in support.

"We, together, are going to make the Reverend Harold Scuffington vanish!"

"Oh!" said the Vicar inside the cabinet.

"You can help me do the count, and when I say the magic word, he will be gone – in a flash! Are you ready? One..."

And everyone joined him, "TWO... THREE..."

Standing behind the little curtain, feeling claustrophobic in the little box, The Reverend Harold Scuffington nervously wondered how he would 'vanish?'

"Caramba!" Marvello stepped on a switch to trigger a blinding flash.

WHOOOOSH!

The fuse box gave up the ghost, and the hall became pitch black... The audience didn't take long to become restive! Stamping of feet and booing had already begun.

2 SCUFFO's FIRST LIFE

Oh, no! thought the Reverend Harold. *Not the fuse box again. What's happening out there?*

What could he do? Leaving this magic cabinet to help would surely spoil Marvello's performance, but how quickly could Archie Mitchell do the repair. Was the magician's act already ruined? What a way to end the day, and it had been shaping up to be a remarkable success too, and what if the electrics can't be fixed?

Money should have been spent long ago, of that Harold was certain. The next committee meeting would require him presenting some hard facts. *It couldn't go on like this – everything hanging on a thread!* And how long should he remain standing like an idiot in a little cubicle in the dark? It was pitch black.

I should be out there, organising things, he told himself.

The sudden brightness nearly blinded him, so he kept his eyes closed for a few moments. That always worked. *Hooray, it's fixed*, he thought, and breathed a sigh of relief.

Thankfully, he'd be out of the confounded box in a moment or two.

"Ricky!" a female voice called out. "Come here quickly!"

Harold opened his eyes slowly – to see an almost-naked female standing with her hand at the light switch, in what was obviously a bedroom.

"Oh dear," he tried to say, but nothing came out. She was staring straight at him, totally unabashed, as if she regularly stood in front of a minister of the church wearing only skimpy underwear.

"How did you get in?" she asked, starting to come over. "Ricky! Would you get through here right away, please?"

Oh-oh! This could be awkward, me being found here by her partner. Me, with a semi-naked female – and I'm in her bedroom! I hope they realise that it's all part of the act!

"Ricky!"

Oh, dear... Is Ricky her husband? Is he a big fellow? I've never liked fisticuffs...

She had started to move towards him, cautiously.

Harold wriggled uncomfortably. Trying to speak to apologise wasn't working – he was unable to say anything, and how could he possibly explain if he couldn't speak? It happened regularly when he was young. Couldn't get words out. "Nerves," his mother used to say. "Don't worry... You'll grow out of it," but he was nearing thirty. *Why was it happening again?*

...And how the heck did I get here? Must have dropped from the cabinet through the floor.

He looked to the ceiling for the trapdoor.

There was nothing there, and why? Because the church hall didn't have any building underneath! So, where was he and how did he get here?

The female moved slowly closer, reaching out with her hands – but why was she aiming at his knees? And that's when he saw the reflection – of the back view of a surprisingly calm semi-clothed female, and of his position. Or rather, where he should have been – but wasn't!

There was a ginger cat with its tail waving slowly – and it was where he was standing!

As he looked, suddenly he realised, his view was different. The world was on a different level. He was seeing everything through the eyes of the cat! He tried again to speak. *Miaow...* Then realised he was trembling. *He was the cat!*

"Oh, you poor little darling," she said. "You don't have to be frightened of me."

She bent down, carefully picked him up, and held him close. As the warmth of her body permeated the fur, Harold found himself relaxing. She was a lovely girl and this was very comforting... Having his head in this position hadn't happened since that little incident with Monica – he remembered it well, because it wasn't something that he'd had the chance to do often...

Purrrr... Purrrr...

"What a lovely collar you are wearing. Did you get lost?" Her fingers played around with his ears. *Purrrr...*

"You like that, don't you..."

Purrrr... Purrrr... Oh, yes, that's nice, thought Harold. Don't stop.

"Someone must be missing you, my little pet. What does your collar say? Oh, can't read it. Need my specs, I'm afraid."

She swung about and moved quickly but being whisked around the room by this scantily clad young lady as she searched for her glasses made Harold feel quite dizzy. He hoped he wouldn't be sick. It would be a shame to be moved from this comfortable position.

"Ah... Here they are." She knelt, and placed Harold on the bed, put her glasses on and reached for his collar. "Scuffo! That's an unusual name," she said.

As she bent over him, Harold looked up at the delightful view. That's when a bulky male appeared at the bedroom door. Feeling guilty at being caught ogling, Harold leapt off the bed and shot to the corner of the room, to hide at the side of a bedroom cabinet – the natural reaction of one who'd been 'caught at it!' Anyway, this bloke looked threatening – obviously into body-building!

Then Harold remembered he was not his usual self. He was a cat – called Scuffo!

He peeped out.

"Look, Ricky. Isn't he lovely," she cooed.

"Lovely, my arse. Smelly, messy, flea-ridden nuisances. How the hell did it get in here?" Harold could sense that Ricky was not a lover of felines. "Get rid of it!"

"I wonder whose it is. It doesn't say on the collar. Just a name. Scuffo."

"Sounds like it belongs to a right weirdo, I'd say, and there are plenty to fit the bill in this block."

Harold was taking a real dislike to this guy. If he could have spoken, he would have told him off about his language, especially in front of a lady – especially when she was only partly-dressed. *Anyway, what wrong with the name, Scuffo?*

"Come here my little darling. Oh, look Ricky, you have frightened him. I'm sure he understands every word you've said."

"He's a ruddy cat, so stop being so stupid! And don't lift it. You'll catch something."

This guy might be considerably bigger than me, thought Harold, *but I'd punch his ruddy nose if I had the chance.* He felt really protective of this female and he didn't even know her name. *How could she team up with an oaf like this?*

"Come to Mummy," she said with feeling. She obviously liked Scuffo, and he wouldn't mind another cuddle, so Harold decided to be brave, and came out from behind the cabinet, leapt onto the bed again, and crawled cautiously over to her – with one eye on muscle-man.

"Its claws will mess up the downy," was Ricky's next grumble. "And you've just bought the bloody thing. You'll not be getting another new one if it does damage it, and if later I find a flea..."

The woman lifted Harold again. "Scuffo... Hmmm, yes, I like you," she whispered as she rubbed her cheek on the top of his head. "I'd love to keep you..."

When Harold had seen people being all soppy like this with an animal before, he'd always felt pity for them, mocking them – not openly, but in his head. However, experiencing it now from a cat's point of view – it was great!

Harold had to be careful with his aforementioned claws. He was no expert at behaving like a cat and it would have been so easy to accidentally draw blood with so much bare flesh exposed!

"Let's get you a spot of milk and some food. You look as if you have been starved."

I look starved? That was totally unnecessary, thought Harold, feeling a little hurt. *That's me she is talking about, and I looked pretty good from what I saw in the mirror,* he told himself. He also remembered her rear view. That was nicer... Anyway, being pampered by a partially-dressed – or was it undressed – female, as was now happening, felt alright, so he wasn't going to object.

Out of the bedroom and into the kitchen he was carried.

But there was something odd? Shouldn't it be late afternoon, and yet breakfast dishes were still lying on the table? Not exactly a competent housewife then, he guessed. Harold was surprised that, even though the window was wide open, it felt really warm in the room, and then he noticed that the heat was coming from outside, because there was bright sunshine. It was like summer. Strange... and the trees that he could see – they were all green and in full leaf! In mid-winter? When the Christmas party started, it had been bitterly cold outside – everyone who'd arrived had commented, that it was nice to be inside on a day like this. On top of that, it was dark outside even before Marvello began his act, but here, now, it's...? *What, in the name of goodness, is happening?* he thought...

How did he get here? The view from the open window was familiar, but the trees seemed larger than he'd expect them to be. *Yes, he was in Woldenham, but seeing it from a new perspective. This was a tall building, but there weren't any tall buildings in the village – and this flat was at least four floors up! To crown it – he was a cat!*

Harold was baffled. Was Marvello a real magician? Had he performed real magic? No, of course not, he told himself. *He was being silly, but more importantly, would Marvello be able to change him back? I was happy when I was just The Reverend Harold Scuffington...*

A scowling murderous-looking Ricky had appeared in the doorway!

...Marvello, please change me back, before this human mutt does me an injury...

"He's on the bloody table!" Ricky yelled. The partly-dressed lady had placed Harold there, and said she'd be back in a moment, so, it wasn't Scuffo's fault!

Harold opened his mouth to explain that simple fact to Ricky. *Miaaaoow...*

But Ricky wasn't interested. "Come here, you disgusting pest!" He lunged forward and made to grab him.

Harold took exception to that and leapt back out of reach, and claws appeared without him even thinking about it. Harold was now displaying a threatening look, he thought but, as he'd never done this before he had no way of knowing. *Hisssss...* His back arched. This was cat-fighting mode, and Harold realised he was into auto-pilot, because, he was Scuffo, staring ferociously at this hulk whose muscles were twitching and eyes were flickering, as a little human brain tried to decide the safest way to get this cat. Another grab!

But Harold was too quick!

No! Not Harold – it was Scuffo who reacted – Harold's reactions were always as slow as an old carthorse... Ricky's arm shot out – and found Scuffo's claws, and that drew blood. The muscle-man was now more determined to dispose of this uninvited creature. Suddenly another swing and he tried to sweep the cat off the table but, again, Scuffo was too quick, this time leaping in the air and grabbing the lampshade.

The large tear that appeared in the shade only enraged Ricky. He seized the empty cooking pot. He was not going to let a pesky cat make him feel a fool. He swiped at the cat hanging there, hit the shade and smashed the lamp!

Scuffo had seen that coming, and with excellent timing had avoided the blow, leaping over to the work surface near the window, but another swipe was on its way. A leap sideways avoided it. He was near the sink now, and he could see the start of another swing of the pot.

Scuffo's brain was the faster one and it was a quick decision. *Hide behind something!* The water taps at the window would give protection. He leapt onto the window sill! *That would stop this idiot swinging that cooking pot about!*

Hearing the noise, the party-clad lady rushed back into the kitchen, just in time to see Ricky, his blood boiling, give the metal cooking pot a ferocious swing that broke off the top of the cold-water tap. The sudden blast of water that caught Scuffo's chin, knocked him off balance and, with nothing to grab, suddenly he was falling – from the fourth floor... All Harold could do, as he dropped, was close his eyes!

3 NOW... WHERE WAS I?

It was the sudden beams of light appearing above his head, and the piercing yell of "Hallelujah!" that convinced the Reverend Harold Scuffington that he had safely reached Heaven – which was strange because, although a 'man of the cloth', he'd never previously bought into the 'Heaven or Hell' philosophy that he preached...

"So now, if I pull back the curtain..."

Good gracious! Harold recognised the voice immediately – and it wasn't God – it was Marvello! The magician's cabinet – it was still in middle of the stage, and he was still in it. Light was shining through the top edge of the box. He was alive, he couldn't have... *What was happening?*

Harold couldn't see out. "...And you will observe that our volunteer has vanished!"

The empty cabinet was exposed by Marvello with the flourish he always used at this point in his act, usually to a massive round of applause. This time, nothing. Not surprising, considering it had taken five minutes to repair the fuse. He closed the curtain again.

"Rubbish!" came from the audience. "You fused the ruddy lights deliberately. He walked off in the dark!" This comment just encouraged mutterings and grumbles from all around the hall.

It had to be admitted that on odd occasions, tricks had not turned out perfectly for Marvello the Magnificent, but a dicey fuse-box had never been the challenge before. Failing in the middle of the grand finale had been most unfortunate.

"Sir, maybe I should have put you in the cabinet instead," Marvello called out to the heckler, and at least got a small titter. "And anyway, there could be a bigger problem. Our volunteer, your dear Vicar, has been away for a lot longer than usual, so it might be difficult to bring him back again – or would you rather I didn't?" he asked teasingly.

"Who cares!" came back from the heckler, gaining a titter from his pals.

"I do!" It was Monica Winter. She stood up and faced the heckler. "He has to be Santa Claus at the Little Tot's Party on Tuesday – I've got no-one else..." Everyone laughed at that.

Of course, The Reverend Harold could hear all this. Getting support from Monica had been heartening – but it could have been for a better reason – surely!

"Ah, someone who cares, and that's given me an idea. Perhaps this lovely lady would be my glamourous assistant and help make the magic work." The magician had the audience's attention again. "I've always wanted a glamourous assistant." He went down into the audience, took her hand and brought her onto the stage, encouraging a round of applause.

Monica stood there, red-faced, a rather uncomfortable volunteer.

"Tell you what," said Marvello, "You could pull back the curtain..." and Monica stepped forward, "...but not until I say the magic word!" and Monica froze! Marvello's aside to the audience, "Wants to take over the act, she does..." got a laugh, and made Marvello happier to be back in control – but caused another flush of Monica's cheeks.

"Oh, you didn't tell me your name, young lady. I can't have a glamourous assistant, without a name, can I? To put on the posters!"

She wished she'd never opened her mouth, and anyway, if the Reverend Harold didn't come back, she could probably ask Tommy Sinclair. He was old enough to look like Santa and always badly needed a shave, and with a bit of red material...

She coughed, feeling uncomfortable being in the spotlight. "It's... Monica."

"What a lovely name. So, Marvello the Magnificent and... Monica will now show you what real magic looks like. When I say the word, Monica, you do the magic!"

She was tense.

"Caramba!"

Monica leapt forward like a trained dog, whipped back the curtain – but nothing again... The cabinet was bare. Going to have to be Old Tommy then, she thought sadly.

"Told you it could be difficult," Marvello said to the audience, and closed the curtain once more. "Monica, I think you and I should call upon the power of the audience. Will you help us please?"

He guessed he'd regained control because all the youngsters, and some of the adults, yelled back "YESSSSSS!"

"Here we go then. One..."

And they all joined in the count, "TWO... THREE... CARAMBA!"

Monica instinctively leapt forward again, whipped back the curtain and there, in glorious three-dimensional super-duper technicolour was her hero – The Reverend Harold! She'd done it. And she couldn't stop herself. Her arms reaching out and enfolding him, and, the big kiss being planted on his cheek, let the Reverend Harold Scuffington know that he was definitely in the land of the living.

"I have a Santa!" Monica cried out triumphantly.

He'd had high hopes... but, Sunday was disappointing.

The day of rest for everyone – except him, with only a meagre group of dedicated churchgoers appearing in the pews and spreading out in the usual way to make the numbers seem even fewer when viewed from the pulpit. So much for yesterday's event being an attraction for the Church Service – even after his little commercials on Saturday. Demoralising. Maybe next time...

It was now Monday. In retrospect, Saturday's annual get-together had been a success, but it had taken nearly twenty-four hours to become an acceptable fact in his head, and what about that crazy spell in the cabinet? *A cat, for goodness sake? All in my imagination, of course,* but at the time, to him, it felt so real...

This was more down to earth, as there he stood, talking to himself, in front of the full-length mirror, in the Santa Claus outfit.

Helping Monica Winter would be reality. Underneath he was wearing his stripy pyjamas – he'd get dressed and have breakfast in a moment, but a decision would have to be made.

"So, what do you think?" he asked the reflection, but no answer... It was times like these that made him wish he'd met someone suitable to live with. Having a second opinion would have helped.

Last year he almost melted away at the Little Tot's Party while wearing this outfit on top of his normal clothing. He remembered, with distaste, being seated in the tiny grotto that Archie Mitchell and young Freddie had knocked up, and the choking sensation of his dog-collar making him feel hot and sweaty, and then experiencing claustrophobia for the first time. Most uncomfortable! Then again, it could have been just something wrong with the heating controls in the hall.

Of course, his streaming cold being at its worst hadn't helped. His popularity dropped a notch the following week, when all the children who visited the grotto became infected.

This morning, standing admiring himself in the mirror, he felt healthy, but, who knows, this might be the year that they get their own back – he might catch something from them, and, with the electrics playing up again, it's anyone's guess what might happen.

"So, what should I do? Would Monica help me decide?" he asked the red shape in the glass. *"She was really pleased to see me in that cabinet, wasn't she? And the hug and the kiss – I enjoyed that, maybe more than she did though..."* He never could tell for certain with Monica.

Ring...

Someone at the door? This early?

Ring... Ring... Ring... Ring... Ring...

Pretty insistent! *Remain calm,* he told himself. *It will be someone with a problem, and they're coming to me for help.* Forgetting the fact that he was dressed in the Santa costume, he opened the door.

"Vicar – Vicar! Come quick! The hall's on fire!"

"What?!!!" and out he went, following them, running as fast as he could, bearing in mind that the elastic of his pyjama trousers was not as effective as it could be, passed the front of the church, to face smoke billowing from the little window of the kitchen.

"The fire brigade! Has someone...?" The approaching sound of the fire-engine bell answered that question, but he should have brought the key. He turned around and galloped back round the front of the church, into the house, went to grab the key from the hook in the hall – but it wasn't there!

Oh no! Where is it? I put it in my pocket as I left the place yesterday... My trousers!

Upstairs he ran, looked for them – remembered that for once, he'd been tidy and hung them up in the wardrobe – found them, removed the key, and rapidly retraced his steps – to find that the rear door had already been forced open by the firemen...

"You're a bit late, Santa," they chorused. "Been feeding the reindeer?"

"Why does life have to be so complicated, Monica?" Harold asked glumly.

She'd come back round with him, feeling almost as bad as he did. She'd planned the Little Tot's Party and, other than her panic on Saturday at maybe having lost her 'Santa', the arrangements had been going reasonably well – until now.

Her skill with children was appreciated by the Vicar, but making tea was also a skill that Monica was renowned for, certainly in the abode of the Reverend Harold Scuffington, so Monica was busy downstairs now – well acquainted with his kitchen.

He'd gone upstairs, to put on some normal clothing, and now the Santa outfit lay on his bed – being the least of his worries.

What a start to the day. He was feeling a little stressed. *Relax,* he told himself. *Think nice thoughts...*

He remembered liking Monica from the moment he met her. At the time, he'd hoped that she felt the same, but so far, the relationship had only been displayed as a sense of duty. That had been disappointing for him – for five years! Sadly, the bond was still very loose.

"Ready when you are!" she shouted from downstairs.

"Hmmm... Yes..." he mumbled to himself, wishing that the shout was telling him that it was for a different state of readiness. He put on his dog collar. *Behave yourself, Harold. Make do with a cup of her strong sweet tea. That's all that will be available.*

As for the present problem, what was to happen about the Little Tot's Party? Not surprisingly, it was the hall's dicey electrics that caused the fire, and though not a lot of physical damage had been done, the place was stinking of smoke, and the lighting was totally kaput. Definitely no chance for tomorrow.

"Monica, is there a Plan B?" asked Harold, as she poured out the tea.

"Well, Vicar... I thought about the school hall, but the older children are still studying. Or, we could deliver the presents by hand to all the children at home – no party games, but at least they would be getting their little presents."

He was listening, but thinking of something else. There was something he had to say...

"Monica... We've known each other for a long time. Isn't it about time that you stopped calling me Vicar, I have another name, you know."

There was a pregnant pause.

Has it been bad timing, he wondered, now wishing that he'd concentrated on the subject in hand?

"Well, to be honest..." Monica started to say, with a shy smile.

"It has been almost five years..." he added, and smiled at her. *Yes, it was the right moment...*

"I know," she said, "Five years and, ever since I learned it, I've wanted to call you it."

"Monica!" *This was it!* Both their smiles were now beaming. "Say it to me, dear Monica, please. Shout it out loud!"

"Oh yes! I will," she said with obviously great enjoyment. Then, at the top of her voice yelled, "SCUFFO!"

4 ON THE ROAD...

He was hanging on like grim death, convinced that this lorry was travelling well in excess of the speed limit, but it did feel quite exhilarating – the wind blowing fiercely through his hair – or rather, his fur!

It had happened again... The pitch-black darkness of a cardboard box that was being bounced around was where he'd found himself this time, and, he'd known right away that he had been reduced in size by the sense of it being a rather small box. Of course, another clue in the darkness was the fur, when he touched his face – with a paw! He'd made his way out of the box easily enough. Claws are great tools when used properly...

That's how he discovered that he was on the back of an empty open truck, travelling at a disturbing speed. The empty cardboard box had since gone, blown into the air and into the lorry's slipstream, dropping onto the road to be cautiously avoided by other traffic, initially, before being flattened by another heavy truck.

Thankfully, the feline transition wasn't as severe a shock this time, though it was still an extremely strange feeling. How he'd arrived on the back of a speeding lorry he'd no idea. Other than having had that little glass of the amber fluid before opening the newspaper to read in bed – on his own.

Arriving in the cardboard box had been about half an hour ago, as far as he could judge, but for Harold, the time of day was confusing. *Had the change occurred while he slept? This vehicle was racing along in broad daylight? Was this the following day? Had he slept soundly through the night?*

Another thing, all these cars?

He had thought himself knowledgeable about cars and would dearly loved to have been the owner of one, even an old banger, but being a humble minister, he couldn't possibly afford that, and anyway he couldn't drive. However, for years he'd taken an interest in all vehicles, and he'd thought he was up to date on the latest models, but today he was unable to recognise most of those being overtaken.

Where am I? Whoa! There's a clue! A signpost was glimpsed as they roared along. *Preston By-Pass? Oh! That's unfortunate, he thought. I live nowhere near Preston!* The lorry was going away from Woldenham, entirely the wrong direction for him. Maybe he should get off now – but, how could he?

No use asking the driver to stop, of course, him being in the cab. Even if Harold shouted very loudly from the back of the truck, there would be no chance of being heard. Anyway, it was extremely unlikely that the driver would understand what a cat was meowing about.

The lorry was travelling on a wide road with two lanes, and lots of other vehicles, all moving very quickly in the same direction – but not as quickly as the lorry! It was the same going the other way – on the other side of a continuous grass patch down the centre, more fast traffic on the two lanes.

The Preston Bye-pass? Wait a moment. Wasn't there something? Last night, while reading in bed... Yes, new roads for the future, it said. Money to be spent on a new Bye-Pass at Preston – but that was to be in four years' time? Maybe they've pulled it forward. No...! That's being silly. Am I in the future? Of course not! Now I am being really silly. This is a dream. Me? A cat – and in the future? No. Of course I'm not. I'll wake in a moment. Shouldn't have drunk whisky...

Whoops! He dug his claws into the wooden floor as the driver swerved to avoid something on the road. *If this is a dream it's a very realistic one!*

Dust swirling around the floor of the lorry was getting into his eyes. He raised his head back into the wind. That helped. This road looked different to any road he'd travelled on. He'd never been out of the Britain to see for himself, but it looked remarkably like the pictures in the Guardian, last night, of German autobahns, with their double lanes and wide central reservations.

Of course, it's a dream. Reading in bed... glass of whisky... This is what happens!

Wow! His paws lost contact as the lorry bounced over something that the driver had this time failed to avoid. Scuffo banged against the side. *Some dream!*

Wonder if the driver knows I am here... Maybe I'm being kidnapped? Harold had found that if he leaned out, he could look in the side rear-view mirrors, and see what was happening in the cab – but it was a death-defying position with the wind threatening to tear him loose. The driver was not alone. A mate sat beside him, just about to get his teeth into his very, inviting-looking sandwich. Harold felt as if he hadn't eaten for a fortnight and would have loved a share of that food.

Should I feel hungry in a dream?

The man had a newspaper on his knees and was unfolding it. The thought of anyone reading on a moving vehicle immediately made Harold queasy. He'd found out to his cost and had to get off a bus in the middle of nowhere, but not everyone suffered the problem it seemed, because the paper was opened. Harold tried to see the front page for the date, but that bloke didn't even glance at that. An inside page was where he was going.

Trying to see it, Harold felt his stomach react and looked away rapidly, but he did catch the title. Not one he recognised.

'The Sun'? The Guardian was usually Harold's choice, a newspaper that was a fairly serious read, so he almost lost his grip when he looked again. The mate was holding the paper to show the driver the inside page.

What! Harold blinked. *That lady! She's... displaying her assets! She's bare! No! She couldn't be! No, no. I must have been mistaken!* His queasiness had been forgotten. But she was! A bit of a prude was probably how most people thought of Harold. "I do have standards," he'd say when pushed on the subject – but he was also rather curious, and peeped again, but the page had been turned, and that's when he noticed the wasp! So, did the driver's mate.

It must have been sitting dormant inside the cabin before they left, because no wasp could ever go fast enough to reach the speed of the lorry and catch up. The alternative of coming from the opposite direction would surely have meant 'splat' against the windscreen – however, it was inside the cab and the driver and his mate didn't like it at all.

The mate's hands were being swung back and forth in the cab, then the newspaper became the weapon of defence. A newspaper to swot a wasp is fairly normal, but, the combination of watching who the wasp was about to attack, whilst dodging the blows of a newspaper being swung about by a passenger utterly terrified of wasps, was not conducive to safe driving!

"Mind what you are doing, you flipping idiot!"

"Stop the ruddy lorry! Stop! Stop!" yelled the panicky mate.

"Wind down the window!" yelled the driver.

The lorry was swinging from side to side.

"It's going to get me! I'm getting out!"

"Don't open the door, Stupid!" yelled the driver, as he

swung the wheel to the left, and the vehicle veered towards the verge.

Swinging over to the inside lane and off the road was, of course, the only sensible thing to do before stopping, but safe only if there is no other vehicle in the way. The driver of the E-type Jaguar was not happy! Almost having his front end crushed in again, after it being in for a major repair, was not what that gentlemen considered to be fair play!

The Jaguar's driver was already in a rage as he left his vehicle, and he certainly didn't notice the cat. It was gawping from the back of the now stationary lorry that had tried to flatten him, and it wasn't gazing enviously at him – it was the car! Mouth wide open, and drooling! Harold could not believe how magnificent that vehicle was.

He'd always admired sports cars, but the Jaguar that had screeched to a stop was surely the epitome. He'd never seen this model before. *Must still be on the secret list, maybe on road trials. The company would not be pleased at it being exposed to danger like this and having uncontrolled publicity. A car like this must surely be meant to be kept under wraps – for positive PR!*

Luckily, both vehicles did manage to stop without actual damage, but all three men were now standing at the side of the road. A calm discussion, it was not – an almighty row was developing.

While that was going on, other things were on a cat's mind. Harold had, with difficulty, torn his gaze away from the fantastic car, and it was Scuffo's need for food that had taken over. That tasty-looking sandwich had been abandoned, lying there, inside the cab, doing nothing... *What a waste,* thought a hungry cat – *we can't have that.*

The three-sided kerfuffle on the verge, was becoming more heated.

Scuffo dropped onto the ground, crept along the side of the lorry, with one eye on the arguing humans, and then leapt into the cab. He'd done it without being observed – he thought, but he was wrong.

Hmmm... This is good, was what Harold mumbled to himself, but what came out was actually a rather muffled, sounding-satisfied *Miaow...* Muffled because his mouth was full. He took another bite, thinking again about that sports car.

Thank goodness it wasn't damaged, he thought. It's a beauty! The sandwich was certainly tasty, and there wasn't much remaining, then he remembered – the mate's newspaper, a chance to have closer look – *purely for investigative reasons, of course – and just a little peek at Page 3!*

Yes, a very interesting picture.

That's when he saw the newspaper's date – 20 January, 1971.

He was in the future!

5 UNDERSTANDING...

Thank goodness I have someone who'll sit and listen to my ramblings, thought Harold. *It would drive me mad if I couldn't get it out of my system.*

That someone was Monica. She sat opposite him at the kitchen table, a slightly quizzical look on her face, hoping that her dear Vicar was not starting to suffer from the strain of all the pressures associated with his little parish.

Oh, dear, she thought, *he seems to be talking a load of rubbish, the sort of silliness they show regularly in the big city cinemas.* "Oh yes," she'd said, nodding tolerantly. He'd been to the future... She'd seen films about that – going to the future, but she'd never liked that sort of stuff – too fantastic!

Harold had wakened this morning, standing in his pyjamas in the kitchen airing cupboard – no traces of any fur, though he did have some buttery crumbs on his chin, and none the worse for wear, other than a slightly sore head. He felt back to normal and remembered it all very clearly.

"Yes, Monica, it said 1971! That is twelve years from now! And it was a strange newspaper, called The Sun, and, inside on page 3, it had a photo of..."

No, he couldn't tell her about that!

"And, you'll never guess how much he had to pay for it!"

Monica was not even going to try. She reckoned that she'd already been patient beyond the call of duty, but the poor girl hadn't the heart to stop him going on about it.

He'd already recounted most of what had happened on two occasions when he was a cat. *He needs help*, she had concluded, but then he'd sworn her to secrecy, and she'd foolishly agreed. It was only him and her that were destined to know, and rather than scream at the craziness of it all, she did the next best thing – she made fresh tea!

"I didn't think they'd seen me nipping into the cab of the lorry, but they had and stopped arguing. The driver's mate rushed over because it was his sandwich – it was delicious! I saw him coming. It was a good job because he was in a really vile mood, already in the middle of a serious argument – it would have become physical, if they hadn't noticed me. So really, I did them a favour."

Monica was pouring out the fresh brew and wishing that she didn't have to listen to him wittering on. *Maybe he's lacking sleep*, she was thinking, *but why had he been trying to sleep standing-up?* She couldn't believe that he'd wakened in the airing cupboard!

"It looked as if he was about to take it out on me! So, I scarpered. I jumped out the driver's window – and landed right in front of another lorry travelling very fast.

There was nothing the driver could do. He was going too quickly to avoid me. He tried. It wasn't his fault, and that's when he..."

The picture of a flattened cat immediately flashed into Monica's head! And she froze!

"Are you all right?" asked Harold.

She put down the full cup she had lifted, added three sugars, and tried to remain calm.

"Yes," she said, and gave a sigh.

"And that's when I found myself in the airing cupboard," continued Harold.

What worried Monica most, was that the Reverend Harold actually believed it had all happened. As he spilled it out, it seemed that he was also enjoying telling her about it. *The man's going crazy,* she reluctantly concluded, *just when we were getting to know each other a little better...*

"How many lives do they say a cat can have? It's nine, isn't it?" If he had noticed Monica's eyes rolling skywards in despair, he might have desisted, but he did not. "Well, I think I have used up two and it makes me think that..."

Monica was not hearing him now. She was hearing music. She was a famous ballerina. She was dancing across the stage, in a tutu, just as she used to, at the dancing class – then she realised he had stopped talking. He was standing in front of her, giving her a strange look.

"Are you all right, Monica?" he was asking.

"Oh, sorry," she said. "What was that last bit again?"

"I said, each time the cat was bumped off it was to let me come back here again. Isn't it weird?"

You can say that again, she thought. *I've had my fill of your cat-life!*

For the Reverend Harold Scuffington, it was the opposite. He wanted more. He knew that he'd been there and he'd done it. It was the 'how' that was now the puzzle! *What caused the transformation? Could he choose to become a cat again if he wanted? Did darkness have something to do with it? Perhaps there was a way of...*

At that moment, Monica could have been a very effective fortune-teller. She could tell that his imagination was going into overdrive. Unfortunately, there'd be lots more to come. It was so obvious, and she dreaded having to listen to any more of this nonsense. *He's a lovely man, and I really do like him, she told herself, but I might have to leave the country!*

The Reverend Harold's mother had been a major influence in his life. He remembered his father, but only just because he was very young when his mother decided that enough was enough.

Whisky ruled his old man's life, and that was not acceptable to her. That had been clearly stated on many occasions when he'd staggered home after partaking, but, the writing was on the wall when Scuffington Senior was barred by the pub for causing a fracas for the third time. Unfortunately for him, that was closely followed by more trouble with a wife who had reached her limit. The result – kicked out, never to be seen again. Harold was barely six years old. Any comments that his mother made about him in later years, tended to be preceded by, "Remember that drunken slob, how he would..." However, there must have been some regret because, invariably, the comments would end, "...God rest his soul."

Hence Harold's feelings of guilt when he was daring enough to try a drop of the stuff that had caused his little-known father's downfall. He'd never dared to try even a sip of 'that obnoxious liquid', as his mother described it, when she was alive, and it was a long time after being ordained as a minister that the 'Tasting Test' occurred.

That's when Harold understood. He tried a sip. Liked it. Tried another, and then appreciated why his father had difficulty heeding his teetotal wife's advice!

Before that little taster, from the pulpit he had always encouraged his flock to avoid strong drink. Afterwards, out of feelings of guilt, he stopped any mention of the subject in his sermons. To be honest, he actually drank very little, but the fact that he was drinking alcohol at all, made worse by doing it secretly and alone, made it feel so wrong.

It was amazing how it preyed on his mind.

What was also amazing was how quickly a bottle emptied, even though he only had the occasional glass! It goes without saying that the purchasing of another had always to be done with caution. Didn't want that sort of gossip getting about!

On these occasions, the dog collar was removed, and the collar of his coat turned up, but that was not enough. He bought a soft hat to wear, and always added the false moustache and, of course, the purchase could not be done in Woldenham. Oh no! He had to travel to Codgestone for that.

"How are you today, dear?" was asked of him by the same woman shopkeeper each time. "Feeling the cold, are we?" and, much to his annoyance, "You'll want the usual then?" because he didn't want to be remembered! The usual, indeed! "The Glenlivet?" she'd continue, "The large bottle? That'll be..."

Monica was aware of a lot about Harold's life, but not of the secret drinking – at least, that's what Harold hoped...

The weeks went by and nothing untoward happened... That is, if you can describe the burst pipe in the upstairs toilet causing flooding in the hallway, that afterwards caused Monica to slip and fall on the wet floor and break her arm, as nothing untoward.

Had the cat gone for good? It certainly seemed like

it. Harold had begun to think that perhaps Monica was right. Maybe he had been dreaming. So far, there had been no return of Scuffo, his cat persona, not even in a dream. It was most disappointing. He'd been looking forward to it happening again. It would have been something new to tell her – a special little secret between the two of them, and it would make him less boring in his own head.

Then a thought occurred... *Maybe, if it is going to happen, I'd have to instigate it. Could I do that? Could I prove that it is real, and not a dream? I could try. Why not tonight?*

So, a plan was hatched!

A small measure of whisky would be required. He would also concentrate his mind on his nickname, Scuffo, which was also the name on the cat's collar. The reading of the Guardian would be given a miss tonight. He would simply sit upright in bed, with eyes closed, and concentrate on saying, "Scuffo, Scuffo, Scuffo," as a mantra.

He did...

It didn't work. Not enough whisky, was his conclusion! So, he poured another little measure, and tried again... Nothing! Hmmm... Still seemed a good idea though – so he tried yet again. Still nothing! Maybe another little measure of...

He fell fast asleep in an upright position and, in the middle of the night, *it happened*...

6 WHO's WHO?

Harold awoke with a start. He could see nothing and felt a bit groggy, but he also felt a bit – fluffy? He was still in bed, but under a sheet and a blanket and in the middle of a bed and, my goodness, it was hot! He suspected that this bed wasn't his own...

Have to get out of here, or I'll suffocate!

Ah, daylight!

He stretched himself and gave a big yawn, unhooked his claws from the blanket and straightened up. He'd no idea where he was. An arrogant wipe of his cat's whiskers showed how proud he felt, then he jumped to the floor of a strange bedroom.

And how did I do it? Strong drink!

Sorry Mother...

Now, his apologising to a long-gone Mother might seem odd, but not as odd as him now being a cat! He'd done it. He'd wanted it to happen. He'd willed it, and, voila! Success!

Yippee, he yelled at the top of his voice, but the only sound was a happy *miaow...*

Was he in the future, again? He padded around looking for a clue. *Where was he this time?* He'd managed to convince himself that his first escapade as Scuffo had been in Woldenham.

Didn't seem so at the time but, when he'd thought more about it and talked it over with Monica, and then visited the very spot that Scuffo had looked out at from the high window, he was able to pin-point exactly where those flats were going to be. Several old sheds would be removed, and flats would be built – right there! In the future!

It was daylight in this bedroom. He jumped onto the window sill and looked out. No, he couldn't see any Woldenham landmarks that he recognised this time. What he did see was that he was on the ground floor of a flat or, from the look of the tidy garden, a private house.

He felt good, and there was an arrogance to his movements as he prowled around. Mirrored doors took up the whole face of one wall, mirrors waiting to be used, and he didn't resist. He jumped back onto the bed – much better view.

How do I look?

He turned this way, then that. Just admiring himself. *What a lovely cat I am, maybe a little bit ruffled from being under the bedclothes...* He stopped and did a little personal grooming, something that he never did as the Reverend! Ah, that's better...

He was sitting on the bed, instinctively licking a very personal area, when the door opened.

"Kitty! Don't do that!" said the voice. "Dirty! Dirty! How many times have you to be told? And look at the mess! What have you been doing on the bed? You haven't done a pee-pee on it again, have you?"

The covers were lifted and inspected.

"No. Thank goodness..."

When Harold got over the shock and embarrassment of being caught licking his private parts, he had the chance to take in what had happened. A middle aged, attractive woman had entered, lifted a magazine from the bedside table and left the room again – without questioning who he was, or what he was doing here! Rather strange... She hadn't seen anything odd about him, but he had noticed her though, and she was wearing a very, very, short skirt!

Surely that is not a future fashion! Monica would never dare to wear anything as short as that! She'd say it was indecent, and probably extremely chilly! Quite attractive though, thought Harold.

And she called me Kitty... That's a name for a female cat – so she didn't see what I was licking! Thank goodness for that!

He stopped and listened. A door was opening – an outside one.

"Bye, Kitty. Be a good girl now and look after the house, please. I'll see you later." An outside door closed with a bang.

There it is again, he thought. A tendency for cats to be treated by their owners as responsible human beings – as if a dumb animal could understand a word that was being said! Oh, except in my case, of course.

Bye... he shouted back automatically, which sounded rather like *Miaow...*

The house was silent.

I've been left on my own – how fortunate. I can look around at my leisure, he decided, but before he could venture from the bedroom, a movement at the window caught his eye.

Another cat, and it looked very like he did. Making sure the window was closed and that there was no chance of trouble, he jumped up to the sill. It was a very odd feeling, looking at what appeared to be a mirror image, but with one difference. The collars. His was blue and had a tag saying Scuffo. That cat outside had a red collar. The name on it was, Kitty!

Oh! I'm in her home. She won't be very pleased about that. Hope she doesn't think I did this intentionally. He tried a friendly smile, though he wasn't sure that it looked like that to the other cat, but he couldn't remain on the window sill all day, staring out at the face staring in, he had things to investigate!

"Bye Kitty. I am glad you are on the outside!"

He jumped down and squeezed passed the bedroom door, into the hallway. The front door was at the end of the hall. He went from room to room – there were two bedrooms, plus a room with a dining table and sideboard. There was a bathroom, and a kitchen with a lot of strange and expensive looking gadgets. Interesting, yes, but he was trying to find a clue to the date. She lifted a magazine earlier. That would have a date, but he couldn't find it and had to conclude that she had taken it with her. No calendars hanging around either – no clues.

A date would have to be found. He felt quite proud of himself at discovering a way of becoming Scuffo again – that had been smart, but he didn't know for how long he'd last like this, so, the date was most important. It would be sad to return without knowing what year he'd visited.

If it can't be done from inside this house, I'll have to go out. Bound to find lots of clues outside, but how do I get out? A window? He went in and out of each room again, but all the windows were closed. *That was disappointing. It looks like I am stuck in here until that woman returns!*

Then he noticed it, on the door! Why hadn't he seen it before? *A cat-flap! There's my exit!*

Unfortunately for Scuffo, that flap wouldn't open from inside. He didn't know it, but it was a new idea Liz Smith was using. A flap adjusted to let Kitty enter the house only. Kitty was inclined to wander off at the wrong times for her mistress. When at work, it seemed a good idea to let her cat have shelter if the weather turned bad, but the one-way flap gave control of when she was allowed back out and that was usually after food.

For Scuffo, no escape that way. *Scuppered! So, what to do?*

Simple. Sleep! A soft spot was selected, circled a couple of times and, after lots of careful prodding to ensure comfort, he flopped down. *This is the life*, he thought drowsily, and promptly dozed off...

"Hi Bro!" said a female voice with an American accent.

Scuffo opened one eye, then the other – rather rapidly, because in front of him, nose to nose, was his reflection again, but very close up this time, and no glass!

He gave a surprised little squeak of *miaow*, followed by an even weaker *miaow*... Sounds that definitely lacked confidence.

The identical cat, but with a red collar gave him a funny look.

"Talk in Catspeak, maaan. What's wrong wit' ya?"

"I..." Harold was dumbfounded. "I..." He started again and stopped. He blinked a few times and took a deep breath. "I can understand you!"

"Natural, maaan. Why shouldn't ya?"

"You are... Kitty, I presume."

"Says so on ma collar, man, so dat's ma name. An' you, who be you den?" Kitty looked closely at the blue collar. "Yo-ho man. *Scuffo!* Dat be a real cool name! Yea, dat A like!"

"It's not a takeover of your home, in case you think I am trying to muscle in," offered Scuffo, delighted that it wasn't fighting talk. "But it's a complicated story."

"No big deal, hunn. Take yore time cos A am listenin', man. Dere be no getting' out 'til Liz gets home, so we have aaaaall day, man. Juss me an' you, baby..."

"Are you American?" asked Scuffo. "I sort of hear an accent."

"Nooooo man! Doggone it, yo are way, way out! , No, A'm from right here, man. Bridish through an' through. Liz watches a lotta American TV, an' A kinda liked da way dey taaalk."

"What year is this?" Scuffo had to ask that right away.

"It's 1968! Where yo all been, man? Not knowing' dat?"

"Oh! I..." Scuffo tried to reply, but Kitty was in full flow.

"Everybody says dat one day, dey'll call dis Da Swingin' Sixties – an' dat's for sure, man! Ah know, 'cos ah can swing! An' you? You gotta ged in da groove... Be cool, man. You inta da Beatles?"

"Beetles?" said Scuffo, thinking how Harold had found them one day in the larder, all over the butter. He shuddered. "Hate them!"

"Da Stones den? Great moosic, man."

"Stones? Music? Sorry, Kitty, I am not quite up to date – I am from 1959. Also, I am normally, a human male, a minister of the church, to be precise."

"Whadya sayin', man? Are you *on* somethin'? Speed? LSD? Cannabis? Which are ya usin', man? It must be gooooood stuff! You are one cooool babe!"

Scuffo was confused. *What was this cat with the strange accent on about?* If Kitty was referring to drugs, Scuffo knew that Harold was reluctant to even put an aspirin down his throat.

"No, man," Scuffo replied, feeling that he should attempt the lingo.

"But yo'll be inna free love, a'd guess," added Kitty. "Everybody is, an' you sure look da type to me, man."

"I am not," he replied indignantly. "Monica and I are just good friends, very good friends – and I don't pay for it either!" was added hurriedly.

And that is the way it went on, until the sound of the key in the door caused the cessation of Catspeak.

Liz was home from work and that meant food. Surprisingly to Scuffo, she didn't even raise an eyebrow at seeing her cat's double, or at finding two cats in the house, and she automatically prepared two dishes of food.

"Brought a little friend home with you, again?" she said to Kitty in a gooey voice, expecting a response, but both cats had more important things to consider! Food! Scuffo, especially, he was starving and gulped it down – and liked it.

"Out you go, the two of you," was next from Liz. She was in control. "Go and be clean girls, and Kitty, I want you and your new girlfriend to remember the rule – *next door neighbour's garden!*"

As she opened the door, Scuffo stopped to point out his gender, because she still hadn't noticed that he was a boy, but only a *Miaow* came out, of course.

It was a pity he delayed, and very unfortunate that Liz had since opened all the windows, because the strong draught caused the heavy front door to slam shut – before Scuffo was totally out!

7 TOGETHERNESS...

"Ouch!" Harold relived the moment that ended his escapade.

Scuffo, losing part of his tail in the door, had been the shock that brought Harold back to the present. "And I ate cat food! Yugh!"

Monica winced too as he recounted his visit, and, as he talked, she was becoming a little less sure that this was, as she'd first thought, the result of a disturbed mind. Neither was it dreaming. Too much detail being remembered – that was not the sort of thing that happened with her dreams.

Today though, she was asking herself – did she really want to be so closely involved? *He could be just making it all up to impress me,* she thought uncharitably, which was most unlike her, but it was one of those days. *Thinks he'll get me as excited as he is about it – and maybe I'll let him have his wicked way with me...*

Suddenly she felt terrible. *No, no, no! Not Harold!* She chided herself for these unkind thoughts. *How could I think that? He's not that type of man.*

"And Monica, it was unbelievable! That cat... Kitty! Suggesting that I was on drugs!" Harold was quite indignant about that. "Me?!!"

Yes, that was the real Harold. Don't suggest

medicine to him....

"Isn't it incredible though, that cats are able to talk and understand each other? Do you know, when Kitty tol*d me that she...*"

Wait a minute! This is going a bit far, Monica thought. *Harold, talking to a female cat with an American accent? No, no, that's too much. He can't expect me to believe that. Anyway, I am not sure I want to hear all the detail.*

But she had not been told it all. He'd held back on one bit of information – the method used to achieve the transformation, the drop of the hard stuff – more than one drop in fact. That was definitely not for her ears. He doubted that she'd ever speak to him again, if she found out that. *I hope my breath doesn't still smell of whisky.* It was a sudden panicky thought, because she seemed in a bit of a mood today!

There was something else that he wouldn't be mentioning to Monica. A clandestine visit to Codgestone. The whisky bottle, it was empty. The sooner he went the better, but he'd have to be careful, because Monica was visiting his place rather a lot these days. He'd have to have a good excuse for a visit to town – a believable cover story.

Harold had another problem. An old feud in the village. It had been going on, since he arrived in Woldenham, between the Russells and the MacGregors, and it was rearing its ugly head once more. Dan had asked for his help.

Dan Dixon, the local police constable, was a man who liked a quiet life, and, if possible, someone else to do the dirty work for him. The arrangement had worked in the past. Dan and Harold would talk over a problem that had the potential to become a police matter, but rather than let it reach boiling-point, and lead inevitably to official action, the Reverend Harold Scuffington would have a quite word in someone's ear.

It wasn't always successful, but most times it was. Harold would usually speak quietly with whichever relative, or pal, that he thought could influence matters – and cross his fingers. If that didn't work, he would try and convince the one causing the problem of the error of their ways. Two individuals that he spoke to recently, actually decided to attend church each Sunday as a result of his involvement. The shock and surprise of being successful was so great it almost caused Harold to have a bad turn...

Unfortunately, he was at a loss for the current trouble developing. It seemed that all members of each family, young and old, were becoming bitterly entrenched, and that his usual method of mediation was unlikely to succeed.

"Should I dodge this one, Monica?" he asked her. "Avoid getting involved? They can be a rough crowd. I can't see them thinking that Sunday church attendances would be the perfect answer. Do you?"

However, dodge it, he could not. That would be against his principles and he would have had it on his conscience not to at least try. But how?

The Russells were a close family. Samuel was the father, Mary, the mother, and they had four tough kids. On top of that, there was Samuel's older brother who still lived in the village. He would be part of their army if it became physical.

The MacGregor family consisted of the father – Wee Willie, and the mother – Bella. They had three rough young ones. Backing them up were Granny and Grandad MacGregor, who lived next door, both pretty formidable characters.

What could he do? Invite them all to come to the church hall for a cup of tea and a wee chat? Hmmm... Or organise a quiz game that they could all compete in? Hmmm.... Could he ask the two fathers to meet him in a neutral area to talk peaceably to him? Hmmm... What about a boxing match – and get the two mothers to put on the gloves? Definitely not! But, he'd have to come up with something!

"Any ideas, Monica?" was asked tentatively. He was not expecting any – in her present mood...

"Do you really want to know? I'd use the church hall. I'd give them *all* boxing gloves and lock them in there until they killed themselves off!"

"What a good idea!" he said, but of course there was

a better way, and Harold eventually thought of it. He wrote a little note for each wife, and Monica helped, then did the legwork and delivered them.

Now, Harold was having second thoughts. There he stood behind the oak tree – disguised! He'd donned his trench coat, his soft hat, and his false moustache. Incognito! Didn't want recognition for the good work he was about to do, though it had crossed his mind that he could be a really good spy. Would it work...? He looked at his watch. Almost three.

They'd be arriving very shortly if the ruse was successful. And there they were, coming from different directions, of course. Bella was the first to reach the bench. Excellent – and there's Mary now.

Boxing gloves wouldn't be involved after all.

He'd sat and composed the letter, with Monica's assistance, directed at the mother of each family. 'Dear Bella,' it started, 'it seems a shame that our relationship hasn't developed in a friendly manner. I am full of regrets, I blame myself and would like to make amends. It would be lovely if we could meet and discuss things, and it would benefit both our families if we could talk things over peaceably. You and I, as young women, are more likely to reach a compromise than our short-fused husbands. Could I suggest that we meet in the village park at 2.00pm on Wednesday, when the children are at school, and our husbands at work? If you are willing, we could get together at the bench in front of the Old Oak Tree. Forgive and forget, is my motto. Yours hopefully, Mary Russell.' The one to Mary had the same content, but with the names changed.

Behind the tree and keeping out of view, Harold smiled. They'd both sat down. This was it! There was silence, except for the chattering of a blackbird that had spotted a roving cat. It was an uncomfortably long silence between the two women, as far as Harold was concerned, so he was relieved when Bella spoke.

"Right. What have you got to say?" The tone was confrontational.

"What? Me? You say sorry first," demanded Mary.

"Why should I?" Bella responded.

"It was you that sent the letter, remember!"

"What letter?"

"Apologising!"

"That was you!"

"I didn't send you a letter!"

"Well, what's this?" and Bella whipped out the envelope and displayed the contents.

"That wasn't me. Here's your letter!" and out that came.

"I didn't send you that! Do you think I am stupid, or what?" Bella asked.

"Should I answer that?" said Mary, face now flushed

It disturbed Harold that they now were sitting face to face, with both their noses getting dangerously close!

It wasn't working correctly he realised. Have to do something – quickly!

"Ladies..." he said, stepping into view, "perhaps I can help." His attempt at a pleasant smile was met with a frosty glare from two pairs of beady eyes...

"Ladies, I wrote the letters. I wanted you here to put a proposition to you."

Suddenly, Harold realised that an immediate bonding had taken place between the two females – against him! Oh!

"Did you hear that, Bella? He is trying to proposition us!"

"No, ladies, please don't misunderstand me. Now that you are here, I was going to invite you to my place for a coffee..."

"He's trying to organise a threesome, that's what it is, Mary. I've heard of his sort!"

"We are respectable married women, I'll have you know."

"He's one of these park perverts that I've read about," said Mary. "Look at the trench coat he's got on. Probably intending to flash his tackle no doubt!"

"Just get lost, you dirty devil!" shouted Bella. "My friend and I will be reporting you! Come on, Mary, dear. Let's find the constable."

At this point, Harold turned on his heels, and walked away from them, then thought it wiser to break into a run, and appreciated the nearness of the trees.

Harold hurried home. It wasn't all a lost cause in his mind. The dislike displayed for him seemed to have a binding effect on the two females, unintentionally though it may have been, and they'd hurried off in the other direction, together at least. How long would that bond last?

A visit would come shortly no doubt from PC Dan Dixon, with the bad news of the complaint, but with any luck he'll have recognised my success, thought Harold hopefully. I've reduced his problem. Unfortunately, Harold had inadvertently created one for himself. He should have checked that the trench coat had been buttoned up to his neck, or else he should have removed his dog-collar!

He was outside the front of the church hall, about to lock the door, and go to eat his meal when they appeared. Fourteen of them – the combined Russell and MacGregor families.

Wee Willie MacGregor was anything but wee! "You!" he shouted, as he approached the gate. "You have been harassing our wives."

"Yea!" chimed in Sammy Russell, "and we are not happy!"

"Go, get him, lads!" came from Grandad MacGregor.

"We're coming to teach you a lesson, you naughty boy!" shouted Granny MacGregor.

"You have misunderstood..." Harold started to say, then thought it wiser to move inside the hall out of harm's way, but didn't move quickly enough. He closed the door but couldn't lock it. He rushed into the hall. He was standing, undecided, at the far end when they all poured in together at the other end. Their shouts echoed terrifyingly.

Obviously, no sense in trying to explain, but where to go? Into the passage he went... Where now? The toilets or the kitchen? If he'd had the key for the kitchen door he could have escaped out that way, but he didn't, and it was locked, so he couldn't...

Pushing and struggling to get through the door to the passageway, while shouting and screaming, came the combined force of Russells and MacGregors. They charged into the kitchen – to find it deserted!

"He must be in the toilets!" yelled Bella MacGregor, and there was a rush for there.

"Grab him and put his head down the loo!" cried Mary Russell.

"What the...?" was the only comment made when the toilet doors were thrown open, and the place was found to be empty. There was no sign of the Reverend Harold Scuffington.

In the corner was a shivering cat, obviously terrified by all the noise.

"Aw... Look... What a wee dear," said Bella, and Mary couldn't resist – she had to lift it and give it a little cuddle.

"I do like cats," said Mary, "Do you, Bella?"

"Oh yes, Mary, and this one is lovely..." and their chat continued.

The little ginger cat, with the unusually short tail, was quite pleased, and happily added a *Miaow... Miaow...* as it was carried to the hall entrance and turned loose.

"We've done all that was needed, Charlie," said Sammy. "Scared the shit out of that pervert! Calls himself a minister?"

"Yes, he'll not try that again," agreed Wee Charlie. "Come on, mate – fancy a pint?" and, as one big army, they all trooped out of the church hall.

That was togetherness...

The ginger cat, watching from a distance, gave a relieved, *Miaow...*

8 ALL CHANGE!

A moment ago, he'd been a church minister for whom an act of kindness had gone seriously wrong, standing quivering in a locked toilet cubicle that he'd guessed was about to be bashed open by rather angry people who were after vengeance.

The next moment...

There he was being loved, by all and sundry, as a fluffy little pussy cat called Scuffo, with almost everyone wanting the chance to pet and cuddle him.

It had been a bit of a surprise, but he certainly wasn't complaining.

Getting out of the church hall without being manhandled by two irate husbands was not the outcome he expected at all, but he now realised that his idea that alcohol was the trigger to cause the changes in his shape was incorrect. It may have worked before, but it wasn't the only way. This time it had been sheer terror!

Another surprise – he was not in the future. *Can't wait to tell Monica about this,* he thought, but no rush. Let the dust settle.

He was sitting on the high boundary wall of the church grounds, watching the MacGregors and the Russells exiting the church hall, and delighted to see that they'd decided to leave and not wait for his return, but, more delighted that they were calm and peaceable and mingling happily together, and chatting as if the feud had never existed.

Yes, I have done some good, he thought to himself. *Having a common enemy can be such a blessing...*

WOOF!

Suddenly, Scuffo's pondering was disturbed, and his already depleted tail had to be whipped clear of teeth that snapped and just missed. So much for calming down! He had naturally sprung to his feet, back arched, ready to retaliate with sharp claws, when he realised that he was looking down at Tess – the nice, friendly, Border collie, that he would meet regularly when he went to the local shops. He always patted her, and she would lick his hand. So, he relaxed.

"Hello, Tess," he said, in a nice gentle manner. "What's got into you today, eh? We are good friends remember. What's all the noise for?" All Tess heard was *Hissss... Hissss... Miaow...* and leapt yet again!

Oh! I am a cat, Harold remembered.

"Tess, surely you can jump higher than that..." shouted a female voice. "The minister must have a new cat. I've never liked the man. It'll be his, Tess. Go for it! Kill! It'll annoy him, and he'll never know who did it."

And Tess gave another massive leap, which came rather close, so Scuffo jumped from the top of the wall onto the tree branch – out of sight and much safer, but he was horrified! Not for the closeness of the teeth... The woman's voice, it was Elsa Middleton – the church organist! *Good gracious! That woman! She's both blood-thirsty and two-faced! I didn't know that!*

Must go home. It will be safer inside, decided Harold. *Did I leave the door open? Darn! I didn't! Oh! Never mind. I am a cat. I can climb in through a window.*

Scuffo checked each downstairs window, but no luck – then he remembered the attic window might be open – *yes!* Now, he'd never tried climbing up ivy before, and it was reasonably easy, until he reached the upstairs window level, and looked down. Oh! Harold's poor head for heights – it affected him as Scuffo too!

Ohhhh...! Miaaaaooow......!

Luckily, being a cat, hitting the ground didn't hurt too much.

Surprisingly, it didn't change him back! He was still a cat, a cat that had to sleep outside that night, hungry and thirsty, and who felt really sorry for himself in the morning.

Harold only ever slept outside once in his life, when he'd run away from home, aged seven. "I didn't like it. I'll never do it again," he'd promised his mum, and crossed his heart.

Though he hadn't run away this time, he certainly hadn't slept in his own bed and he liked it even less! Last night, his much-disturbed sleep had been on the ground, outside, under a bush near the front door.

Someone knocking on the door wakened him.

It was Monica popping round as usual, and, by the aroma, she had brought something tasty with her from the baker's. *Relief, thank goodness.* Scuffo stretched, and left the bush.

"Morning Monica, glad you came today. You'll never guess what happened." The *miaows...* made Monica look down.

"What are you doing here, little fellow?" she asked, bending down and stroking his back, "...and whatever happened to your tail?"

"I couldn't reach the door handle and there weren't any windows open, so I have been sleeping rough all night. Didn't like it! And as for my tail... I told you about that. Don't you remember?"

The *miaow... miaow...* seemed to indicate to Monica that this cat liked being petted so, she bent down again and stroked it for a few more moments, then stood up and rattled the letterbox.

"Come on, Harold," she muttered. "What's keeping you this morning? You obviously can't smell these rhubarb tarts."

"Oh, but I can, Monica. Monica... Are you not listening?" Miaow...

Monica pushed open the letterbox and peeped in.

"Strange... He must have gone out early. He usually tells me."

Miaow...

"You are a persistent cat. Well, what's your name then, little chap? Lost your way, or are you just being nosy?"

Miaow...

"Let's see your collar... Scuffo?"

She stopped and stared down at him.

"...Now, that's a coincidence."

Harold gazed up at her.

Monica, it's me! Harold! Miaow...

He was being given a blank look.

Miaow... He moved closer and rubbed his body against her leg. *She wouldn't be able to resist that. She'll realise what has happened, in a moment. It's so obvious! Come on! I'd really appreciate some food and drink, Monica... Miaow...*

But there was a frown on her face.

"Scuffo... So he got the idea from you, did he! He has been making up stories," she muttered, looking straight into his eyes. "Yes, he's pretending that he becomes you," she confided to this sweet innocent cat, "and then tries to impress me by telling me big whoppers." A little bit of a sneer was appearing now. "Not enough for him to be trying to fool me that he's been a cat. Oh no... Mr Bigshot has been to the future, as well! Harold Scuffington! You have disappointed me, big style! Just wait till I see you..."

"You are seeing me now, Monica! The stories... This is the proof! It's all true! It's me!" he tried to tell her.

Miaowowow!

All Monica heard was a cat howling in despair. At least that won her sympathy.

"You sound unhappy and you look hungry, little fellow. It's not your fault. Let's go back to my place. I'll get you a bowl of milk. I'll eat the rhubarb tarts myself!"

Harold said nothing this time – what was the point?

9 MONICA EXPOSED

All the way along the road, the aroma of the rhubarb tarts was tantalising – his favourite, but it was unlikely that he would be getting a share, in his present 'condition'.

This is all wrong. It doesn't make sense. If I'm a cat I should only be in the future, surely! I should have changed back, but I mustn't panic... It should just be mind over matter, he told himself, so he stopped where he was and close his eyes tightly.

Make it end! Now!

But nothing changed. He tried again, but he was still a cat! It had been a novelty at the start – after he'd got over the shock – but not now. Now this was worrying! He had no idea what triggered the changes because it seemed different every time.

Monica was walking ahead, oblivious to the ginger cat having stopped. Her thoughts were on rhubarb tarts...

Sticking with Monica had to be the sensible thing to do, so he tried running to catch up.

Ouch! That wasn't wise. What would his body feel like when he changed back to his own, if he was feeling it painful in Scuffo's?

Although it wasn't far to reach Monica's, he didn't feel brilliant having to go that distance after the fall.

He was stiff and sore, having slept under a bush, plus, being wakened really early by a blackbird squawking loudly. That had been really annoying, and almost prevented him getting back to sleep! Even worse, he was realising that there was not a smidgen of a chance of recognition by Monica.

The journey wasn't all bad though, because he realised, that he hadn't viewed Monica from this angle before. So, he whiled away the painful journey gazing up at her neat little behind, jiggling merrily, as she strode it out. She was obviously eager to get home and get stuck into those rhubarb tarts!

He made it too, but when he got there, he hadn't realised just how thirsty he was, or that it was possible for him to drink so much milk or, that he could make such a mess doing it! *Sorry Monica,* he said. She immediately brought out the mop to clean it all up, and for some reason, that irritated him.

"Monica, you are a right fusspot!" he declared as loudly as he could, knowing now that she couldn't possibly understand him – *Miaow...!*

She stopped and looked at him sternly.

"Oh! She did hear!" and he panicked! But he was wrong. She was wondering what to give him to eat. Opening a tin of sardines was her solution. He was grateful and it tasted nice but, for him, the fishy smell rather spoiled the aroma of the rhubarb tarts.

However, it didn't stop Monica scoffing two, her own

– and his! Things couldn't get any worse, surely!

He went for a roam around Monica's place, in and out of the rooms, hoping that something dramatic would happen and surprise him, and make him return to his normal self. Not being able to talk was becoming frustrating, and even trying to make cat decisions this morning was difficult. He definitely needed a nap, but should it be on the settee, or the bed?

He chose the bed! The pillows were particularly soft, and had a lovely perfume – an even more pleasant smell than the rhubarb tarts, so he curled up contently...

"What are you doing!" was the sudden scream, and he leapt up in alarm.

"I was only..." Miaow... But, obviously, Monica wasn't interested in him being 'only'...

"Get off the bed!" and she made a swipe at him.

A snooze on the hard wood flooring of the kitchen was the best he could do...

Harold woke to the mutterings of Monica. He'd never realised how much she talked to herself. *Happens when you live alone*, he decided. *Hmm... I live alone – do I talk to myself?*

"You will have to move, Scuffo, my friend. Outside for you, back to wherever you came from, because I am going back to the church to see if Harold has reappeared yet. So, out you go."

He was unceremoniously bundled out of the front

door. She followed him and, after locking up, off she went and left him sitting on the doorstep, feeling forlorn.

"What about me?" he shouted. *Miaow...*

She didn't even look back. It was not pleasant being ignored, so he followed, first at a discreet distance, then he went a bit faster and caught up with her. Thankfully, his pain had eased after the snooze.

Monica and the stray cat trailing her were crossing over the grassy area of the little park when Elsa Middleton appeared. Yesterday's incident was one of the things Harold had wanted to tell Monica about. *That woman, she speaks with forked tongue! And as for her dog!*

Oh-oh! Where is it? She is carrying the lead... That means the dog is...

WOOF!

And out of nowhere it came! Running straight for Scuffo!

WOOF!

"Good Girl!" yelled Elsa. "Get it this time. You can do it! Kill the pesky cat!"

What else could a cat possibly do, under the circumstances, when no trees or high walls are close enough for safety – other than leap onto the shoulders of the nearest person! Who happened to be Monica!

"Arghhh...!" she screamed.

WOOF! WOOF!

Miaow!!!!! Hissss!!!

"Leave it, Tess," shouted Elsa Middleton, just as Tess was about to leap on Monica as well. "You are getting too darn slow... missed your chance," and off she went, saying unpleasant things to her pet.

Monica stood there, petrified.

Scuffo jumped down. He thought he would have changed immediately – the suddenness of it had been rather dramatic. He should have returned to being Harold. *What a disappointment,* then he noticed Monica. *What's wrong with her? She's gone as white as a sheet. Hmmm... Bit of a drama queen!*

Poor Monica remained frozen in shock, before eventually discovering that she was still alive, and could walk, so that's what she did – being very wary of the cat that now was strolling, calmly, beside her.

Monica rapped again. The incident in the park had shaken her and she needed some comforting.

"Why don't you answer...?" she mournfully asked the closed door.

"And why would someone answer the door, when that someone is the cat that is standing beside you?" Harold was feeling sorry for himself too and, sadly, becoming sarcastic. He'd had enough of being small and furry. *Miaow...*

"He's not back yet," Monica muttered.

"Surprise... surprise..." said a smarty-pants cat. *Miaow...*

Monica gave up knocking, turned on her heel and headed back home. It would normally have been mealtime for her, but having a cat suddenly jump onto her shoulders seemed to have lessened her appetite. Getting back home without further incident was a relief, but it disturbed her that the troublesome cat had traced her footsteps again to her front door.

"Go away," she said firmly. "Go home. Stop following me!"

Miaow... Miaow...

"Oh, come in then."

That was a close shave, thought Harold. Another night sleeping rough was not appealing, so he was thankful to be back inside.

"I'll try not to be irritating," he promised. *Miaow...*

"I am going to have a little sherry," she said out loud. "And I don't want you clyping to anyone, especially not the minister," she said, looking down at Scuffo and smiling at her own joke. "As if you could! He doesn't know that I like a little tipple now and again, and he'd be shocked if he ever found out. He's so blooming strait-laced!"

"I won't tell a soul..." Harold promised. *Miaow...*

After her meal, she sat down with another glass of sherry, and that did shock him, but he sidled up to her, and rubbed his fur against her ankles. She liked that, and she bent over and tickled his ears – and he liked that.

She turned on the radio, searched around the stations until she found one suitable, and the sound of music filled the room. Monica began to dance. Harold wondered if this was always the way sherry affected her. He'd never seen her dance around before, but she was very graceful. As she passed him, she stooped, and scooped him up in her arms, and danced around with him held close. Much as he enjoyed the sensation of being cuddled to her like this, his problem with heights and fast movement returned, and she was spinning as if she was a prima ballerina. He was getting very dizzy, and...

"I mustn't be sick," he told himself. *"I'm already in enough trouble!"*

He was relieved when the music stopped and she flopped down into a chair, still holding him in her arms. It was a tight grip. He couldn't move, but he wasn't complaining. A cuddle from Monica was not unwelcome, and she smelled nice, even though it was strongly of sherry, and then he realised – she was fast asleep.

That too, is when he fell asleep...

It was the high-pitched scream of a panicky female that woke him, and the reason was obvious – he was no longer Scuffo. A full-size, back to normal, Harold, was lying with his head on the bosoms of the lady who was screaming.

The lady was Monica!

10 WHEEEEEEEE!

"Not yet," said Monica, peeping through the curtains, watching the actions of the neighbour across the road. "Wait until she takes in her milk. If she sees you creeping out of here at this time in the morning, she'll be rushing out and knocking on all the other doors to tell them! Nosy cow... And you know, as well as I do, what she'll be telling them!"

"Monica, that's not like you at all," chided Harold.

Monica's unusually grumpy mood was as the result of a) having claw marks on her shoulder from yesterday caused by that stupid cat, b) suffering the after effects of two large glasses of sherry taken last evening, and c) being awake all night hearing Harold go on about the genuineness of his condition.

Now, it was almost 7.30am and the Reverend Harold Scuffington had been about to open Monica's front door to leave. He'd stopped and stood awaiting further instructions. He had to agree with Monica, because he too knew the woman across the road, she *was* a nosy cow, though maybe he wouldn't have used Monica's terminology out loud...

They'd been together all night, Monica and her favourite minister, and, certainly, it would look to any outsider that there had been some hanky-panky going on. Harold would have loved that to have been the case – but there hadn't!

Surprisingly, Harold didn't feel bad – rejuvenated, almost... Well, he was back to being himself, and he'd succeeded in proving to Monica that his other self, Scuffo, did exist, and – the part that was most pleasing, he'd spent last evening lying spread-eagled on top of Monica. It was as a cat admittedly, but that was the most intimate they'd ever been.

As for the subject of strong drink – there was no mention. Well, Scuffo had promised Monica not to tell Harold of her taste for sherry, so it would have been ungentlemanly to comment, even in jest. That might have led to him having to admit to liking a drop of the hard stuff himself. He certainly didn't want that to be known by anyone, even Monica.

On the positive side, Monica was now convinced that, incredible though it was, Harold did have an alter-ego – a cat, and as that cat, he had been to the future...

"Right! Go now! Quickly!"

As she watched him, through the curtain, scurrying off guiltily down the road, she couldn't stop herself calling out loud, "Next time, take me with you!" but Harold didn't hear...

Being handy with his hands had almost been a necessity for a minister of a church that was in a severe state of dilapidation, and Harold's skills were largely with thanks to his mum. From an early age she had encouraged him, and, in turn, he'd helped her around the house. If he wasn't capable of tackling a task, she'd do it herself but, she'd show him how it was done. So, hammering, sawing, electrics, decorating, they all came as second nature now – the only thing he was less than confident about was plumbing.

He liked to think that he was as fit as he could be for a young man who was barely thirty, and probably was, but he noticed that after episodes of being the cat, he tended to feel as if he had been many rounds in a boxing ring, and lost!

Today, however he was feeling good and sitting on top of the garden shed in the sunshine. Why on top, you ask? Replacing the felt! It was the original stuff put on when old Tommy Sinclair built the shed. The same Tommy who refused to give in to old age and who still claimed to be as capable a joiner as he'd always been. He'd wanted to do this job, but Harold knew that it would be on his conscience to let him, particularly if the effort killed the old guy.

Also, being an old building with a roof that leaked for many years, the wood could have rotted. Harold could visualise someone climbing on top and confirming the rot – by crashing through it! He reckoned that if that was to happen, at least he had a better chance of survival than the old fellow, but, he could imagine old Tommy standing and grinning at him lying there.

"Should have left it to me..." he'd say.

So, Harold was doing it himself, on his own, and happier that way. Much better not to have the 'expert' looking over his shoulder. He'd checked the state of the structure, and it had proved to be safe because he was almost finished. Just a few more clout nails along that edge, he told himself, and you'll have done a good job, young man.

"Hello Harold!" It was Monica. "Apple tarts this morning!" she called out. "Hope you are being careful with that hammer. You know that my dad once lost a thumbnail because he hit it with a..."

He knew he should have been concentrating on the job in hand, and not on Monica... or the apple tarts... or her dad's lost thumbnail, because...

"Owwww!!"

Opening his eyes, he found that he was no longer on the shed roof, but on the pathway of a lovely little country cottage surrounded by an abundance of colourful blooms. It was silent and peaceful, and though it was obvious what had happened, it surprised him as usual. He was having to get used to rapid changes of scenery. For him, sitting there in those surroundings would have been idyllic, had it not been for the throbbing pain.

Yes, it had happened again! He was the cat – and suffering! It was the front left paw that was sore – almost as if he'd hit it with a hammer!

As he sat there, feeling sorry for himself, there was a roaring noise in the distance that disturbed the peaceful atmosphere. It became rapidly louder, and a large motor bike with an empty sidecar appeared, being driven by a leather-clad figure. The vehicle was swung off the narrow road into the drive. Harold watched as the rider dismounted and parked the bike.

The silence of the countryside had returned, but now felt threatening to Scuffo, as did the figure in the heavy leather jacket, leather trousers, and heavy boots. The crash helmet with the smoked visor showed nothing of the face inside, and to a small cat who was in pain and not able to run off quickly if chased, the figure looked menacing.

Miaow!

He shouldn't have tried to move. The sound had slipped out by mistake because the paw was very painful. Scuffo had been noticed!

The gauntlets were removed as the rider came striding towards him. The boots crunched the gravel with each menacing step. Still wearing the helmet, the figure bent down to inspect the furry source of the noise. Scuffo shrunk back... The reflection of the odd-shaped cat that Harold saw on the plastic hood, was looking extremely sorry for itself!

The shape looming above him, was overpowering to a cat with a painful paw. Scuffo made to back away... *Ouch!! Miaow!!*

"Oh," said a muffled voice. "You are limping. What have you done? And your tail! You've had a tough life! Let's get you inside."

The figure turned and reached into a pocket for house keys, and that's when Harold saw the back of the jacket. HELL'S ANGELS, it said in bold Gothic script. To a minister of the church – even though a cat, this was a strange message. What was about to happen inside? He knew all about the reputation of both Heaven and Hell because he preached it, with tongue in cheek admittedly, but the message on this jacket made him slightly queasy. What Satanic horrors awaited inside? *Nothing sacrificial* he hoped!

The door was opened. Scuffo was lifted and carried into a little hallway, and then through a door, into a large comfortable looking room where he was placed on a soft seat.

All right so far, Harold thought. *I'm being treated better than I expected.*

He said a grateful, *Miaow...* and wriggled about a bit on the cushion, being cautious with that left paw, and was about to settle, when...

"SURPRISE!!! Happy birthday, Gran!" and up from behind the furniture appeared, what seemed to Harold, to be hundreds of heads, that started to sing, "Happy birthday to you..."

As the helmet was removed, the beaming smile of a little old lady was exposed. This was someone who was obviously delighted to be surrounded by a noisy family singing their heads off and everyone was in party mood! Her large family had gathered secretly to celebrate the birthday of this eighty-year old 'Gran', and it rapidly developed into a joyous occasion – except for Harold...

Scuffo was really out of place, and vulnerable. He shouldn't be here, and with the shock of the sudden noise, on top of the pain of his paw, he felt proper poorly... He cautiously jumped down from the chair and made his way towards the door. He'd leave them to enjoy their surprise party. His paw was throbbing!

"Just a moment, my little friend. Where are you thinking of going?"

Harold paused. He didn't feel like anyone's little friend – he felt nauseous, and his *Miaow....* was rather pathetic. *"Just leave me alone... Please!"* *Miaow...* But he was scooped up by the spry eighty-year old.

"Let's see what's on your collar. What an unusual name. It's Scuffo? Don't know how you got here, but you looked lost out there. How about staying with me, little fellow?" she said, nuzzling him with her chin, "At least for a little while?"

How could Harold resist? He had a sore paw and someone cared. The shouting and the laughter was continuing all around, but, for a moment Scuffo was in a little dream world – with only a sweet little old lady and him, and he was being cuddled and loved. Sublime, until...

"Gran, which is the cat's sore paw?" asked little Susanne innocently, reaching up and grabbing.

YOWLLLLLL!!!

"Oh!" said Gran, pulling him closer and out of reach, for which he was extremely grateful. "Let's get it bandaged up for the little chap. Susanne, you can help me."

"Oh! No thanks," Harold decided. He'd rather suffer the existing pain than have the help of that little brute. *Miaowaow...!*

"Hear that," said Gran, "he thinks it's a great idea."

And it didn't turn out too badly. After the paw was carefully bandaged by Gran, Scuffo was able to join the party and have a great time, by annoying Gran's grumpy younger brother, who hated cats!

The cottage was so different when the family left. Peace and tranquillity returned.

Scuffo was bloated. He'd gorged himself on such an assortment of food – food that was surely not meant for a cat, but no-one had stopped him, so he'd gone wild. Back home for Harold, a little glass of Alka-Selzter would have solved the problem, but that was one thing that didn't appear available.

Gran was now seated on her favourite chair, smoking.

Harold had avoided smoking all his life, even though he had been tempted many times. Having been surrounded by those who did smoke a lot, he'd had to accustom himself to stinging eyes at church meetings in his little office, so, seeing Gran, sitting there puffing away with a contented look on her face, was nothing extraordinary.

What was a little surprising, when he was sitting beside her, was her talking to him as if he was his normal human self, and not a short-tailed cat with a bandaged paw. Even more surprising was the explanation that this was no ordinary cigarette she held in her hand.

"Live for today, for tomorrow you may die!" she'd proclaimed as she struck the match. "I like having friends who supply me with these," she confided in him. "I'd never have believed it myself. Me, at my age, smoking a joint – and loving it!"

This sweet little old Granny was not quite the perfect relation that her family thought her to be. Harold was amazed. Eighty years old and living it up in a way he hadn't come across before – her riding a motor-bike, and being in a gang with the strange name, and having mates that supplied her with drugs! Wow! She seemed so at ease with life – not a care in the world and looking as if she'd last forever.

For Harold, sitting on the arm of her chair like this, it was a little like being at one of his own church meetings – smothered by the smoke of others. Different this time – he was experiencing the same effects as

Gran! It may have been all in the mind but, no matter, he was becoming more relaxed by the minute.

"A cat's life is such a happy one," he told her, feeling quite euphoric. *Miaaaaaaowww...*

Gran lifted him and held him close. There they were, nose to nose. A happy Gran and a happy cat, and she was grinning as she exhaled all over him.

Scuffo took another deep breath...

Next day – a trip to the coast.

Scuffo was seated in the sidecar as Gran sped along, justifying her Hell's Angel insignia by some of the manoeuvres. Due to the many shocks to his system on the way, at any moment he'd expected to return to his own time and body, and, reluctantly, to leave Gran behind, but that had not happened.

So, here they were, safely parked on the top of the cliffs, gazing together at the blue sky stretching all the way to the horizon. Gran was sitting on the grass with her back against the sidecar wheel and Harold by her side. The paw didn't feel quite so painful, and having been so well wrapped up, and the bandage being so white, he was being very careful to avoid dirtying it – it seemed the least he could do!

He had been amazed at the agility of a woman of her age, sitting down on the ground so easily, then springing up again as an afterthought to fetch something from her bag in the sidecar, as she'd done moments before. What had she produced? In her hand, and being lit, was another of her gifted joints! He should not really have been surprised – but he was.

Today, she was very relaxed as she talked.

She'd chatted to him for a long time last evening, saying nice things about her family, and how lovely to have been surprised by them. Lots of treasured memories had spilled out too. Unfortunately, the way she'd begun mumbling, and the secondary effects of the joint on him, meant Harold's memories of what was said were rather vague, but sitting next to her, in the open air, this time he was not suffering the same way, so he was able to listen as she began to talk seriously. She was mumbling a little, but this time he was able to hear her words.

"You are a very wise cat, Scuffo," she said. "I can see it in your eyes. You understand every word I say – almost as if you were human. We have only been together for a very short time and yet it seems as if I've known you forever."

As she talked to him, philosophising, and giving him lots to ponder – and perhaps to use in future sermons, Harold felt the usual sense of frustration that a human obviously feels when in the body of a cat... He would have loved to respond properly, but all that came out was the usual, *Miaow...*

"Will you stay with me to the end, my little friend? I haven't told anyone else this, but, the end is nigh!"

That's a bit hackneyed, thought Harold! *The end is nigh!* He expected better from her than that, but she was part way through another joint...

"It's sad, isn't it, that, in this day and age, they still haven't found a cure for everything."

Why is she talking like this, he wondered, *is something wrong with her?* He'd read in his Guardian of unbelievable leaps forward that were expected to occur in medicine. 'The next thirty years could see incredible success', it had said, and it would be nice to return to Monica with confirmation of that, but had that forecast been wildly optimistic?

Then it occurred to him that he didn't even know what year it was. He might have travelled only a few years ahead.

"The doc broke it to me gently, I suppose. I couldn't tell the others though – not during a birthday party."

Miaow...

"Yes, you are the only other one who knows. 1995, and still they can't stop it happening."

The date! He was nearly thirty years into the future! He was glad she'd mentioned that.

Miaow... he said happily... and then realised that Gran was telling him that her doc had given her a death sentence. Thankfully, she hadn't noticed his wrong reaction. He realised sadly that the 'forecasted medical successes' couldn't have been achieved for *all* ills.

"But I am going out with a bang," she said with

determination.

That's the spirit, thought Harold. *Miaow...*

"I am going to do a Thelma and Louise!" she announced. "Will you stay with me? If I pretend to be Thelma, will you be Louise?"

Who are Thelma and Louise, he wondered, *and what did they do? Miaow...*

"Oh, thank you," she mumbled and gave him a hug. "I knew you'd stick by me."

At that, she stood up – a little unsteadily perhaps, but she was still capable of kick-starting her trusty motorbike. As she sat there revving, she called out to him. "Climb aboard, little fellow, unless you have changed your mind."

He jumped into the sidecar. *No sense in being left here on my own, he decided. Let's get back to the cottage. She was happier there anyway.*

But, that's not what happened. She revved the engine, started to move homewards, then swung the wheel around and, travelling at over sixty miles an hour, shot off the edge of the cliff!

"Wheeeeeeee!" she cried...

11 A LUCKY BREAK?

"Don't you want one of these then?" Monica shouted, holding up the paper bag that held the two fresh apple tarts. "I'll have them both if you are a not quick!"

Harold doubted his sanity! He'd just transferred and his head was throbbing, but he was sitting on top of the shed that he'd been repairing – as if nothing had happened! In his right hand, he was holding the hammer. He looked at his left. Hadn't he just hit it with that very same hammer? Surprisingly, it didn't feel as if he had, but on his thumb – a bandage! A spotlessly clean bandage!

"Good grief, Monica! You'll never believe this, but..." As he spoke, he was moving excitedly backwards to come down from the roof, and stretched with his foot for the ladder, managed to miss his footing, and toppled backwards, luckily falling onto grass.

"Ouch!" he said as he smacked the back of his head. He passed out, but only for a moment, and he hadn't fallen far, but it made an already throbbing head worse.

Being aroused by Monica slapping his face, perhaps a little too vigorously in her panic, did not make him feel better, but he was grateful to have her assistance to reach the settee. He lay there, feeling sorry for himself, as she made a special cup of tea. That, and the cold-compress she held on his forehead did revive him sufficiently to make sure he could claim one of the apple tarts.

"Thelma and Louise? No, never heard of them," said Monica. "Is it a song?"

"Don't know. She said she'd be Thelma, if I'd be Louise. I said yes, and that's when..."

Last time, when Harold claimed to have been to the future as a cat, Monica had eventually been convinced that it had happened. The actual cat, called Scuffo, had been there, sitting on her lap – hadn't it? Well... Unless, after those Sherries, he'd been just taking advantage! This time his story was even less believable. Hadn't she been standing in the garden talking to him when he hit his thumb?

Could he be kidding me again? I didn't actually see him smack his thumb... He banged down the hammer, yelled... and where did the bandage come from? He could have had it ready to slip on his finger! He never even left the shed – although I'm not certain about that...

"And her last word before she hit the water was *wheeeeeeee!*" he said.

"And you didn't even get wet?" Monica's question was asked cynically. He wasn't winning her over that easily. She was almost inclined to add, pull the other one.

"And, she was smoking a joint as she died... You know what a joint is, don't you Monica?"

"Of course," she replied, having only the vaguest

notion, but was not going to admit it.

"I wish you'd been there to see for yourself, Monica, because I am not sure that you are believing me... And did I tell you that she had a jacket that said Hell's Angels on the back. She was a member of that gang? I did tell you that, didn't I?"

"Yes. You did!" Her reply was a bit curt. No, he wasn't convincing her.

It was fortunate, for a lonely cat stranded on the window sill of the high-rise flats, that Morag Johnstone kept her spare blankets in the cupboard in the back room, because it was freezing outside, and forecast to become even colder as darkness fell. What made it worse for Harold was remembering an earlier occasion on a window sill that led to disaster!

"What the...!" the woman exclaimed. "How did you get there?"

Harold could barely hear what was being said through the double glazing, but would have happily explained his unfortunate predicament to this woman if she had been able to hear him – and, of course, understand!

His current quandary was his own fault.

Why on earth had he allowed Monica to help?

She'd insisted that she was lighter than him and therefore it would be safer if she stood on the wobbly chair. Of course, his giving in to a sudden urge and tickling her waist, while she was stretching to put the box of books on the highest shelf, hadn't been sensible. He remembered trying to dodge the box as it slipped from her hands and fell towards him...

As a consequence, it had happened again and here he was, Scuffo once more, shivering uncontrollably while perched precariously on a very high window ledge, and feeling really sorry for himself. *"If only I could control the changes..."* If he'd been able to talk normally, he would have sounded so whiny! But, he was a cat... *Miaooooowwww...*

What a pitiful sound, thought Morag, as she struggled to open a window that was rarely used.

"You poor wee soul." She lifted him into the warmth. "You must be freezing."

He was, so he appreciated some tender loving care. *Miaow...*

Through to the living room he was taken in her arms, where a young boy and his little sister were seated, but neither looked up or paid any attention to his arrival. Both were too concerned with the object in their hands.

"Look what I've got," said Mum, but total concentration of both remained for the devices.

"Not just now, Mum," said the boy, without lifting his eyes.

His little sister said nothing and continued to give the object in her hand her full attention.

"Both of you – switch off now please," instructed Mum.

"I've switched off, Mummy," said the girl, giving her brother a sideways glance.

"I've switched off, Mummy," mimicked her brother, in a funny voice, again without looking up.

"Gavin...! Do as you are told!" said Mum in a more determined manner, and that got a result.

"Mummy, you have a kitten!" said Sarah, suddenly realising.

Harold thought it was nice to be noticed – at last.

"Is it ours? Can we keep it, Mummy?"

"We'll see, when your father gets back," said Mum, knowing for certain that there was little chance of him agreeing to that. "Scuffo, he's called. It says so on his collar, so, he must already be someone else's pet, and he's frozen."

"Scuffo? That's a stupid name!" scoffed Gavin. "And look at its tail. He has only half a tail. He looks ugly! Anyway, I don't like cats."

Mum ignored the comments, and placed Scuffo on the floor and left the room. She had other things to do.

"Gavin, there's a bandage on its leg," said Sarah. "Do you think it's sore?"

"I know how to find out," said big brother, and leaned forward and prodded the paw.

"You little...!" Yowlll!!!

Claws at the ready, Scuffo backed away from the boy.

Dare to do that again!

The wicked grin on the boy's face, when his mother came rushing back, told her the story.

"Ga-vin!" was said through clenched teeth.

"He only touched the paw, to see if..." started Sarah, coming to her brother's defence.

"You little tell-tale!" came from a brother who didn't want her help.

"Gavin! Leave – the cat – alone!" said Mum and left the room again.

But he didn't...

Sarah had followed her mother. It was just Gavin and Scuffo!

First, it was an attempt to grab the remains of Scuffo's tail. That went on for a while, but the cat was quicker than the grabbing hand, so that failed. Then, he tried to hit the cat with a thrown cushion. That failed also. Then all the cushions were used to try to barricade Scuffo in a corner, but that failed too – and Gavin got bored.

Harold felt exhausted. It had been wearing, him being under pressure from the boy and having to be constantly on his guard. That had been on top of becoming the cat again and the disturbingly cold arrival spot, so he was delighted to see the boy go to the table and retrieve the object his mother had told him earlier to 'Switch off!' It was on again, and Gavin became totally engrossed in it once more.

Scuffo relaxed.

Harold would have had a few nippy words to say to this annoying child if he'd been his normal self but, he decided instead, that he would to take advantage of the hiatus and curl up in a corner, but then, curiosity took over.

What was the toy in the boy's hand? He crept onto the back of the seat, unnoticed, and looked over his shoulder. Moving pictures, in colour, on a small screen, just like on TV! But, tiny pictures! It was smaller than a camera and it was showing moving pictures, but not taking them! And the boy seemed to be able to choose whatever he wanted. This was incredible. Something else to tell Monica...

"Gavin!"

Gavin jumped, and almost dropped the mobile!

"I told you to switch off!" Mum was back. "Leave that phone alone! Now give it to me," and into her pocket it went. "Do something useful," was her instruction as she left the room again.

But Gavin didn't! Crawling round on hands and knees, chasing Scuffo in and out of the furniture was the nearest the boy got to 'useful'.

Enough was enough, Harold decided. The cat said, *Hisssss....!*

Gavin didn't hear this as a warning – more of a challenge!

Scuffo stopped running.

Gavin didn't, and when he appeared round the corner of the settee for the umpteenth time, Scuffo struck! As the claws caught the end of his nose, the "Boo!" that had been intended by Gavin, turned to a squeal of pain – just as Father appeared on the scene...

"Dad! Dad! Look what that cat did to my nose! The horrible cat that Mum brought in!"

"Morag! What's going on here?" shouted a horrified Dad. This was 'his boy', and with blood on his nose. "Where did this cat come from, and what's it doing in our house? And look what it's done to my poor child!"

"Ah..." said Mum, coming into the room, and seeing the blood. She grimaced. "You've been asking for that, haven't you Gavin?"

Gavin was holding his nose and didn't agree. Though he cowered behind his father, there was a determined look in his eyes that Harold recognised. There would be trouble, later...

Mum didn't easily convince her husband where the fault lay. Anyway, 'my son' could do no wrong in Dad's mind, so it must have been the cat to blame!

However, it was cold outside, he was glad to be home from work, and, after the meal he would be settling down for some peace and quiet and some relaxing television, and so he would tolerate a cat in the house for this evening, provided it didn't cause poor Gavin any more trouble!

Tomorrow, it would be out the door!

Scuffo now hoped that, with both adults about, he might get some peace. A chance to relax, and sleep...

Oh my goodness! What the...?! Who...?! Miaow!!
The blast of noise wakened a dozy cat. "And now," the loud voice continued, "a very important event for followers of our longest-running soap. A special occasion for the nation's favourite family show, Coronation Street, because tonight it's notching up its eight thousandth performance."

The voice was coming from a very large screen sitting on a low table, on which beautiful moving colour pictures were being displayed. Harold gazed in wonder. This looked better than Codgestone cinema – and in this family's front room.

"Started in 1960, long before I was born," boomed the continuity announcer, "and still going strong. So, what are we waiting for...? Let's see what's happening tonight..."

"Alexander, turn the volume down!" came the shout came from the other room. "I am on the phone to your sister!"

The sound immediately reduced, with hardly any movement from anyone other than Alexander's hand rising and being pointed at the screen. *Magic,* thought Harold, *how did he do that?*

"Sorry, Sandra," continued Morag. "Couldn't hear you for the TV."

A modern television set! Harold hadn't viewed much TV back home, but any sets he'd seen had not looked anything like this! Normally it was a big box, a big cumbersome box. *But this is so thin – like a large flat board, and enormous… and where's the tube?*

Incredible! Miaow…

How is it done? Miaow…

What must it have cost? Miaow…

"Be quiet, cat!" said Alexander.

"Will I chase it for you, Dad?" asked a bloodthirsty youngster.

"No. Leave it. Come and sit beside me."

Music was now playing – music that would soon be part of the lives of all, as titles and credits appeared. It was the first time he'd heard it, but Harold could tell that it would quickly have the nation hooked – *especially Monica! Surely though, it must get boring after eight thousand episodes,* but he began to watch it and became as absorbed as the other two, the male members of the family. *Odd that it's them…* thought Harold, but half-way through, Mum appeared, delayed by putting Sarah to bed, and asked to be brought up to date.

For Harold, the adverts that interrupted were an even greater attraction. So seductive! Especially the ones with females advertising holidays, walking about with hardly any clothes on, and in parts of Europe he'd only ever read about! As if it was normal!

Then back to 'The Street"…

"Wow!" The end of tonight's episode took them all by surprise, but held Gavin's attention only briefly. He was eyeing up the cat again. Scuffo would have to be ready.

"Alexander," said Mother, wanting to talk to Father. Alexander reacted immediately and performed magic once again. The picture continued but with no sound...

"Have you checked Wednesday's lottery?"

"Of course I have," he said confidently, and then he hesitated. "Oh! Maybe not."

"Would you like to then? I have a feeling that 2012 is going to be our year," said Mother. "I think the cat on our windowsill could be an omen..."

That sounded nice to Harold, being looked on as a good luck charm. *Miaow!*

Gavin's beady little eyes focused. How to get back at the cat? The cushion again! When his dad left the room to fetch the Lottery Ticket, and his Mum was gazing into space and wondering what to have for the main meal tomorrow night, Gavin threw it! This time he caught Scuffo off guard.

It hit fair and square, with enough force to knock him off the back of the settee. Scuffo had to twist as he fell, and although a cat, Harold felt a sharp twinge! Then being smacked by the little picture, knocked off the wall by another cushion, didn't help!

My ruddy back again, Harold thought angrily. *Yowl!*
"Gavin?"

"What Mum? It's that silly cat," he said innocently, as

Dad returned with the ticket. That proved sufficient distraction to save Gavin.

"Is this the right one?" Dad asked. "14 November, last Wednesday?"

Margo nodded. "...And I've got the results," she said, looking at her mobile. "Now the numbers? Read out what you chose."

"Fourteen..." said Dad.

"Yes," said Mum.

"Fifteen..." said Dad.

"Yes," said Mum again.

"Seventeen..."

"Yes, good. Now give me another correct one."

"Excellent," said Dad. "Something for three correct numbers, anyway. Twenty-nine..."

Morag hesitated.

"...Yes," she said, with a smile developing on her face, "Hmmm... That's four correct!"

Alexander read out the last two chosen numbers, followed by the bonus ball, but to no response from his wife.

"Ah, well," he said, with a smirk. "At least we've won something for a change. How much for four?"

Morag looked up at him. It was strange look. Her mouth opened, but no sound came out.

"Mum, are you all right?" asked Gavin, totally forgetting the cat. She just gave a blank look.

"Morag! Say something!"

"We've won the big one..." she said in a very quiet voice. "Six numbers and the bonus ball..." She had forced herself to stay remarkably calm...

But then she lost it! "I love that cat!!!" she screamed, as she jumped up and down on the settee flapping her arms. "It's made us rich!"

It was Alexander's turn to stand white-faced, open mouthed, and silent.

12 POWER CORRUPTS!

"And you brought this back with you..." said Monica. It was a statement, but said in a way that made everything that he'd told her to be thought untrue.

Monica had never seen a National Lottery ticket before, and incidentally, until his previous visit, neither had Harold. How could they? The National Lottery didn't even exist! This was 1959.

"And how much did you say this is worth? More than six and a half million pounds?" She held the ticket up to the light. "Hmmm... That's an awful lot of money!"

There it was again. The expression on her face, the same suspicious tone to her voice. Harold was pacing the floor, feeling greatly agitated. The pain in his back had become worse too.

"Maybe you would like to run it by me again?" she suggested. "Sad that they've lost it, but... the fact is, these people were taking part in something illegal. Betting and winning money in that way is wrong! I know that for certain, and you... Being a minister too!" She tutted. "You should know better than most what is right and wrong!"

"But, Monica, betting's made legal in the future. Remember, that's where I was – in the future! 19th November 2012, to be precise, watching Coronation Street! The eight thousandth episode too!"

"Hmm..." She sounded tense, as if she'd suffered too many of his stories. "As you say, watching Coronation Street... Whatever that is!" She made it sound as if that was a sin too.

What he would really have liked at that moment was a little drop of alcohol. It might have brightened things up and eased the pain in his back. Maybe even offering a little whisky to Monica would have improved her mood. Unfortunately, the bottle was empty.

"Answer me honestly, Monica... Do you believe anything I'm telling you?"

"No!"

Harold sighed. *Maybe he shouldn't have asked! If only he'd stuck with suspecting it – less painful than the truth.*

"You stole this money, you know, from someone in the future – probably a crook too."

Wait a minute! Now, I stole it in the future ...and I am a crook!

"No, Monica. That's not what I said." Unfortunately, he was beginning to have doubts himself. *Did any of it actually happen, and would telling the story to her once again make any difference?*

"I want to believe you, but it is difficult. Now, if you'd taken me with you..."

"How would I manage that?" said Harold. "I can't even control what's been happening to me!"

"Alright tell me again." She sounded a bit more

sympathetic now. "What happened after they found they'd won the money?"

Harold sat down, closed his eyes and imagined he was still in the room with the Johnstone family, and told Monica once more...

Morag and Alexander had double-checked the results, then triple-checked, and then phoned the Lottery Organisers to be given the news that they had won, and that it would be a substantial sum. "More than six million," said the man at the other end.

"Six..." Alexander gulped, and took a deep breath. "Did you say... million?"

"Yes," said the man, "Over six million, in fact... Hello... Hello, are you still there...?"

Morag, it was, who took the phone from Alexander's hand and carried on the conversation. Someone had to remain calm. Alexander sat where he'd dropped onto the chair in severe shock, sipping from the glass of cold water that his son fetched.

"Right," she said, as the call ended. "Where's that bottle of Prosecco?"

Little Sarah had appeared, unable to sleep, with all the noise her mother had made.

"I love that cat!" Margo reiterated.

If a cat could blush, then that's what would have happened with Scuffo. Instead he gave a bashful, *miaow*...

Harold felt good, other than the painful back, and delighted to be sharing in such a happy occasion, but the amount of money, regularly being mentioned by both husband and wife, was so enormous in his mind to be meaningless. Two glasses appeared, both filled to the brim, which were emptied – and refilled, and, as it was a very special occasion Morag thought, the cat should have some too. A saucer was laid on the floor and some poured onto it. *Cheers* – thought Harold, but unfortunately, although he would have been delighted to drink their health and prosperity, Scuffo wouldn't. Bubbles up his nostrils didn't appeal! It was so tempting that Harold exerted all his willpower to get Scuffo to sup at least some, and won – but one lick was all that he got.

Someone, who shouldn't have, did sup! The troublesome Gavin! After his Mum and Dad had had a few glasses of the bubbly, they progressed to the wine. Gavin lifted the not-quite-empty prosecco bottle and drained it!

Harold saw it, but only too late. Another claw to the nose would have stopped him, he told himself. Little Sarah had seen him steal the drink too and whispered, "Oh, that's naughty, Gavin." She'd gone over to sit with a slightly tipsy Mum, who appeared to now be suffering from nervous exhaustion. Dad's energy was totally drained. He'd already dozed off on the settee.

Gavin's eyes sparkled. With parents out of the picture, here was his chance to get back at that pesky cat. He knelt down and crawled menacingly towards Scuffo.

"You scratched my nose," he snarled, with his face inches away from the cat's nose.

Harold held his temper, but Scuffo was ready. He'd happily scratch that nose again, or run, depending on the direction of this nuisance's attack. The move came suddenly, as an arm swung out! Scuffo just managed to dodge it. It swung again, and another fast move by the cat avoided that blow too, but the sore back was slowing down reactions. *Hisss...!*

"Don't hiss at me, you horrible creature," spat Gavin.

It was more than just a good telling-off that this one needed! He'd probably be locked up in jail one day. Just making cat noises was doing no good, so, the next time the boy's arm swung, it connected with a paw – and exposed claws.

"Ow!"

Blood on his finger! The boy froze, shocked. He started to cry and turned for help to his father, who was lying in a sound sleep. Gavin's second-best choice, Mum, was slightly tipsy and sitting happily singing a little song in her own head, as Sarah slept on her lap. No help there obviously, so therefore...

Harold recognised a change in attitude immediately by the look that appeared on the boy's face, a superior look. *You are only a cat,* it said – *so why am I getting upset? I have a Mum and Dad, who are ridiculously rich, and they've been shouting out loud about it. That means I am rich too. I can do anything!*

Gavin stood up. He was only a young boy but, upright, with that superior look on his face, he looked enormous to the little cat. Harold had a memory of a garden party he'd attended as a penniless young minister, years ago, where he'd been taken down a peg or two with a few snappy words from a very wealthy financier. This felt uncomfortably similar...

With the calm superiority that comes with enormous wealth, Gavin, reached out and lifted the winning lottery ticket from the table, leaned down, and started to wave the ticket in front of Scuffo's face.

"This, you ugly little cat, is what makes me more powerful than you. I could stand on you and flatten you, I could throw you out of the window. I could get someone to do it for me, because I don't have to bother about you. You are nothing! I can do anything I like to annoy you. I'll have your claws pulled out! I'll ask my Dad – he'll do it for me!"

That was it. A cat, who is a minister, can take only so much from a horrible child – and then it reacts...

Scuffo's sudden move caught the boy by surprise. His head darted forward, his jaws grabbed the ticket, and he was off – sore back or not. Harold knew it was the wrong thing to do, but he was dealing with a naughty child. This was a very valuable item to the family. It might be damaged if he wasn't careful, and he didn't want that to happen, but he just had to teach this young brat a lesson...

Through the open door, he went, and dashed into the kitchen. He had a plan! He jumped onto the kitchen units. *Quick – choose somewhere high, somewhere the boy can't reach. No, none in here.* Scuffo was leaping about the kitchen surfaces with the lottery ticket still clutched tightly in his jaws, just keeping out of reach, as the boy chased after him.

Into the hall they went. Nothing suitable here either. He needed to leave it in a spot beyond the reach of the boy, but the family must still be able to find it and claim their winnings.

Scuffo shot into Sandra's bedroom – nowhere there, then Gavin's – same again. All the rooms had fitted wardrobes including the parent's. Scuffo was having to watch for Gavin grabbing at him as well as search for a suitable spot, and all the swerving and dodging was not helping his back!

The spare room was all that was left, and there it was! A grandfather clock! *Perfect!* It told the wrong time because it was tall, dusty, and unused. On top of that would be beyond reach. All Scuffo had to do was leap from a nearby table, and that's what he did, but failed! He'd tried desperately to grip the top edge, but couldn't – and smacked on the floor.

Harold was hoping that all the aches and pains that were developing wouldn't remain in his human form.

Scuffo was gasping. He leapt onto the table and tried again – at a run. This time, success, but only after a tough scramble, and after creating a legacy of many scratches on the varnished surfaces!

He looked down at the boy. He was staring up at him with all the hatred he could muster! A young boy shouldn't have these nasty feelings – certainly not for a poor cat, Harold thought.

I'll leave the ticket here then... Oh! A slight problem. It was caught on his incisors. He couldn't get it off – not without ruining the ticket! He tried again. *Oh dear!*

Down he leapt from the top of the clock, shot out of the room and into the hall, ticket still in his jaws, but undamaged, and into the living room to get help. Mum, or Dad, could remove the ticket safely – but, even though he ran over them lying there and waved the ticket in their faces, all they wanted to do was continue sleeping.

The young boy was right behind and getting more and more annoyed. He'd grabbed a cushion again, and started swinging it, trying to hit Scuffo on the move.

This is not working out, Harold realised. *What now?* Distracted by a movement on the TV screen right above him, the picture still showing with muted sound, he hesitated and marvelled at how wonderful television had become... and that's when the cushion came flying through the air!

It had been hurled with great force by a supercharged enemy – and struck the modernistic floor-light! It toppled over, hitting the back of the TV, which in turn began to tip over too...

All this appeared to be in slow-motion to the cat mesmerized by the screen, as the skyscrapers of New York and the bustling city traffic that were showing, came tumbling towards him... and the TV crashed down!

Young Gavin stood transfixed. What had he done?

"And that is..." continued Harold, "When I found myself, still a cat, but back in real time, sprawled in the darkness under my own bed!"

"Still carrying the winning lottery ticket..." added Monica, who sounded as if this time she had found less fault in what he'd recounted.

"Yes, but worse still. It was a delayed reaction. The change took place then, and there's not much space for a grown man under my bed. What a struggle to get out, but at least I was able to use my hands and remove the ticket from my mouth. I can't say I liked the taste!"

"The ticket does look as if it has been chewed a bit," Monica added.

"I feel terrible," said Harold.

"Oh, please don't start on again about your back, and all the other painful bits," pleaded Monica. "I can't cope with that!"

"No, I feel terrible for what's happened. That family... I've taken away their chance of luxury living – never having to work again – forever on holiday..."

"Let's look at it in another way," said Monica, with a sly little smile forming. "You could keep the ticket until you grow old, and then claim it! It would only be another fifty-three years to wait. I'd like you so much more if you were rich!"

Harold looked at her in horror. One moment she was suggesting he was aiding and abetting crooks, and next, she was looking at him becoming her sugar daddy!

"Monica!" he exclaimed. "How could you!"

"Well, what else can you do? You can't make amends."

"If only there was some way I could get it back to them. I'll never sleep again with this on my conscience!"

"Oh, there might be a way." She said that with the sly grin developing again.

"Oh?" he said. There would have to be a catch. She looked smug...

"Use the same method as before. I'll hit you on the head with the box of books!"

13 REVENGE

"Dad! Dad! Dad! Wake up Dad!" yelled Gavin in the sleeping man's ear, but although Dad grunted something and shifted position, he remained in a drink-induced sleep. "I got that cat, Dad! I killed it! Dad! Dad! I hit it with the telly!"

His shouting wakened his little sister who'd been lying awkwardly on her Mummy's lap, but little Sandra was used to her brother's behaviour. She ignored him and slipped back into her bedroom, back to her own comfortable bed.

The way that Morag Johnstone was lying did not look comfortable. One eye opened. "Go to bed, Gavin," she grunted to her son. She'd been disturbed by his shouting, but for only a moment, and went back to sleep in her chair, still in that same uncomfortable-looking position...

Outside, as dawn broke, it was bitterly cold, exactly as forecast, and there, back where he'd started, on a window-sill that was very high up in a block of flats, was a cat.

Same window-sill. Same cat. Same predicament!

There were differences. Monica had hit his head with a little too much enthusiasm, and although, as hoped, it had caused him to transform and, it appeared with any luck to have given continuity in time, Harold now had a splitting headache, and was absolutely freezing!

Oh God... I hope someone finds me soon. Miaooooow...

If someone doesn't find me, I am going to jump, he decided. The downside was that he had no way of knowing, in choosing to lose one of this cat's many lives, if it would trigger his change back. For him it would be literally a leap into the unknown...

There had been a long discussion between Harold and Monica, before she hit him.

"We don't know if I'll return to the same place, and, if I don't, how will I ever find that family again?"

"And it might be a different timeframe," offered Monica. "They might not even have bought the ticket yet!" To Harold that comment, although negative and troublesome, did indicate that Monica was believing all he was telling her. That was a step forward!

"And we don't know anything about how it happens. You could get lost in time," she added. That seemed like adding another nail to the coffin!

Though nothing positive was coming out of this discussion, Harold remained determined.

"Whatever it is, at least I'll know I tried. I'll regret it forever if I've ruined their lives."

"What if I kill you?" worried Monica, holding the box with two hands. "Sometimes I don't know my own strength."

"Just do it!" he'd said, gritting his teeth, and biting into an already well-chewed lottery ticket...

When the sun arose, Scuffo was still on that window-sill and now, absolutely freezing! The sun had eventually melted the hard frost, but there was still no apparent activity inside the flat.

Thoughts of his conversation with Monica returned. Harold had arrived at the right place, but was it the right timeframe? Was this the dawn of the following day? He fervently hoped for continuity, but there was no way of telling.

He was trying to avoid looking downwards, but could see that the fresh breeze was causing papers to swirl around in the street below. He felt it fluffing his fur. That worried him because, after all this trouble it would be ironic if the ticket was dislodged from his teeth by the breeze and blown off into the distance and lost.

He had survived the cold in the night, and for that he was relieved. Anyway, he wouldn't have jumped! He realised that in the early hours. He was too much of a coward.

Goodness, what time is it? I must be patient, but it would be nice if someone opened this ruddy window. Miaow!

In the living room, two adults were looking at each other, feeling a little foolish about their own behaviour last night, especially in front of the children, but also feeling slightly delirious with the realisation that an enormous amount of Lottery money was just waiting to be confirmed – and spent!

"All we have to do is present the ticket. They'll do all the rest for us," said Alexander.

"Hmmm..." said Morag lying back with a satisfied grin. "Let me touch that ticket again. Isn't it wonderful? We don't have to imagine. It is real. We are multi-millionaires!"

The ticket? Alexander had to think – where? It was only when he looked up and around the room that he noticed something different.

The television – lying smashed on the floor.

"Did you do that?" Alexander asked Morag. "You were sort of..."

"I don't think so... But it doesn't matter anyway. We can afford a new one. We can afford one for every room, Alexander. We're rich. We can afford a new house – a castle if we want! So, where's the ticket?"

There was some consternation five minutes later when no ticket was found.

"The children wouldn't touch it, would they?"

Into little Sarah's room went Mum and Dad.

"Oh no, Mummy," she said in a sleepy voice, having had to be wakened.

Into Gavin's room – to find him using his bed like a trampoline.

"I – killed – the cat! I – killed – the cat! I – killed..."

"Gavin. Stop! Why are you saying that?" said Mum.

"Be – cause – I – did!"

"Gavin, stop jumping. You'll break the bed!"

"You can – buy me – a new one! You – are – rich!"

"Gavin! Stop!" That was Dad, so he did...

"We will only be rich if we can find the lottery ticket," said Mum. "Do you know anything about it?"

"The – cat – ate it!" He'd restarted bouncing. "Cat – under – T – V!"

He was left to bounce on, as the parents rushed back to the living room.

The damaged TV was lifted gingerly from the floor by Alexander. He was afraid to look. He didn't like animals but, even more, he hated to see dead ones. Morag knew that she was the one who'd have to deal with it.

But there was nothing there!

"Oh, Gavin..." sighed Morag, with relief, "I wish you wouldn't fantasise."

Smiles returned. For Alexander, no body! For Margo, her 'lucky' cat should be still around. Then the realisation – the ticket was still missing.

Everywhere had to be searched, but without success, until they reached the spare room, however they were so engrossed looking in all the places it could never be that it was ages before they looked through the window – and there it was, outside! The Winning Lottery Ticket.

In the jaws of the 'lucky' cat!

"For goodness sake! It took you long enough," complained a cold, stiff, grumpy Harold, but *Miaow...* was all that Scuffo said, just grateful to be lifted off the window sill by Margo. He would have made his own way – if he hadn't been almost frozen solid.

"How did you get out there?" asked Margo, as she nuzzled him through stale alcoholic breath! Harold would have preferred avoiding that part. "You are really cold."

Alexander's concern was about a much more important matter.

"The ticket, Margo. Get the ticket!"

"You've been looking after it for us all night, my little darling! Oh, you are a lovely little pussy-cat!"

I hope Monica never thinks I smell like this, thought Harold. Miaow...

"Margo, get the bloody ticket!"

Scuffo's mouth was prised open and the ticket removed.

"Phew... Got it..." and in relief, Alexander dropped backwards onto the old bed, and didn't care in the slightest about the funny noises that came from an ancient old spring mattress. As he lay, slightly more relaxed, a thought occurred... "I don't understand how that cat finished up on the outside of a securely closed window – unless..." He rose and moved purposefully towards Gavin's room.

Although there was a slight feeling of pity for the young lad about to be wrongly blamed for opening a window and putting a cat on a ledge on a cold night – with an extremely important winning lottery ticket in its mouth, Harold was delighted that his nemesis was getting a good telling-off! He deserved it! It made up a little for last night's discomfort.

Scuffo could relax – or could he? What would I do if I was ten years old, and a cat was considered more important to the family, a cat that had thought it got the better of me? To Harold, that answer was so obvious! I'd get back at the cat!

He'd have to keep his wits about him, but he'd done what he set out to do – the winning ticket was back where it belonged. If only he wasn't so tired. He felt spent. He'd suffered the cold while outside during the night, had a bad back and a head that were still aching, and was desperate to lie down, be left in peace, and sleep – for a week! But what chance was there of that?

The lecture in the bedroom had ended. Gavin had been instructed to stay in his room but, as the bedroom door was closed, his Dad could hear that Gavin had started using the bed as a trampoline again. This time he just shrugged and left him to it.

"Don't know what to believe," he said, when he returned to Margo. "He is consistently blaming the cat!"

"Oh, no," said his wife, holding Scuffo closer to her. "How could he blame this little darling?"

Harold thought, at this point, that perhaps he should contribute and added a sweet little *miaow*... That earned an extra hug.

"We'll have to watch that boy. I think he is developing a wicked streak..." said Dad.

"No," said Mum, "Gavin's just a normal boy. Boys make up stories."

"But," said a disappointed father, "I thought that my boy would..."

"Not a day to be thinking negative thoughts, Alexander. There are phone calls to be made, and lots of money to be spent. Oh, I am going to enjoy this!"

Two cushions had been put in the middle of the settee for Scuffo and he was gently placed on top. A position of both comfort and honour.

"You can have a rest while we have showers, then we'll all have breakfast, and... oh, we can do anything we want – thanks to you Scuffo!"

Harold wondered if cats could smile and tried his best attempt. *Miaoooow*...

Relax... He had the room to himself. He was being treated like a prince. What more could he ask?

It was almost half an hour before the first interruption occurred, which was really of no consequence. Little Sarah appeared, in her pyjamas, carrying in her hand her mobile phone. It was actually her mother's old one but that didn't matter to Sarah, as long as it allowed her to play all her favourite games.

She was sitting beside him and he could see the little screen quite clearly.

To Harold, coming from the days where a telephone had to have a curly wire attached to the wall before it would work, the object she held was incredible. In fact, like when her dad held up his hand and controlled the TV screen last night – what she was doing with that toy was pure magic! Even better than that Marvello guy last Christmas!

He felt much better now. Having had a little snooze, and now being able to concentrate on willing Sarah to make the correct choices in her game – *yes, that's what life should be about. Nothing too exciting...*

Suddenly, it all changed!

First one cushion was whipped away from beneath him, and before he could even catch his balance the other went. Gavin was back in action!

"I don't think you should do that to Scuffo," suggested his little sister. ""Mummy will..." but that didn't stop Gavin's arm swinging out, as he tried to hit a cat that had regained balance and leapt aside. Yes, Scuffo was back in action too. Gavin missed.

Footsteps in the hall.

Gavin jumped onto a seat.

"Oh, wasn't it comfortable enough for you, Scuffo," asked Morag, still in a dressing gown and with her hair wrapped up in a towel. Then she noticed her son sitting looking overly innocent.

"Ga-vin?"

"He was only..." started Sarah, but the look from her big brother stopped her.

Mum stood looking at him for a few moments, but no comment came. She left the room again.

"Where's your phone, Gavin," little sister asked.

"Dad's got it – because of THAT!" and, as he said that he leapt at Scuffo.

Too slow," said Harold. Hissss...!

And that is the way it went on. Boy chasing cat. Cat dodging boy.

Sarah was oblivious to it all. She was winning her game...

Scuffo had perked up. Harold's back didn't feel so bad, and the headache had gone. That snooze had worked wonders. Being chased around the room was not doing him any harm. He was in total control and had avoided all danger.

Then the pressure was removed.

"Gavin! Sarah! We're going out. Get ready, please," and off they went to their bedrooms to put on suitable clothes and shoes, which left Scuffo in peace again.

"We need a new television," declared Dad. "We could get a bigger one."

"Yes!" chorused the children, but Mum shook her head.

"But that will cost a lot more than this one did..." she started to say, then realised that the penny-pinching days were over. "We'll get an enormous one!" she declared. "Look after the house, Scuffo. We'll see you when we get back."

Scuffo settled himself on the cushion where it had fallen on the floor, in front of the defunct television now set back on the cabinet. He was ready for yet another snooze. Harold heard the front door open. They were going. *Peace...* He shut his eyes, but the door hadn't closed.

What's stopping them? He opened his eyes – to see a broken television set comes tumbling down on top of him, like last time...

"Gavin, where are you? Come on! Oh, there you are. What have you been doing?" asked Mum.

"I was killing the cat again," he replied cockily.

"Gavin!" said an exasperated Dad. "What did I tell you about making up stories?!"

...And the door was closed.

14 SHOPPING...

Sitting astride the roof of the church hall was not the sort of behaviour the villagers had come to expect from their local minister, and as the word got round, more and more of them were appearing in the street below to stare unbelievingly.

"Always knew it would come to this..."

"Yep, I don't like repeating gossip, but, I heard he has a problem with drink..."

"At least he can trust in the Lord..."

"And it's the closest to heaven he'll get!"

"Needs a good woman, he does. A good woman would keep him in check. Wouldn't allow him to cavort about like this. Look at him!"

"He's going to ruin his trousers!"

"Bit of a show-off, isn't he?"

"Do you think he'll jump? It'd liven up the day. Nothing ever happens here..."

The sound of the fire-engine in the distance, coming closer, was a relief to Monica. She'd phoned the moment she found him up there, but wished that he could have climbed down of his own volition. It would have saved all this fuss and no-one other than her would have known, but he was terrified.

Couldn't move.

Even the rhubarb tarts that she'd brought with her couldn't tempt him to try.

Monica was able to talk to him privately from ground level, but only for a few minutes. It became impossible when the first villager appeared – and that had been almost immediately. At least he'd shouted down to her that he didn't go up there deliberately. That would have been really disturbing. He'd been in the future, she knew that, and once more his return had been out of control. All this chopping and changing between man, and cat, and back again, must surely be taking its toll...

The crowd down below did get their money's worth, because the firemen failed to coax Harold onto their ladder to climb down on his own. He had to be blindfolded before he would release his grip on the flagpole, and allow himself to be moved carefully onto the rungs and helped, step by slow step, towards the ground.

When he put his foot on terra firma, and the blindfold was removed, the first thing he did was to throw up, bringing up the little food that he had in his stomach – and it stunk of fish! That performance quickly dispersed the crowd.

Monica had to step in quickly to prevent the firemen from using their hose to wash down the Reverend Harold Scuffington – that being a technique that the local chief had decided was a good dissuader for suspected potential suicides.

That's when Monica intervened. Harold was sent inside by her, and instructed to run a hot bath immediately, and she took over. The story she concocted, about how the vicar had been doing a good deed associated with a pigeon and a nest, because he cared so much about wildlife, sounded so ridiculous to the fire chief, that he tore up the report sheet and left her to clear up the mess.

A few buckets of cold water thrown by her did that, clearing most of what Harold had spewed, then back into the house, upstairs, and straight into the steaming bathroom – to give Harold the shock of his life. He was thankful that he'd just immersed himself completely in soapy water as she appeared.

There was no standing on ceremony for her today.

"The cloth!" she demanded. "The soap!" and she proceeded to wash his back, a pleasure he had rarely experienced since his student days. "You can do the rest," she said, and left him alone. He breathed a sigh of relief. *It's surprising what the promise of a juicy rhubarb tart did for morale…*

After the bath, getting dressed in clean clothes made him feel much better. How it would feel when he had to face all the people who'd seen him on the tiles, he had no idea.

Of course, it wasn't only those who saw him, the whole village would be aware of his escapade by now. Word travelled fast in Woldenham.

"You did a great job," said Monica, as he sat down opposite her.

On the roof, making himself look a complete idiot? Didn't feel like it.

"I mean, you did return the Lottery Ticket, didn't you?"

Harold sat more upright. *Yes, he did, didn't he? But that was all done in secret. None of the crowd that laughed at him this morning would get to know that. They'd never give him any credit for the real reason he was up on the... Ah, well...*

"It wasn't all sweetness and light, Monica. That boy. He'll be a worry for his parents. Young Gavin, hater of cats – and probably all animals eventually, and with money no object, he's the kind who'll probably grow up and spend his parent's cash by shooting rhinos and elephants for fun. Either that, or he'll feel guilty for bumping me off, and he'll try to make amends by building a cat and dog home. Unfortunately, I know what I'd bet my money on."

"My dear Harold! What's this about betting again? You are the minister. That National Lottery thing seems to have given you bad ideas, and if that does happen as you say it will, it'll probably turn us all into a nation of gamblers. That will be sad. But... I have something else to do today, so I'll have to leave you. You are feeling ok now, aren't you?"

He nodded and smiled. "Thank you, Monica."

He had something to do too, something that he had been intending to do for a while but could never fit it in. A visit to Codgestone. The bottle was empty and, under the circumstances, he could do with having access to a little snifter. He could need that to boost his resolve and his ability to face the villagers.

The local bus was due in half an hour. Enough time to sort out the outfit. That he did, and with bag packed, off he went.

It wasn't the usual conductor, the one who lived in Woldenham and had done the job since Harold had arrived in the area. This was a new man that Harold didn't recognise, but he seemed to know him.

"Good day, Vicar," he said.

Was there a smirk on that man's face? He's heard! But it was the dog collar, of course! The man was just being polite, he realised. *Must remove it when I get there.*

Being able to walk incognito around Codgestone had always been enjoyable. This anonymity was a relief to someone who was so well known throughout Woldenham. Of course, he'd now be notorious there after the roof-top incident. So, he made the most of wandering leisurely around, gazing in shop windows. No rush, and it seemed even more of a friendly town today. Passers-bye were giving him beaming smiles, and he was smiling back, a little self-consciously, though. Nice, when it is like that, he thought, with people being pleasant to each other, but what will it be like next time he walks around Woldenham. He wasn't looking forward to that. It would be mocking grins in the village!

Relax! He told himself, and he did. He even spent time in the park. Sitting on the bench beside the duck pond, watching the ducks coming across, hoping that he would reach into his bag and bring out some food for them. *No chance, sorry – my disguise is in there, and it was time to move.* He couldn't afford to miss the next bus, and he wasn't just here for a relaxing walk, some shopping was required before he went back.

Along Main Street he went, smiles still coming his way. He was trying to look casual, until he reached the usual place, a deserted alleyway. He'd never seen anyone else ever use it. Perfect for changing outfit. Then back along Main Street he went. He was pleased to be unknown here, and perhaps this disguise was unnecessary, but he didn't want to take any chances, especially after today's earlier problem.

Stopping outside the shop was a precaution. He always did that to make sure everything was in place – by looking at his own reflection. The dog-collar had been removed, the trench coat buttoned up to the neck, soft hat in place at a slightly jaunty angle, and finally, the false moustache, firmly glued.

Into the shop he went. No-one else in today. He was glad of that. Only the usual assistant. She was one of the few people in Codgestone who recognised him – but only in his disguise of course, and the one who, annoyingly, always remembered what he was after.

"Good day, Sir," she said. "Nice to see you again. I thought you'd decided to buy elsewhere, and we wouldn't have been happy about that, now would we?" She smiled at her own little joke.

Get on with it, he always wanted to tell her.

"So, what will it be today then?"

"I'll have a bottle of..."

"No, wait! Don't tell me. Let me guess. Would it be *The Usual*?"

"Yes, please," he said, smiling awkwardly because he didn't want the moustache to come loose. The same routine every time.

"Yes, it's a large bottle of The Glenlivet for you, isn't it? Hmm... Price has gone up since last time," she said. "Mustn't leave it so long until the next time... Only joking!"

Harold heard the door behind him open and close – the bell operated for both directions.

"There you are, then," said the annoying assistant.

It was the same price as last time, which was fortunate, because that was the amount he already had in his hand. He took the bottle, now hidden by the brown paper, and placed it carefully in his bag.

"Right dear. That's you then... Next!"

Glad that the little episode of being served had been completed, Harold relaxed a little, knowing she didn't pick solely on him.

She gave everyone the same treatment.

"Oh, here's another well-known face. How are you, love? Some more sherry is it?"

"Yes, please," said the voice behind him – a voice he instantly recognised!

"The usual...?" she was asked, and as Harold turned away to leave, he glanced cautiously.

It *was* Monica.

"Yes..." she nodded to the assistant. She looked just as uncomfortable as he felt at having to do this, but, at least she was able to give a proper smile in response to each comment.

"A bottle hardly lasts any time these days, I find," added the assistant. "It's obviously the same for you."

Does that assistant have to be so loud and so damn knowing to everyone? He could see that Monica was a bit embarrassed about her likes being made so public. She smiled shyly to him as he passed, and he was about to comfort her with a few words and say that he'd see her outside, when he realised that she didn't recognise him.

He continued to the door, opened it and the little bell rang. "See you again," shouted the assistant to him. "Don't leave it as long next time!"

As he left, he had to ask himself, *why do I come back here?* The door closed behind him, and inside, the little bell rang again.

At least Monica doesn't know that I like whisky, he told himself. *A good job she didn't recognise me, because I'm not supposed to know that she likes sherry.*

The Main Street alleyway was on his route to the bus stop. A quick change, then he'd buy the local paper on the way. *Have to hurry, don't want to miss the bus.* Into the alleyway he went and quickly changed back to normal clothes. *"Ouch!"* Pulling off the moustache in a hurry was painful. The coat and hat were hurriedly stuffed back in the bag. *"Next... a Gazette,"* he mumbled to himself as he turned out of the alleyway, and almost bumped into someone.

"Oops, sorry," the person said. "Oh, it's you again, Vicar." It was a beaming smile. "Good work you did this morning. Anytime we can help again, just give us a shout."

It was the Fire Chief and he was being very pleasant.

"Right," replied Harold. That man hadn't seemed so happy this morning? "Must hurry. Bus to catch."

Into the newsagent he went, grabbed the evening paper, and held out payment.

"Well done," said the newsagent, holding his hands up and refusing the money. "Nice people like you don't have to pay. It's on me."

Harold was surprised. "Thanks," he said, and hurried out and over to the bus stop, jumping aboard as the driver started the engine.

Monica was sitting in the front seat.

"Oh hello," they both said.

Monica's bag was on the seat beside her. She moved it to let him sit there. Harold lowered his bag to the floor in front of him, hoping the bottle wouldn't clunk – it was at the bottom of the bag which was stupid, he realised. Luckily the noise of the bus moving off covered any giveaway sound it made.

"Bought the local paper," he said.

He felt awkward, having been right beside her moments before, though she didn't realise.

"Can't read on the bus though. Makes me feel queasy," but his eyes caught the picture on the front. It was him!

15 NAUGHTY, NAUGHTY...

"Well, it wasn't all porky pies! You are making it sound as if there was no truth in what I told him." Monica's feelings were hurt.

"Look Monica, I am really grateful," said Harold. "You did a great job, but I wasn't beside you. You did the talking and sent me inside, remember. Anyway, I am pretty hazy about being up there at all. Did I really do what you've said? How much of it was true?"

"The bit... uhm... where you were up on the roof."

"And the rest, you made up?"

"Well, I couldn't tell them that a few minutes before you'd been a cat that had just returned from over fifty years in the future. I had to tell them something they could believe."

The picture of Harold hanging onto the church hall's flagpole was on the front of the newspaper, the inside page carried the short report. Also, on that page, was a head and shoulders of Harold arriving at Woldenham five years before, when he still had his boyish charm, taken from the newspapers archive.

He read it once more.

A YOUNG VICAR'S BRAVERY.

Earlier today with no thought for his own safety, the Reverend Harold Scuffington risked life and limb on the steeply angled, slippery, dangerous roof of Woldenham Parish Church Hall to save the lives of two tiny pigeon chicks. They'd recently hatched, but had been knocked out of their nest by a marauding cat. The young vicar saw it happen and climbed out of the vicarage attic window, jumped the four-foot gap to get onto the church hall roof, and chased the cat away. Picking the chicks carefully from the guttering where they'd landed, still alive, he then went up the dangerous tiled surface to replace them in the nest. It wasn't long before they were joined by a grateful mother pigeon. After finding his access window had closed behind him, and that he had no means of getting off the roof again, Codgestone Fire Service was called. They then assisted the vicar in his descent from his precarious position. The Fire Chief later commented that the Reverend Harold had a particular dislike of heights and, to carry out this heroic task, he'd had to overcome his own very real fears. He added "Isn't it nice to have people like this in the community – people who care." The Vicar's spokesman said that the Vicar was a little shaken but would not let this stop him from doing more good deeds, as soon as he felt strong enough in the future.

From Readers and the Gazette staff: Thank You, Vicar! You have our admiration.

"And you are the Vicar's spokesman, I presume."

"The reporter was desperate. It was a really quiet news day, he said, so he was delighted that I gave him something. Anyway, look on the bright side. You are now being seen by all of Woldenham and Codgestone as a hero – and not a spineless twit, as it might have been..."

That was a bit harsh, thought Harold. Couldn't she have put it a little better? But Monica was right. She had prevented serious embarrassment for him, and that was proved the following day. His confidence returned when he found that he was able to continue his normal duties in Woldenham, without having to dodge around corners when he met anyone.

Life became fairly humdrum for several weeks, and with no recurrence of the cat experiences, it looked like he was back to being totally normal.

"I think all Scuffo's lives are used up," he suggested to Monica.

Anyway, he'd had enough, even though he had never discovered what caused the transformations and was still curious. He'd been to the future, he'd been the cat, and if those adventures were now ended, he didn't mind.

"That's it – all done."

It had been interesting, sometimes a fun experience, but each time he had suffered after-effects from some of the cat's mishaps, and his brain had been getting slightly fuddled.

After weeks of nothing, he felt much fitter and was having none of the headaches.

One of the other reasons was – no strong drink.

The bottle of whisky, bought on the same day as Monica's sherry, was lying unopened. Not a drop had been drunk and for that he was proud, and each day of resistance, he had marked the calendar accordingly. It must be admitted, each day also, he had looked longingly at the full bottle – but resisted. He was proud of that and would have liked to have shared his achievement with Monica, to maybe help prevent her going down that same slippery slope, but he didn't. He couldn't suggest that she should stop the odd glass or two, because he wasn't supposed to know in the first place.

He liked Monica, a lot! Sometimes he wondered if things could ever become more serious. Perhaps it was destined to remain platonic, but surely there had to be more to a relationship than just regularly enjoying rhubarb tarts together.

Maybe he should do something about it...

The weeks passed, then one day, a special mark appeared on the calendar. It would be nice to say it was the day Monica succumbed to his charm – but it wasn't.

It was Harold who'd succumbed – to the whisky! He'd found it so easy to remove the cork, even easier to pour some of the golden fluid into a small glass, and absolutely sublime to, once more, actually swallow some and sit on his favourite chair in the front room, with the Guardian, and read.

Tonight, he'd decided that a second little glass wouldn't go amiss.

It was bedtime, he'd already changed into his pyjamas, was on his own, and comfortable, sitting deep in the soft seat. It reminded him of being Scuffo, how he would pad around a soft, plush cushion, and prod it many times before plonking himself down, prior to a snooze.

But no snoozing in this chair tonight. Oh, no! Before going to bed, the newspaper would be read from front to back. There might even be an attempt at the crossword.

He did try hard, but his eyes kept closing. He shook himself and turned another page, but it was very dry reading. As he dropped off to sleep, he was murmuring to himself, "Wonder if 'The Sun' will be more exciting?"

Then it happened...

When he'd changed to Scuffo before, the place he'd stopped at several times in the future, had been in somebody's bedroom. He'd been either on a bed, in a bed, or near a bed. Not of his choice, of course... This time he was under a bed, and he'd been fast asleep.

Scuffo rubbed one eye with a paw. He could see nothing. Must be night, he presumed, and wondered how far into the future he was, this time, but he was in no rush to find out. There was no sound, so, if there was someone in the bed above, they were asleep, or maybe there was no-one in the house at all. It would be easy enough to check, he knew, but he still felt sleepy. So, what should a cat do in that case? *Snooze on!*

He was still dozy when he heard the front door being unlocked. Someone was entering, and a bright room light came on that only partly reached where he was under the bed.

Should I say hello?

His view of the room was limited. He could only see what was happening from below the knees, and it was a female, wearing high heels that were kicked off and left where they'd fallen. The heels looked ridiculously high and very thin. *Surely she couldn't walk far in these,* thought Harold. Looks torture! She padded about the room switching on some lamps, then switched off the centre light. The lighting effect changed to become a warm glow. Harold tried to guess her age. He wasn't exactly an expert on women's legs, but he could compare them to Monica's – he'd noticed hers. At a rough guess he thought this woman could be of a similar age, about thirtyish.

As the legs appeared at the side of the bed again, the shoes were tidied away, by being kicked under the bed beside him. It seemed to be the favourite place to store footwear, for there were many more pairs around him that had already gathered dust. Being a fairly low bed with not much space underneath meant Scuffo struggled to sit up straight, and that made Harold feel a little claustrophobic. The sooner he could get out the better.

Would now would be a suitable time to say...?

A man's voice called from the hall, so at least two people were in the house.

He hesitated...

Perhaps not!

The woman sat on the bedside chair, and as Harold watched the legs, the stockings were removed, first the left then the right, but they weren't nylons. When they dropped on the floor, the legs were joined at the top. *So, this was the future?* Now, he couldn't claim to be an expert about what females wore under skirts, but this was not like the nylon stockings that he understood Monica to wear.

Has that made suspenders redundant? Hmmm... Don't like that!

The tights were dropped to the floor and left there, then as an afterthought, kicked under the bed, to join the shoes.

"Pour out some wine, Honey, and bring it through," the woman called. "I'll have the Pinot Grigio."

Should I give a friendly miaow...? I don't want to frighten anyone by popping out suddenly. No, maybe not yet.

"We'll have to be quick, Honey. My dear husband James will be back by eleven, so you'll have to be out of here long before that." As she said that, a shiny red dress dropped to the floor.

Why was she was taking off her clothes? Harold felt uncomfortable. Going to sleep, maybe?

Uhmm... Certainly not the time for introductions. Maybe best if I slip out of the room when she's in bed. I'll sleep elsewhere. She'll probably snore!

That is when the remainder of the lady's unmentionables were dropped. Harold closed his eyes – it was the least a gentleman could do...

"Hurry up, Honey," she called. "What's keeping you?"

The mattress above Scuffo's head sagged. She'd sat down on the side of the bed. Harold could see her legs, and feet, and her painted toes. *Hadn't she put on a nightdress? Surely she wasn't sitting there on the bed, without clothes? Naked!*

Harold decided he'd leave the room when the lights were put off.

It wouldn't be right to see her! I may be a cat, but I am also a man!

Another pair of legs, covered in trousers, now entered the room.

"Leave my drink there, Hon. It's you I'd rather have." That was said in a rather husky voice.

The male sat on the same bedroom chair. First the shoes were taken off and dropped on the floor, and Harold noted that he didn't untie the laces.

Tut! Tut! That's a bad habit!

Trousers came next and it was bare legs on view.

Compared to the ones he saw before, these were hairy and most uninteresting, and he was wearing two different coloured socks, one with a hole in the toe! They were not removed. Male underpants joined the rest of the clothes on the floor.

"Ooh, Honey. You are big tonight..." was said by a huskier female voice.

A few buttons must have popped off his shirt in his rush and then the shirt floated down. Harold was glad he couldn't see any more of the man standing there. The hairy legs, still wearing socks were more than sufficient!

The female legs were no longer dangling over the side of the bed. They'd vanished from view and the shape of the mattress changed as she wriggled into a new position.

"Come to me, Baby," was a whisper, and the mattress changed shape again, this time to sag considerably more in the middle, as 'Honey' or 'Baby' joined her.

This is embarrassing. I hope they are not going to...
But they were!

Scuffo's hearing was so much sharper than Harold's, and goodness! The sounds they made... He missed absolutely nothing. *Why, oh why, had he landed under this bed?* One thing was obvious – no matter what date this was, good old hanky-panky hadn't changed.

This guy, so obviously not the husband – much too friendly! Anyway she said James would be home at eleven. So this is adultery, and I, a minister of the church, am having to suffer this. I should be doing something! This is naughty – but what can I do? I'm a cat!

That's when he had a wicked thought.

What would happen if I jumped onto this guy's back and 'miaowed'? Yes, now's the time to say hello! That'll soon put a stop to their shenanigans. Save them from themselves!

With that pious thought, Scuffo took a deep breath to strengthen his resolve, and raised his body – but he shouldn't have hesitated, because the considerable activity now going on above was putting great strain on the mattress – and that's when a spring went 'boing!' and burst through the cover and struck poor Scuffo's head – but before he could 'miaow' in pain...

Whoooosh! Something strange happened!

Oh no...!

This wasn't the way it should be! Suddenly, he was no longer a cat sitting crouched under a creaking bed! He was a church minister in striped pyjamas being squashed and bruised with every move that occurred on the mattress above, and with an excessive bounce, Harold's nose was squashed, face down on the wooden flooring, causing an involuntary "Oof!"

That gave the game away. The movements stopped.

"That noise?" said the male voice. "What was it?"

"Honey, you can't stop now!" she cried out angrily. "Not when I am nearly..." She'd obviously been enjoying herself too much, and hadn't heard anything, Harold realised.

So, if I just keep quiet...

Harold certainly couldn't move, even if he'd wanted to, because the weight on the mattress above was flattening him. Then that weight moved, and a face appeared at the side of the bed, upside down, and gawped at him! *The man!*

"Sylvia! How could you!"

The face disappeared. There were rapid movements above, then the legs with mismatched socks appeared in Harold's view.

"Sylvia, I am disappointed in you! You are not only two-timing your husband, you are doing the same to me!" Hands reached down and grabbed discarded underpants and trousers.

"What do you mean?" she squeaked.

Game over, thought Harold. *I'll have to get out of here - fast, the other way.* He turned his head with difficulty - to see a female face appear, upside-down, at the escape side of the bed.

"Eeeeek!" She screamed, as she saw the body below her bed, and it moved!

That should have caused Harold to jump out of his skin, if he hadn't been totally squashed.

"I am so sorry to interrupt..." He contributed in a muffled voice, "But..."

"Help! Help! Help! It's a man!" she screeched at the

top of her voice. "Call the police, Terence! Quickly!"

Why does she have to screech so loudly? Harold was glad he no longer had Scuffo's extra-sensitive hearing – his own ears were suffering enough!

"I can't do that!" said Terence. "I am not supposed to be here!"

"But what are you going to do about him?!" She was still screaming at Terence.

"A male, in pyjamas, under your bed, you randy woman! I'd suggest it's more – what have you been doing with him?"

Someone else had acted swiftly. There was banging on the front door, and the call of "Police! Open up, please!"

Now, this flat was in a nice neighbourhood, was very comfortable and had been a reasonable cost. However, there was a downside – the sound proofing was abominable! The couple upstairs had done the needful. They'd thought that someone was being murdered.

Banging at the door again!

Bare legs appeared in Harold's vision, her arm appeared and grabbed the red dress, and she slipped it on, and rushed to the door

"Oh, do come in, Officer. Thank goodness you're here. I have an intruder – a burglar, I think."

She came back into the bedroom, followed by a very young constable.

"My neighbour from next door came round to save

me. I was so grateful," she gushed.

"What neighbour?" The policeman saw only an empty bedroom, until Terence came out, sheepishly, from behind the curtains.

"This your shirt, sir?" asked the policeman.

Terence just gave a silly grin.

"Is he the intruder then?"

"Oh no, Officer," said Sylvia. "That's Terence, my neighbour. My other one's under the bed."

Harold tried to give a friendly smile, as a policeman's upside-down face appeared.

"You! Out!" was the officious command.

Now that the mattress had been vacated, Harold was able to move a little easier, but it was painful to stand. Also, he wished that he'd bought a smaller size in pyjamas. The trousers felt too slack.

"Don't try anything funny," said the policeman. "Hands in the air. What's your name?"

Goodness, it was true that the older you get, the younger the policemen seemed – he's just out of Primary School and look at his uniform. It hasn't half changed over the years. Where's the helmet? He looks ready for baseball. At least he still uses a notebook.

"The Reverend Harold Scuffington."

"Just give me your real name, sonny. You could get yourself in trouble fooling around."

"It is my real name, and another thing, young fellow, I am from 1959..."

"That's a lie," shouted Terence. "These flats only go up to 106."

Harold felt vulnerable. His pyjama trousers, they were slipping. He cautiously lowered his hands.

"Hey," shouted the policeman. He whipped out something that Harold thought, at first, was a gun, then saw it looked like that magic thing they used to change TV programmes. "Hands up, I said."

The trousers... They were going to go any moment. He could sense it, inch by inch, they were moving.

"Excuse me," said Harold, "I'll have to..." and his hands grabbed for the dropping trousers.

That's when the Taser was fired!

16 EXPERIMENTING

Today, seeing Monica, when she arrived with the usual morning goodies, was a very pleasurable experience.

Earlier, Harold thankfully found himself back where he started, in the soft seat, wearing his pyjamas and ready for bed, with a crumbled newspaper lying on his lap – and an empty glass beside him. Almost as if he'd slept there all night and never been away – except for the pain!

By the time Monica arrived, he'd washed and shaved with enthusiasm, and welcomed her with a mischievous peck on the cheek. 'It'... having happened again – and being so unexpected, had somehow rejuvenated him and he couldn't wait to share the experience.

"Boy, was I glad to be out of there," he told her, after recounting it all. "But it could have been a less painful exit."

"Go back to where the boyfriend comes in..." Monica urged. "That was a good bit."

Monica was getting a little too absorbed in the detail, Harold thought. *More than previous times. Was it to do with the naughty bits?* He was scared to ask her that, in case the answer was, "Yes!"

He noticed that, this time, she wasn't questioning it being true. Monica had become a believer.

"Don't you want to go back – like last time, to see what happens next?" she asked. "I'd willingly hit you on the head again..."

"I'd probably be taken to jail!" He shuddered as he remembered the young policeman pointing that device at him. The effect, when he'd pulled the trigger, had been like an electric shock.

"Do you know why it happened again?" she asked. "You were so sure that there wouldn't be any more 'cat' episodes."

I might as well be honest with her, he decided. "I blame the whisky!"

She looked at him quizzically. "Whisky...?"

"Two glasses last night – and then it happened."

"What? You... having whisky?" she said, in disbelief. "But you don't drink."

"Well, to be honest, I do – but only occasionally!" he hastened to add. "I think maybe that's why it happened. It's not the first time it's worked like that."

"Oooh..." she said, her eyes glazing over. "I wonder... Would it work for me?"

"I doubt it. Anyway, don't you prefer sherry?"

He immediately regretted saying that. There was an awkward silence.

"How do you know that?" Her voice had a hard edge.

"How do I...? Well may you ask..." he said, playing for time. "I thought that I read in the Guardian..." A lie coming up! "...that sherry was most popular with the ladies. That, and... Martinis! Oh yes, and Sweet Stout."

"Oh," she said, not totally convinced.

"Of course, not everyone drinks alcohol... Bad for you – and I am sure you don't make it a habit. But you do make a very nice cup of tea, Monica, and that's the truth." She was smiling again and took that as an invitation to do so.

Harold breathed a sigh of relief, but, when she returned, she hadn't given up.

"What else is required to make it happen – other than the whisky?"

"Complete relaxation," Harold told her. "Letting your thoughts take you where they want to go."

"I could do that," she said, "but it would have to be at my own place. I couldn't relax properly anywhere else."

Harold wondered where this was this leading.

"Do you have any whisky?" she asked.

"No." He was lying again. It was becoming a habit, he told himself. "But I could buy a bottle if you are enthusiastic to try."

"I would pay for it," she offered.

"No, no, no," he insisted.

"We could try the experiment – together..."

Harold suddenly had a pang of conscience. What he hadn't told her was, that he was wearing only his pyjamas, each time...

The following evening, Harold arrived for a light meal at Monica's. As he stood on the doorstep waiting for her to answer, he glanced over his shoulder. Across the road, he was sure he could see the curtains move. *That nosy neighbour was definitely keeping tabs.*

He had his bag with him, the bag that usually held his Codgestone disguise. Earlier today, he'd been there with that bag, for another bottle, and found most of the people he passed in the street acknowledging him, same as his last visit – the power of the Press... and he'd been through the usual routine at the store, served by the over-friendly, loud-mouthed assistant as usual, who knew him so well, but only in disguise, of course.

But this evening, no pretending to be someone else. The fresh bottle of whisky was inside his bag, together with a clean pair of his striped pyjamas...

Sitting at the meal, his appreciation of Monica and her talents rose another few notches. *Wouldn't it be nice it if this could happen every night,* he thought. *I should really do something about it – change the state of the relationship.*

Be decisive! Take action! Perhaps...

"Super sausages, Monica, and the chips were superb." She gave a shy smile.

Would tonight be the chance, he wondered, so when she washed the dishes afterwards, he took action! He dried them for her...

After that it felt a little awkward. What next? They sat down in the front room. Harold was pleased to note that the venetian blinds on the window would prevent that nosy woman across the road from seeing straight in.

"Music?" asked Monica. She had a new radiogram, all shiny and polished, and a sizeable collection of records. She took one from its dust cover and placed it on the turntable then pressed the button. The arm, automatically dropping into place at the correct position on the record, had fascinated her from the moment she bought this unit. She'd been told by the man in the store that it was a major step forward in technology. He'd demonstrated it there and then, and she'd been immediately hooked. So different from her little Dansette player. She could never place the arm at the start of the disc on that without endangering every record.

"Nice..." Harold commented as the music started, though maybe Bill Haley and the Comets playing Rock Around The Clock was not conducive to relaxation!

"I love dancing," she said.

Harold was about to admit that that was something he didn't know about her, then he remembered her spinning around the room when he'd returned as Scuffo. He'd been seriously close to her that night. Unknowingly on her part – enjoyable for him!

"Do you like to dance, Harold?"

"Well, um, I haven't really tried," he said. He'd always

made the excuse at Church Social events that he had two left feet and had no desire to prove otherwise.

"It's easy," she said, and stood up and started gyrating in the middle of the floor. "Come on. You could do it! Just relax," and she bounced over, reached down, and grabbed his hand.

He glanced over at the window to make sure that no-one outside could see him, and reluctantly got up – and it wasn't easy, he wanted to tell her. Many parts of his body still ached when he tried to move quickly – thanks to that blooming policeman the other evening!

"See! Told you, you could do it!"

She played the same music again simply by pushing a button – she liked that bit, and he forced himself to try harder this time to please her. When it came to an end the second time, she let him sit down. He was grateful and flopped into an armchair.

"What kind of music do you like then?" she asked. "Something fast and good for more dancing?"

It was easier to shake his head than speak. No!

"I have classics, I have pop, and I have jazz," she offered. "You name it. What about Perry Como? He's a super singer."

Harold wasn't really into the music scene any more than he was into dancing, but he had heard of Perry Como. "Yes, I like him." *Oh my goodness,* he realised – *I've lied yet again. I always thought he was an Australian novelist...*

"Want to hear his latest? Just out – Hot Diggity."

"Oh yes..."

That turned out to be a bouncy novelty song, a foot-tapper – certainly not for relaxation, so she had him on his feet again and trying some new moves. They failed, so they agreed that he should stick to the basics.

It seemed more promising when she brought out an LP of Como's romantic songs, and it was – until the scratch!

"Oh no!" That really upset her. A scratch on her good Perry Como Album, and on the very first track. It kept repeating, "*How could anything go wrong? How could anything go wrong? How could anything...*" until Monica rushed over and snatched at the playing arm, and, in doing so awkwardly, made it worse.

Harold was itching to open the bottle in his bag.

"Are you thirsty?" he asked her. "We were going to try an experiment, remember? Would you like a...?"

"How could this have a scratch?" she blurted out, ignoring his question, and making him feel that he'd damaged it! "The first song too. That's most upsetting."

"Sorry!" he exclaimed automatically, feeling guilty. He stood up and went over to look at the various records she had. Doris Day! Now he knew who that was. Everybody knew who that was! She sang nice songs, nice peaceful songs.

"How about this one?" He held it up, and Doris's smiling face on the cover transformed Monica.

"Ah... Good choice. A lovely voice and romantic music. If I didn't know you, I'd think you were trying to..." and there was a sparkle in her eye.

Harold felt uncomfortable now and looked at his feet.

"We were supposed to be getting relaxed," she said.

She's doing it again! Making it seem as if I am the problem – and that was making him tense...

"So, remind me how you made it work the last time," she demanded. "I want some excitement with you."

Harold swallowed. Her enthusiasm was disturbing him.

"Well, being totally relaxed is the most important thing, I think, but remember, I don't know for certain how it happens. I was relaxed, and then I had some whisky."

"So, it's as simple as that then..."

"Well, there was one other thing. I was ready for bed... I was wearing my... pyjamas!"

"Right then," she said. "I'll change into a nightdress. You have your pyjamas with you?"

He nodded, feeling extremely guilty. *She was supposed to say, "Don't be ridiculous." Surely she wasn't going to...*

"You can change in here. I'll change in the bedroom," and off she went.

Harold was astounded. *She was leaving him to... but, 'bringing his pyjamas' was supposed to be in fun! Better stop her now.*

"Monica!" he called. "I should tell you..."

"Wait a moment," was shouted from the other room, "I'm not ready yet. Have you already changed?"

He was in a quandary. *Should he change – for a joke, into his pyjamas? No, surely that would shock her. Anyway, I am the minister. What would people say if they got to know?*

That's when Monica came back in – dressed in a flowery cotton nightdress, that Harold would have said was a little on the short side!

"You're not ready," she said accusingly. "Go into the bedroom and change there. I'll get two glasses."

He did as he was told, and then crept awkwardly back into the living room, holding tightly onto the elasticated waistband of the stripy trousers. He'd had the same problem last night with the waistband, and though these were clean ones, they were the same size. He should have fixed them this morning.

Monica had poured out the whisky. Two large glasses sat there, each containing an over-generous measure. She was standing with her back to him. Harold wasn't sure where to look. Then she turned round and it was obvious, in his mind, where he shouldn't! She sat down. He sat opposite. She took the glass in her hand and appeared ready to quaff the lot in one go.

"No!" he said. "Just sip the stuff. It's strong, particularly if you don't drink."

"But, we have to relax, you said. I'll put on Doris Day."

How the heck can I relax, Harold asked himself, *with her in that nightdress?*

"We have to think nice thoughts, haven't we..." she said, as Doris helped set the mood. "Hmm... I could get to like this," and she gave him a big smile as she took a first little sip.

Next morning, they were still in their original chairs, wearing the nightclothes. Two empty glasses sat beside them, and a whisky bottle sat on the table, with very little whisky remaining.

'It' hadn't happened. They'd been nowhere, either separately or together, and had consumed an inordinate amount of the golden liquid.

Harold woke first, and took a few moments to clear his head a little, then looked across the room and remembered with a jolt where he was. He thought it wise to put a bedcover over Monica, for her modesty and his own blood pressure.

He slipped his clothes on top of the pyjamas.

Leaving her sleeping seemed correct, he decided, and he'd nip back to his own place before she awoke. Save any embarrassment. He picked up his bag, placed the nearly empty bottle in it, and tiptoed to the front door – then, remembered the nosy neighbour. She saw him come in last night, but she wouldn't have seen him leave – because he didn't, but it would have been unlikely to see him in the dark anyway, but there might be a better way...

If he went out the back door, and slipped round to the front again without her seeing him do that, and then banged Monica's door loudly to attract her attention, it would make her think he was just arriving this morning!

That was what he did. Round to the front, checked that she wasn't looking over, and then banged the door loudly, and, not surprisingly, a voice came from across the road.

"Vicar, you are wasting your time. I wouldn't bother," she shouted over. "That one's never up before ten!"

Harold thanked her, turned on his heel, and went home with a smile on his face.

17 A LEAP FORWARD?

"Harold. That nosy cow across the road from me, stopped me on the way here. She said that you were trying to waken me this morning. Do you think she could see what we got up to through my venetian blinds?"

"No," said Harold. "I was outside. I confused her by knocking on your door before I left. She thought I was arriving."

"Oh! Sorry. Didn't hear you."

There was another gap in the conversation. It was one of these mornings.

"Last night, I didn't... Did I?" Monica asked.

"No, of course you didn't," Harold replied immediately.

"That sounded a bit patronising," she said suspiciously. "What didn't I do?"

"You didn't do whatever it was that you thought that you might have done. Or, wanted to do."

"Oh well... That's a relief."

There was a further silence. Two rhubarb tarts sat on the table uneaten, perhaps due to strong drink having been consumed to excess on the previous evening, which could also be one of the reasons why this morning's communication between them had been somewhat stilted, up to now.

"It didn't do it for me. You?"

"No."

"What went wrong, do you think?" she asked.

"Wrong type of relaxation...?" he offered.

"So, it should have been Perry Como? I thought so. If only it hadn't been scratched... "

"Doris Day was still playing when I woke up," said Harold. "I stopped it."

"Hope you did it the right way. It's a great radiogram. You realise it was set on repeat play. She must have been singing all night. Hope you didn't scratch that one."

There she goes again! Making it sound as if I'd done the damage. Glad we don't live together. I couldn't cope!

"Fancy a cup of tea?" he asked, hopeful that Monica would leap into action, as usual, and make one, but no...

"Yes, please," she said, and so it was his turn.

"I've been thinking," she said, after she'd taken a sip of his brew that was obviously not up to her standard and made a face before putting the cup down. "If it didn't work with whisky, why don't we try sherry?"

Harold's stomach had been telling him that he could try eating one of the tarts with the tea, but this new thought of over-indulging on sherry put him off.

"You're forgetting – I don't really know what causes the change. It happens differently each time," he said. "It could be just to do with me."

Monica's face immediately fell. She seemed to have

set her mind on sharing his experiences, even though that seemed highly unlikely, so he had to say something more promising.

"Oh well..." he added. "We could try sherry then..."

There would be another meal at Monica's. The chosen drink would be supplied by her, but as a giggle, now that his liking of whisky was no longer a secret to Monica, Harold decided to use his disguise. Trench coat, hat, and moustache. He looked in the mirror before he left home. "Harold you look good!" he said to his reflection.

"Can I help you?" was the greeting, as Monica opened the door. "Sorry, but I don't buy things on the doorstep from strange men," and closed it.

He knocked again. It was obvious from the time it took to reopen it, that she'd been reluctant to face him again.

"Look! I'm very busy – expecting a dear friend, so, please... get lost!"

"I had hoped that I was that friend..."

"Oh my goodness. What are you doing dressed liked that? It's not Halloween! Come in."

Not an auspicious start to the evening...

Eggs and bacon it would be tonight. He could smell it the moment he entered.

"Hmm... I'm looking forward to this," he said.

"I've already poured a sherry for you," and she pointed to where his glass sat. She had a part empty glass of sherry within easy reach as she stood beside the sizzling bacon. She emptied it and refilled it.

Harold lifted his, but it was sipped very slowly. He didn't like sherry.

"Another?" she asked before he'd finished the first.

"No, I'm doing ok, thanks."

As she carried the food over, Harold thought his egg was going to slide off the edge of a plate that was being held at a funny angle. It arrived in front of him just in time, and still on the plate.

"More?" she asked him as she held up the sherry bottle.

"No thanks. Maybe later," he suggested.

She'd refilled her glass before she sat at the table.

"Hope that'sh cooked well enough," she said. "I shuppose I should practish more."

After food, they sat opposite each other, same seats as last evening, but this time wearing normal clothing. No music. They were about to attempt a silent contemplative session.

Monica had suggested that – but silence it wasn't to be... She couldn't stop. She was rambling on about the future, how it was out there, waiting for her to arrive. Harold tried reminding her about the 'silent contemplation'.

"Why are you talking then?" was her comment. "You know, I should care, but I don't, if I'm not a cat. I would be pleashed to be a horsh! Or even a hippopotomush! I jusht want shomething to happen..." And then she fell sound asleep.

Harold sat on, glad that he'd barely sipped the sherry, and wondered if it would just be a short nap she would have, but two hours later, he concluded that she would sleep all night. He fetched a blanket and put it around her. He would return in the morning and make sure she was alright.

It was dark outside now. He peeped carefully out of the venetian blind at the house across the road. It was in darkness. Safe to leave without being observed. He switched off all the lights, checked once again that Monica was comfortable and closed the door quietly behind him...

It was a short, pleasant walk home, and all the better when stone-cold sober, he told himself.

When he got in, he immediately went up to bed, appreciating the silence of his own home. He was tempted to have a drop of his favourite fluid, but, remembering the effect it had last night on the two of them, he had a glass of tap water instead. That made him feel so righteous...

He wondered, when his head hit the pillow, if something would happen to him again. *My goodness*, he thought, *wouldn't it be strange if Scuffo were to arrive in the future – and come face to face with a hippopotomush...*

Morning seemed to arrive very quickly, and nothing untoward had happened. He felt bright and refreshed. Maybe it would be better, last thing at night, to always have a glass of water. Much healthier.

...Who am I kidding!

What would Monica be like this morning? Not having been to the future as she'd hoped. That would disappoint her, and, he also knew in his bones, that there was little chance of her being as bright and cheerful as he felt. *Maybe I could make her feel better by going round. No silly disguise this time. It hadn't impressed her.*

A lovely morning to be alive. The sun was shining and birds were singing, and he was whistling tunelessly, but quietly, as he strode along, minding his own business, when the voice said, "Pssst...!"

It was the neighbour. He was on her side the road, about to cross over to Monica's.

"Vicar...! I just noticed you there," she said, even though she'd been watching for the last half-hour in case she missed him. "It is you isn't it?" and she adjusted her glasses, leaning forward and peering at him. "I just thought I'd say – about across the road, and you'll know I don't like gossiping but, as her friend I think you should be aware... She's got another fella!"

Harold looked at her in amazement. That was shocking news. He'd known Monica for going on six years and he thought that they were close, and that they could maybe have moved into another stage in their relationship... She'd never given any hint whatsoever that she had another man friend.

"Oh...! She has, has she...? Oh dear... That's not good."

"Are you all right, Vicar? You look a little... peaky."

"Yes, I'll be OK. You go inside," he said. "I'll..." but, he wasn't sure what he should do.

I saw her only last night. Surely she hasn't been keeping him secret from me. Maybe I am only a good friend after all. He turned and, sadly, started to make his way back home. *Perhaps I offended her last night in my disguise...*

Wait a minute! That was me! I was the other fella that nosey cow saw!

He turned back at a run, crossed over, and rattled Monica's letterbox until she appeared, looking none too enthusiastic about life, until Harold grabbed her in his arms – and kissed her!

It took Monica some time to get over the shock. To suddenly jump from it being an almost purely platonic relationship with Harold, to being passionately kissed on her own doorstep... Wow!

She recovered a little when they were inside and he'd sort of apologised for taking her by surprise. He told her how much he had enjoyed that same sort of moment, a long time ago – when she had grabbed him like that –

but he had to remind her when it was!

"In the cubical – Marvello the Magnificent!" She'd clean forgotten. "Anyway, how are you, my dear Monica? Feeling better?"

The look that was returned didn't make it seem so.

"Did you ply me with strong drink again last night?" she said. "I suspected you were trying to get your wicked way with me?"

"No," he said, trying to remain calm, after such a momentous step in this love affair.

"Well, that's a disappointment," she said, sarcastically.

"If I might point out, you plied yourself with..." He hesitated. She wasn't exactly reacting with any fond emotion. "And, I couldn't possibly have had my wicked way because you were too desperate to become either a horsh, or a hippopotomush, to permit anything like that to happen!"

"Oh...? Then you should have tried to stop me drinking the stuff!"

He knew he was on a hiding to nothing this morning. He should have stayed at home.

"But I had a wonderful dream," she said.

"Oh, that's nice. What was it?"

"I was an alligator – and I bit your ruddy head off."

He wasn't helping her, was he? Only time, and an Alka Seltzer would do that. So, as it seemed wiser to leave her to suffer on her own ...he left.

18 ALL CHANGE

It was Monica who, figuratively, tiptoed back to him to say sorry, and brought a peace offering. It wasn't whisky, and it certainly wasn't sherry, but Harold was delighted – a fresh rhubarb tart. It was the simple things in life that mattered.

The moment she entered, the kettle was boiled by her, and without him even having to hint, he knew that an excellent cup of tea would be appear as if by magic. That was more than enough to placate him.

"I am really glad that you are hard skinned," she said, by way of apology as she handed him the cup of hot liquid, with her words being accompanied by an affectionate peck on his cheek.

The relationship had taken a leap forward! For Harold, after more than six years, it was a gigantic leap, and a delightful precursor to the humble pleasure of food and drink, but... "Ugh...!" he spluttered, as he took a sip. *What a disappointment! "No sugar ...and it's too blooming hot!"* which, unfortunately rather ruined the moment.

"Oh!" she said, flustered.

She had to admit that she still felt under the weather and really hadn't been concentrating properly. Back to the kitchen she went to fetch more milk and sugar.

God, I've said the wrong thing! A beautiful moment wasted!

He could have bitten off his tongue, but that was only the start... and how he did it, he didn't know, but spilling the hot tea all over his leg had an immediate dramatic effect!

"Aaahhh!"

Whoosh! And he was on the move again!

Monica returned, to find an empty chair, an uneaten rhubarb tart and an upturned plate on the floor beside an empty cup. There was also a large damp patch on the carpet.

But where was Harold?

She sighed. Off to the toilet... *Perfect timing. A typical man.*

What now? Scuffo's back paws were wet, and he was limping slightly as he moved across the floor. He was in a kitchen.

One that had obviously been refitted recently. It looked shiny and clean, and his paws left a damp trail on the new flooring.

He leapt onto the surface nearest the window.

Ah! A calendar on the wall, and there it was – 2002! He hadn't see it from the floor, and was glad that he wasn't having to search for it this time. Then, it hit him.

Gosh... That'll make me seventy-four. I'll no longer be young!

It came as a bit of a shock. He hadn't thought of the future in that way... about 'getting old'. He looked around this room from the higher level. It seemed familiar. His kitchen in Woldenham wasn't unlike this, but this was quite different in many ways, much brighter, with colours that he would never have thought of choosing, and a lot of equipment. Though work must still be in progress, it was still much tidier than his kitchen ever is. *A stainless-steel sink and look at all the cupboards under the surfaces too. Is that a fridge?* He had hoped that, some day, he would buy one.

His kitchen was cream. Always had been. So boring.

He padded to the window. It was partly opened and had been recently replaced with fresh new wood surrounds. He looked out. The view was immediately familiar. He was looking across at a church and a church hall – his!

He was in his own kitchen! *How about that!*

Oh, but this wouldn't be his kitchen now... *Seventy-four... Have I retired? Of course I have! I'll have been kicked out of here, probably. Obviously, I couldn't have afforded to do all these changes. Looks so much nicer. Someone new must be moving in. Ah well... Good luck to them. Wonder where I've gone?*

There was a piece of paper stuck on the kitchen door. 'Wet paint.'

He sniffed. Not a smell that he liked. *It's all just recently done...*

There was movement outside. Some people were going up the path to the church. Something was happening in there today. He could see black ties, but he could also see a lot of bright colours too. *Is that the top of a hearse that I can see over the church wall? It is. Won't be a funeral with people wearing colourful clothes...*

He jumped down. *Ouch!* He'd forgotten his back legs hurt. *The hot tea – that's what caused it and Monica's brew was usually perfect too. Still suffering from last night, she was! Last night? No. it wasn't. It was forty-three years ago.* He shivered. It was a strange feeling being in the future. It had been a novelty before but, now, he wasn't so sure he liked it.

He squeezed through the part open door, and into the hallway, hoping that the paint was dry and that he wouldn't have a streak of white on one side of his fur. Carpets were rolled up in the hallway, and paint brushes and closed paint pots were sitting beside folded dust sheets. A window was open, probably to clear fumes, he presumed. He stopped and listened. *Was that the organ being played in the church, the same funeral music that that horrible woman, Elsa, used to always play so badly?*

He felt sad, and it wasn't just the badly played organ. Time had certainly moved on and it was an uncomfortable feeling. Someone else now living in his vicarage, and that person would be officiating at the funeral, in what had been his church but was no longer his responsibility. New life takes over on the death of the old one. The unavoidable cycle. How often had he comforted the people of Woldenham when a loved one had passed on? That was someone else's duty now.

He looked around nostalgically. *I no longer live here... This is no longer my...*

Oh no!

It's my funeral! They're saying farewell to me!

He stood there shocked!

But not for long...

What the heck!

Scuffo straightened up. The sparkle came back into the eyes. *That isn't the way at all, thinking nothing but sad things! A positive approach. That's what's needed, and, my goodness, the look that will be on Monica's face when I return and tell her the story this time – provided I get back as usual. It will be worth a fortune. Yes! I'll go to my own funeral!*

And he did...

A latecomer was hurrying up the path, and, because so many were attending what was obviously a very important ceremony, he struggled to find a space.

Yes, a very nice turnout, Harold decided proudly.

They liked me!

As he slipped in, then he noticed the music. Lustily, at full volume, the congregation was now singing a really happy song. It didn't sound like a hymn. *Certainly not music that I would have approved for a funeral, especially mine, he thought. They seemed to be singing, "Can't buy me lo-ve... Can't buy me lo-ve..." It was more like a pop song.* He'd never heard of it.

Huh!

He was inside now. No-one had seen him. He looked around, but his view was very limited, being at the entrance and on the floor.

I could get a better look from the shelf...

The narrow shelf that ran all the way along the side of the church had, over the years, been both useful and a nuisance. He remembered how the ladies who'd volunteered to keep the church clean, had always complained that it was totally unnecessary and should never have been added in the first place – a dust collector.

Yet, those very same ladies would then praise themselves at the Flower Festivals, and at Harvest Thanksgivings, on how well they'd made use of that very same shelf. "Don't know how we'd manage without it!" they'd say.

...They haven't done brilliantly today though. Not a solitary decoration all the way along that same shelf. Did I ever say something to offend them? No! I kept lying, and telling them how clever they'd been. I did it with a straight face too, and this is the thanks I get...

Yes, if I want to see, going along that shelf would be perfect, so up he jumped up onto it.

The singing came to an end and everyone sat down, and that's when the cat, slowly working its way along the narrow shelf, was noticed. The whispering started. *Would someone do something?*

Then Harold heard a voice he recognised.

"Friends, we are gathered here today to celebrate the life of..."

That voice! It was his!

It was his own voice he was hearing. He was taking the service!

I am not dead! Hallelujah! MIAOW...!

The heads of everyone in the pews swung round to see a feline interloper, sitting on the shelf – in a state of delighted shock!

"I'll get rid of it, Vicar," said another voice that Harold recognised. A man stood up. He was so much older looking now. Young Freddie Fulton. Now a fine-looking fellow. His voice had barely broken back in '59.

"No, leave him, Freddie," said the Vicar. "He's not doing any harm, and anyway, Tommy would have been pleased that he's attended today. That cat's been a friend for a long time. It is you, Scuffo, isn't it?" he called out from the front of the church. "I had a feeling that you might pop in."

Miaow...

"Well," said the Reverend Harold Scuffington, if you'd all like to settle back comfortably, including Mr Cat, we'll return to the business in hand."

There was a general buzz, and knowing looks from a few, to indicate to others that they'd been aware all along that this vicar was crazy...

"We are gathered here today, to celebrate the long and eventful life of Mister Tommy Sinclair, a loyal and long serving member of this church, a very good friend to all of us, and a joiner who never really retired."

Nods all round. Everyone knew Tommy well. He'd done work in almost every house in Woldenham.

"He told me that he reckoned he'd had a good innings, and was almost ready to hang up his tools. At one hundred and five, I'd say it was about time."

Scuffo sat where he was and gazed at the man taking the service. Harold, could hardly believe he was looking at himself standing there – bald and fat!

When did I let myself go? He felt quite guilty, because he immediately realised the probable cause – the rhubarb tarts! Daily! They were addictive. That could be a dilemma when he returned. He was sure that Monica wouldn't want to change that routine either.

It was something to think about...

As it was, he was a cat and getting fidgety, and the sermon was being ignored by him, now that he realised that he wasn't in that long box.

Scuffo wanted a better view.

All he was seeing was the backs of heads, so, he stood and slowly made his way along the narrow ledge. Eyes turned as he passed and he was noticed, but the watchers remained silent this time. Working his way along the shelf he could almost reach the front. There he would be able to look back at everyone sitting in the pews and maybe recognise a few more old codgers.

That's when he saw her – Monica! Sitting near the centre passageway, in the front row, with eyes only for the Vicar, it seemed – but, she'd hardly changed. Her hair was a little grey admittedly, but she wasn't plump, like him. How did she manage that? She'd eaten as many tarts as he had!

Scuffo jumped down from the shelf and padded silently along towards her, but every person he passed in the row wanted to pet him, so he had to be tolerant and let them.

"Sit on my knee," she whispered when he eventually reached her. It was as if she too had been expecting him. Together, they continued listening to the wise words of the Reverend Harold Scuffington.

"...And wouldn't stop. Determined until the end he was. The shed, in the church grounds, that he erected more than eighty years ago and said that I was too old to repair. Me... Too old! He wanted to do it himself. 'It is really my shed,' he declared. 'So, I have the right to do it. You hold the ladder.' I told him that I doubted the strength of the roof structure, but he pooh-poohed me – but I was right. When it gave way and he dropped through the middle, I had to tell myself, it was the way he'd want to go. He was a great joiner... Now, we will stand, and link hands, and sing the other song, as he stated in his will for us to use. It's the second one on your hymn sheet. 'We all live in a Yellow Submarine.'"

As old Elsa Middleton struggled to play the introduction on the church organ, Monica whispered in Scuffo's ear, "He liked the Beatle's..."

19 STAYING WITH RELATIVES

The service ended and the coffin was carried out to the church graveyard. The deep hole was ready to receive the casket of a one-off deceased joiner, a casket prepared by Tommy for himself, nearly ten years ago. "Why pay someone if you can do it yourself," he'd told anyone who asked.

Tommy and his wife had no family themselves, and as she had died forty years past and Tommy had outlived all his relatives, the mourners who attended his funeral were all friends and neighbours. They took a long time to disperse after the ceremony but, eventually, a stillness returned to the church grounds.

Monica, with Scuffo cuddled in her arms, had watched from the distance as the Reverend officiated at the graveside. The three of them returned to the house afterwards and Scuffo was placed on the floor. Monica refilled the water dish, lying there.

So, who was moving in then? Harold was curious and would love to have been able to talk to himself, though that would have been a bit strange, but there was so much he wanted to know.

Where were they going if someone else was moving

in? Then it occurred to him, he was thinking of the Reverend and Monica as being coupled – confirmed as soon as he looked at her left hand. Of course. There it was. They were married.

Oh-ho! Wait till I return with that news... My goodness! Young Monica will have something to say! Wonder how and when it happened? I knew I'd do it – eventually!

Monica was removing a necklace she'd been wearing. It looked valuable.

"Aunt Mabel couldn't have passed away at a more suitable time," she said.

"I thought she'd never go," responded the Reverend.

"At least we know where all her money came from, even though she didn't. Good old Uncle Syd refused to tell her how he achieved his initial fortune. She never did find out that we were feeding him winners. I think we deserve it. It was big money in the end and he'd be pleased that we've been able to put it to such good use. Not so sure about Aunt Mabel though..." She gave a chuckle, and then went more serious. "It would have been terrible to have had to give up this place."

"Yes... Love you Auntie Mabel! Wherever you are!" plump Harold cried out cheerfully. "Can't be many vicars who can buy their own vicarage. I thought we'd have been kicked out last year. Now, money is no object."

"Go easy though, Harold," said Monica, with a slightly forced smile. "Remember, although she promised it to us, we haven't had confirmation... yet. Don't go wild."

Scuffo looked around the kitchen. It looked too late to say that. A new freezer, a new fridge, a dishwasher, a microwave oven...

"Never realised how easy it could be to buy on-line," said Harold. "Glad young Freddie showed me how, and nice of him to give me his old PC. Said it would just be thrown out. That would have been a waste, and it's worked for me."

"Don't know how you do it, because I haven't a clue!" she said. "You are not bad for an old fellow Harold."

"It's an iPad for you, next – oh, and one of these large smart TVs for the front room. Have to wait till late tonight to order that, though. Faster speed on the internet then – young Freddie tells me. Ridiculous! For the size and population of the towns now, we should expect a better service! Freddie said that too..."

Scuffo was settling on the cat mat in the corner, taking all this in. *There'd been so many changes over the years, and who was this Aunt Mabel who'd died?* Harold had never heard Monica mention an aunt before. *That's an important question for when I go back, he decided, and if she's rich, getting to know her would be a good idea. Having a rich relative must be nice – I've never had one!*

Time for a snooze. I'll catch up with the gossip later...

Great excitement this morning! The Reverend had left early – to collect his new car from a garage in Codgestone.

"This is going to be fun, Scuffo," said Monica. "He'll be back soon. Wonder where he'll take us for the first run?" Her eyes lifted skywards. "Oh thank you again, Aunt Mabel," she said fervently.

She was like an excited child, going back and forward to the front room window.

"Hope he can remember how to drive," she said with a giggle. "It's such a long time since he passed his test. Must be fifteen years – at least."

Only just getting the chance to prove his driving skills now? Oh-oh, thought Harold. Sounds like a recipe for disaster. Miaow...

"We are both looking forward to this, aren't we? I think you are as excited as I am, Scuffo," and she bent down and ruffled his fur.

Worried, rather than excited. Miaow...

"You'll be going too. The three of us can be together. Together – like we always are."

Now, that confused him a little. Didn't he just arrive with them yesterday?

Miaow...

A horn sounded outside.

"Here he is now. I should have stayed at the window. I did so want to see him arrive..."

The horn sounded again.

"You stay in just now, Scuffo," she said, and out she went.

A shiny new red sports car would be sitting at the kerb waiting for her, like the type he was always admiring in the car magazines. His mature self would not have lost that dream in the passing of time, and if they now have the money...

Back came Monica.

"Right," she said, grabbing a jumper, and giving Scuffo the nod. "Let's go!"

It wasn't a sports car.

Scuffo walked round the vehicle slowly. *What a disappointment. A dull green used Ford Fiesta, with two doors.* Is this all he had to look forward to? A shattered dream... His future – an ordinary little family car? And it wasn't even red!

...But at least I passed the Driving Test.

"Where is he?" The Reverend was eager to get on the move again. "Scuffo! Don't go under the car. That's dangerous."

"Have you looked under there?" Harold wanted to ask the Reverend. *"Have you seen the state of that exhaust? It's about to fall off."* Miaow...

"Nice to have your approval, Scuffo," said the Reverend. "Now, jump inside."

Monica was already in, seat adjusted, safety belt on, and ready to go.

"Hold on tight, everybody," was the warning, as the

engine was started and revved up a few times. Into first gear, and moved forward, and into second, and... Stalled!

"Damn!" said the Reverend, then realised he shouldn't have said that. "Sorry. We'll try again."

Scuffo had landed on the floor, having bounced off the back of the front seat – one of the perils of sitting unbelted at the back, so, he was pleased that the driver was a bit more successful the second time, and they were on their way.

He heard it being mentioned last night that Woldenham and Codgestone had merged. That felt very odd to Harold. He'd always preferred being insulated from the busy town life and living in Woldenham village did that for him. Three miles between the two places, now filled with houses.

As they drove along the main street in Codgestone, Harold was really disappointed to see that almost all the original shops were no longer there. Even the liquor store where he bought his whisky, in disguise, had gone. It was now a Bookmaker. All the big charities that he knew, and some he hadn't heard of, had filled a lot of the spaces, but the place looked very run-down. So much rubbish about too. Shouldn't people complain to the Council?

"How do you like it, Monica? Only one hundred and twenty thousand miles on the clock. Yes, it's what I've dreamed of all my life..."

Hmmm... What a whopper, thought Harold. Miaow...

They went to the seaside, to the cliffs. They stopped and gazed at the skyline for a time, but that was a bad idea – the Reverend had difficulty getting the car going again. Harold was not happy about the Reverend having parked looking out to sea, facing the edge... It reminded him of the Hells' Angel granny, and he was afraid that that was where the story could be about to go, but no. They drove down onto the promenade and parked there. There was no-one else about, it being a chilly day.

"An ice-cream, Harold. We'll have to have one now we're here."

"Of course, dear."

Scuffo was left in the car.

It was a bit nippy outside and no-one was silly enough to be sitting on the benches. The cones were bought in the deserted Beach Café, and out they came again.

"Not inside the car. If the ice cream dripped on the carpets and seats... Sitting on the bench would be nice," said the Reverend, so that's what they did.

Monica managed two minutes, then left him in the cold and returned to the slight warmth of the car, with her cone. Harold lasted another three minutes.

"Want a lick, Scuffo?" Monica asked, and held the cone to his mouth. Scuffo couldn't resist and took a few licks, but Harold thought, *"Giving me a lick of your ice-cream? I am a cat! Hope you are not going to eat it yourself now,"* but she did.

"Just be careful, dear. Drips!" said the Reverend, even though the carpets and seats were well stained already. Hadn't he noticed that, wondered Harold...

"What does that sign say, Monica. That one over there. Can't quite make it out."

Monica could read it quite clearly, as could Scuffo.

"It says that there is no parking on the promenade, Harold. That's where we are, isn't it? Maybe we should move?"

"No need to panic, Monica. Traffic Wardens never come down to this part."

They carried on licking the cones, and then sat gazing at the waves washing gently over the shingle beach.

Miaow!

The Reverend smiled benignly at Scuffo. "You obviously like the car then, Scuffo," he said.

Miaow! Miaow!

"Yes, I know, you like it a lot. I can tell."

Look in the rear-view mirror, you silly old duffer! MIAOW! Too late...

"Excuse me, sir. Would you wind the window fully down, please?"

"Oh yes, Officer. Can I help you?" said the Reverend.

"Have you read the notice across there, sir?"

"Yes, of course, Officer, well, my wife did."

"And you are still here?"

"We were finishing our cones, Officer."

"Oh well, that would make it alright, then..." Scuffo appreciated the sarcasm. The Reverend did not and was about to make another silly comment. Luckily, Monica was in the car.

"It's really my fault," she said in a little girly voice. "It's such a beautiful spot that I insisted he stop here – but only for a moment."

The Police Officer was about to say that he'd been watching from a distance and that her moment had been a very long one, but he didn't get the chance.

"It's where he proposed marriage, and I accepted. Thirty years ago, today, on this very spot. We didn't have a car then. This is our first one and our first outing in it. It would be terrible if my dear husband, (you may have heard of him?) the Reverend Harold Scuffington, a highly respected minister of the church, were to be arrested and put in jail on this very special day."

She gave a slight sob. Harold couldn't see her face but, he was sure that she would have managed to conjure up a little tear. He remembered similar situations, a trick she'd used on him... and it still worked.

"And was the cat your bridesmaid?" was asked sarcastically, because the constable didn't believe a word. "Well... This time, take it as a warning," he said, and gave the car roof a double slap – as policemen do, and walked off.

The Reverend breathed a sigh of relief, glanced at his wife gratefully, and started the engine, put it into gear, and kangarooed off. As they passed the policeman, Monica gave him a wave. He didn't wave back...

It was obvious that the Reverend's biggest problem was getting started from stopped. On the move, his driving didn't seem nearly so bad, but, all the same, Scuffo sat in the middle of the back seat so that he could see out of the front windscreen. He didn't trust his older self's eyesight.

"Could we go back the long way?" asked Monica. "Have a look at the house. Just make sure it's properly locked up. It would be terrible if vandals could get in and do damage. We'll have to make arrangements for the sale, tomorrow. I've made an appointment. The Estate Agent will be there at three."

Going the long way would not have been Harold's choice. He was a bad traveller, even when he was Scuffo, and the Reverend's driving was...

Whoops! That was close! Wonder if he even saw it?

They arrived at the house.

This was where rich Aunt Mabel had lived ever since marrying Uncle Syd. To Harold, it looked like a mini-palace. Various extensions over the years had changed the original shape. It looked spectacular and was complimented by the extensive garden that had been well cared for, too.

The Reverend drove through the open gate and up the long driveway and being able to drive completely around the building was a relief for the Reverend. He knew that he wasn't up to the challenge of a three-point turn.

The front and back doors were checked and were ok, as were all the windows, but when they were leaving, Monica decided that it would be safer if the gates were closed. There was a chain and padlock. Monica had the key, but it was the Reverend who had the struggle. That gate had not been closed for a long time, but he managed, eventually, so it was secure when they left.

Looking back, as they drove off, Harold reckoned that Monica's Aunt Mabel had known how to enjoy her riches.

Sitting in the back seat, ever watchful, Scuffo witnessed several close shaves. Their survival, in Harold's mind, was largely due to the skills of avoidance by other drivers. His older self certainly lacked experience. The roads were really busy, and what a difference in traffic. To Harold, it looked like every person in the country owned a car now! Recognising Woldenham was a relief. Almost home. Hooray! They'd made it in one piece.

"Are you leaving it on the driveway, Harold? It would let everyone know that we own a motor car now," suggested Monica as they approached the church.

"A good idea, Monica," he replied, as he swung the wheel, to pass between the two stone pillars.

Bump!! Screech...! "Oh, shouldn't have gone so close. Get it repaired tomorrow..."

20 HOME SWEET HOME

No return journey yet. Harold was still Scuffo, the cat, and that cat was being nosey...

He would have been happy to be back in real time, in '59, telling Monica all about what he now knew of the future, their future – together! It would shock her, he was sure of that. Instead, here he was wandering around his own home, the home he had been living in for nearly six years, and forty-three years later finding how different it looked. Apparently, all due to a windfall – a substantial one.

Incredible what money can do. The walls were still in the same positions, but he recognised little of the contents. Furniture, carpeting, decoration. Must have been Monica that chose all this. He'd have been clueless.

Something saddened him. He saw the usual collection of framed photographs on display, but they were almost all of Monica and him through the years, but no photos of youngsters. That would have been something to look forward to, but obviously it hadn't happened for them.

He was surprised to find photos of a cat and it looked very much like him. There were others that showed the three of them, Monica, himself, and a cat. It looked like him, but it couldn't be, not Scuffo he reasoned, because

he was Scuffo and he couldn't be two beings at one time
– simple. Except now! Here he was padding around, quite
definitely a cat – while, guess who was lying snoring, in
the double bed beside Monica – he was!

*It makes no sense, but some things I just have to
accept,* he decided. Seeing the enlarged, glossy, black
and white photo of a minister in a dog collar, hanging
onto the church hall flagpole, had been a surprise. It was
the one from when he'd starred in the local paper. It was
nicely framed and had pride of place above their bed. *I
wasn't too proud about that at the time when it
happened but, I must have got over it...*

Something buzzed on the bedside table. A hand
reached out from under the bedclothes and grabbed the
device.

"You promised to switch off your phone at night,
Monica," complained a muffled, grumpy voice from
under the bedclothes.

"Sorry!" she said, insincerely and pleased that it had
wakened him too. She opened the phone's cover – and
immediately sat up straight. "Harold! Read this!" She
whipped the bedclothes off his face and shoved the
phone in front of it. "It's from Gosling and Partridge –
New York."

"Oh, for goodness sake!" He rubbed his eyes and took
hold of the phone and looked at it. "It's from your Aunt's
solicitors, so...?" he reached over to the table at his side
and lifted his reading specs.

"Oh!" said the Reverend. "Not again!"

In the morning, as soon as the London office opened, Monica was on the phone. They'd have to go to there.

"Sorry. Can't be discussed on the phone," she was told. "Could you be here for this afternoon, Mrs Scuffington? A meeting with Mr Bird."

"But we live in..." Monica started to say, but Harold, who'd been listening too, interjected.

"I'll drive you down," he said, confidently.

After the telephone conversation, dressing took very little time. Similarly, for breakfast, which consisted of a gulped glass of cold water from the tap, and a chocolate digestive biscuit each, and it was into the new car.

Scuffo had not been invited this time, but he decided to slip into the back seat anyway. He was curious. He didn't think that they'd even noticed that he was there, such was the panic. The crunching of gears was not a good omen, neither was stalling twice before reaching the road. Then, they were on their way.

Scuffo sat upright and tense. It would take them all their time to get there. Monica would be navigating and had the road atlas open on her knees, but they were moving slowly in traffic that was even heavier than last night. Then there was a clear stretch. The Reverend speeded up, but the state he was in, being quite agitated, didn't boost Harold's confidence, and he could feel, in his bones that it would be only a matter of time before...

No doubt, the group at the zebra crossing were

perfectly within their rights in stepping confidently onto the road, expecting traffic to stop for them, but it surprised the Reverend. He slammed his foot on the brake – his driving instructor would have been proud of him, and the car screeched to a halt, short of the pedestrians, but poor Scuffo suffered.

He shot, like a bullet, in between the front seats, towards the windscreen...

"What..?" Monica gasped and blinked. She could only be surprised by his sudden reappearance. "The chair was empty. I thought you..."

There had been no sound this time, yet there he was, seated uncomfortably in the chair again in front of her, trousers with a damp dark mark that looked remarkably like he'd wet himself, the empty cup and rhubarb tart at his feet.

She forced herself to breath normally again. What a relief! He was safe, but did a transfer have be quite so dramatic? Did nothing for the nerves...

"Monica, I have a few things to report," said Harold in a shaky voice.

Monica replaced his tea, freshly made and, for safety's sake, in a mug that was placed on a little table in front of him. Nothing could be done about his rhubarb tart.

She would gladly have given him hers, but she'd already scoffed it.

"You've been away," she guessed. "And here was me thinking you were in the... Ah, well, never mind."

For Monica, there was no doubt now. Harold really did go where he said he did, and it made her feel a little envious. It always seemed so exciting when he explained what he'd done and seen. To her, the future was fascinating.

"Monica, we get married," he announced, then hesitated. "...So, how do you fancy that?"

"Ok with me," she said. "When is it happening then? But, wait a minute! Harold, aren't you supposed to be on bended knee when you propose, and in dry trousers? At last. It's taken you long enough!"

It wasn't at all the way he'd expected it to happen. There should have been some more romance to it, surely – music and flowers, and an engagement ring! She hadn't even been surprised? He didn't expect her to...

Another thing, he suddenly realised, in the future where he'd just been, she'd lied! In the car, parked wrongly on the promenade, she told that policeman that he'd proposed to her thirty years ago, and on that very spot... What a load of nonsense, but they'd made a commitment now... and painlessly, thank goodness.

Harold was happy. He could relax. At long last, he'd got that out of the way, and it only took him six years to get around to it.

There was another important matter.

"Aunt Mabel," he said.

"Aunt Mabel? What about Aunt Mabel?"

"You never mentioned her."

"No. Why should I?"

"Well, I thought that..." He'd been expecting a simple answer.

"What's my Aunt Mabel got to do with you?" The eyebrows had lowered. Now that wasn't a good sign.

"It's just... You've never mentioned her to me, have you?"

"Then how do you know about my Aunt Mabel then? Have you found out something? Is it naughty?" She was fishing. "Are there still another two men in her life? Charles and Joseph? Of course, one fancy man could never be enough for Aunt Mabel. I always suspected that's the way it would go. Poor Uncle Syd. Sex mad, she is! Anyway, she's never liked me."

This was not the reaction he'd expected.

"Don't know why he puts up with it. Him, a lovely man, away on business most of the time, and her, taking full advantage on every occasion of both him and his money. He must know what's going on ...surely."

"Is she rich?" Harold asked, expecting to be told it's none of his business.

"Not really. It's all Uncle Syd's money she uses. He is. She's about five years younger than him. Her with a constitution like an ox and guaranteed to outlive him. He's not a well man..."

"Do you ever see them?"

"Not since Mummy died. Aunt Mabel's her younger sister – much younger. I told you, she's never liked me. But, wait a moment, why are you so interested?"

"She leaves you her fortune..."

Monica's face brightened up immediately.

"But don't take that as gospel. There could be a snag."

"Don't take it as... A snag?" She wasn't quite so bright now.

"I had to leave before I could find out what happened. There was something about another will, and you might not be in it, and if so, we could end up owing lots of money!" He wasn't doing a good job of explaining, and he didn't like the look she was giving him. "I'm sorry but I didn't come away deliberately. It was that idiot's driving that did it."

"What idiot?"

"Well..." and it seemed a bit daft to him as he said it. "It was me."

It sounded odd to her too. "I thought you were a cat."

"My older self, I meant. I'm a lousy driver it turns out."

He wanted to start all over again. It had seemed a much brighter future than he was managing to explain now. A bit like the village bonfire night, when he was supposed to do the needful and the matches failed to light. He'd lost that spark again!

"And when do I get this fortune... or maybe not?" she asked sarcastically.

"You only have to wait..." and he did a quick mental calculation, then didn't want to say, "...forty-three years."

"Oh, thanks a bunch," she said, as if it was his fault. "So we don't know what happened after you left them? You should have stayed for that bit. It's us we are talking about, Harold! You blew up my balloon, and then you took a pin... It is most inconsiderate of you!"

What could he say? He was only reporting what he'd learned, and to his mind it wasn't so bad. *Something good would be happening eventually – a long way off. Could they maybe improve their prospects and bring the good fortune closer...?*

"Maybe we could... change the future?" he suggested meekly.

"How?" she sighed. She wasn't in the mood for one of his long philosophical discussions.

"Make your Aunt Mabel like you?"

"No!"

That was pretty definite.

"Or work on your Uncle Syd. Show him that you have an astute brain."

"Me? An astute brain? Are you taking the mickey, Harold?"

"Think about it. We know something about the future, we could maybe exploit that. Business is always having to guess about future prospects. Perhaps I could learn what actually does happen and tell you."

Her eyebrows raised at that comment. "And I could

tell him, like a fortune teller? Without mentioning you, or Scuffo?"

"Indeed, and when time proves you right, you get a reward... perhaps."

"Can you find out more?" she was hooked now, and that made him feel a little better. It was a bit hair-brained but it could maybe work. "You can go back can't you? Learn some useful stuff. Like the stock market and that sort of thing? Would another cup of hot tea over your trousers send you off again?"

"I'd rather not try just now, if you don't mind," he said sheepishly, with cold wet trousers sticking to his legs, then he asked, as an afterthought, "Do you want to stay the night?"

21 A PLAN

Harold got short shrift, inviting her to stay. Until he put a wedding ring on the third finger of her left hand, she was only his future wife, and she was resolute. Until they married, she would be remaining virtuous, whether he liked it or not, so it was off to bed alone for Harold. Anyway, a good night's sleep would do him good, but he would have been more likely to have a good night if she'd stayed with him. His back was really painful. *She could have applied embrocation.*

Monica went home alone, and straight to bed. She wouldn't sleep, she just knew. Being destined to be rich, maybe, one day, was praying on her mind. Though, wouldn't it be nicer if that one day was sooner, rather than later? *Could they make that happen?*

Both lay awake, separately, with the opportunity to think of a plan – then both fell fast asleep.

Over the weeks they racked their brains, but neither could think of a good approach for Uncle Syd. Harold would have liked to have been able to choose how far ahead in time he would travel, because it was a venture into the unknown almost every time. Rarely did he return to a specific date.

It was Monica who came up with the idea.

"Horse racing!" she exclaimed one day.

The blank look on Harold's face showed his total ignorance of both horses, and racing.

"Uncle Syd has always enjoyed a little flutter with his local bookie. If we could convince him that I am psychic and able to foresee, for certain, which horse would win a race, he could make a lot of money, and maybe one day become a bookmaker himself, and be in complete control of all his betting. He'd make a fortune that way and be grateful to me."

This was the young lady who'd criticised Harold for even thinking about betting! "Shouldn't we just place the bets ourselves and have winners all the time – make our own fortune?" asked Harold.

"Oh no," said his future wife. "That would be dishonest!"

Harold couldn't see either way as being honest, but agreed that it was worth a try.

"It's simple! All we need is the 1960 version of the Horse Racing Almanac," she declared. "That will tell us all the winners for next year."

"And where would we get that?"

"From the library, or a bookshop – in 1961!"

"Oh! And that's easy?"

"Yes. All we need do, is work out how to get you to the right place, in the right year... We'll have to experiment."

Harold wasn't looking forward to this – he would be the guinea pig.

And the trials began...

Monica requested a current copy of the Horse Racing Almanac. That caused raised eyebrows at Codgestone Public Library, because, to the librarian, neither Monica nor the Reverend Harold Scuffington standing beside her, appeared to be the type to be inveterate gamblers, but it was located and handed over. Of course, the librarian's eyebrows would have risen even higher, if Monica had explained it wasn't for gambling – it was to be used by her to strike the Reverend Harold Scuffington on the head.

Controlled doses of whisky, coupled with Harold being hit unexpectedly by the Horse Racing Almanac, was Monica's idea, but other than Harold having a sore head every night when he retired to bed, it was having no effect.

Then one night, it did work!

Luckily, Monica had been recording the combinations of the various failed attempts, in order to avoid repetition, and

The Glenlivet now was no longer the prescribed alcohol.

Along the way, Glen Grant had also proved a failure, so she was happy when, at last, the combination of three tablespoons of Macallan, followed by two soft taps and two hard ones – using the 1959 Horse Racing Almanac, led to a 'whoosh...' and Harold vanished from under her nose.

There he was, in Codgestone Public Library.

He'd done it – well almost! Scuffo had taken a time trip to 1962. Harold could tell because the librarian always had the date displayed behind her working area. It was on a large board with interchangeable numbers and had been in that position long before he ever came to Woldenham.

It was the correct location and he'd almost reached the correct year.

Scuffo was in Codgestone Library again. Well done Monica! All that he had to do now was find where the paperback copy of the Horse Racing Almanac was. He should be able to collect the two previous years, rather than just one. He remembered from his last visit where the books should be and went straight there. Still laid out the same way. When he found 1960 and 1961, he found 1959 too, and decided to take them all.

Oh dear, not him again, thought the librarian when William Walters approached her. Can he never find anything on his own? All these returns to be put on shelves and he's going to drag me away.

"Miss Jones," he said politely. "Should a cat be in the Sports Section?"

Well, at least it's a simple question this time, she thought, and carried on moving the returned books around as she answered, "Of course not, Mr Walters, it should be in the Animals Section. Someone has been a silly Billy, obviously. If you leave it on the table over there, I'll put it away in the proper place when I've finished here."

"Oh dear me, no, Miss Jones. I am not going to touch it. That's your job."

She froze! How she hated awkward customers, and so many came into her library, but she kept calm.

"Well, just leave it where it is then." That was said somewhat sharply. "I'll be over there shortly."

"...And I think you'd better bring a mop, because I think it piddled on the floor."

"Yes, Mr Walters. I'll do that," she said, carrying on replacing the books. She gave herself a figurative pat on the bag for being so tolerant with him, and then had second thoughts. What was he talking about?

Oh no, he's coming back!

"Miss Jones. You are responsible for the stock in this library, aren't you?"

"Yes, Mr Walters," she sighed.

"And, if books were being removed from the library without you stamping them first, that would be wrong?"

"Yes. Mr Walters..."

"Then, why are you not stopping that cat? It's just taken three books out of the door."

Scuffo had reached the pavement with the three paperbacks in his mouth, which was rather awkward, and was wondering how he'd ever manage to return home with them, when the librarian appeared at the door.

"Stop that cat!" she yelled and ran towards him.

Instinctively, Scuffo leapt off the pavement, into the path of a motor-bike, and *whoosh*...

For Harold, the taste of the wet card of the well-handled book covers in his mouth was not pleasant, but he was pleased with himself. Scuffo had been and got what they needed and brought them back home! Exactly as they'd hoped, and there they sat, on the table – a copy for this year's winners, next year's, and the year after's. The Horse Racing Almanacs. There was a little dried saliva on the covers! So what? They were now in business, and they could start right away...

"Uncle Syd?" Yes, it was the right number she dialled, so she put the coins in the slot, and pressed button A. "Hello. I hope you remember me," said Monica. She was standing in the red GPO telephone call-box in the middle of the village. "It's been a long time since I spoke to you... Yes... I was wondering if we could maybe meet sometime. I've had a wonderful idea..."

For Harold, going to Codgestone Public Library the following day with Monica, felt more awkward than his last visit – which was as Scuffo, yesterday, three years in advance! When he nodded to the librarian on the way in, he was expecting her to shout at him, "You! My books! What have you done with them? You're barred!" but she smiled and said, "Good Morning."

They were here for research because Harold was sure that somewhere, in the not too distant future, betting laws would be changing. He'd remembered reading in the Guardian of a Government plan for a committee to look at the existing archaic rules on gambling. Harold and Monica hoped they'd locate a back copy of the newspaper for confirmation, or at least familiarise themselves with the current details.

"Morning," was said, automatically, by Harold to the fellow approaching the librarian's desk. Recognition came after they passed.

"Miss Jones, if I could have your help? This book..."

"Yes, Mr Walters," said Miss Jones, in a resigned voice, "...and what is the trouble this time...?"

In his time travels, one of the pieces of apparatus that Harold had come across was a photocopier. How much simpler life would have been that morning, if one of these had been available in the library, but no, that would still be many years in the future.

Today, they made copious pencil and paper notes. When they left carrying their notebooks, Harold was relieved that this time no-one chased him.

The meeting with Uncle Syd was to be at his home, only a fifteen-minute journey if she'd used her bicycle, but she'd decided that today it would be by local bus. That took considerably longer. She had to get one into

Codgestone, and then wait for another to take her the four miles to the other side of the town. It seemed to be taking forever because the second bus was late. Standing at the terminus in Codgestone she wished she'd cycled but, even more frustrating was seeing Uncle Syd drive by!

When she eventually arrived, Aunt Mabel was there too.

It was a frosty reception – not from Uncle Syd, but the gap since the last meeting with Aunt Mabel had not made her any friendlier. Monica had expected her to be gadding about somewhere, possibly with one of her boyfriends, but no, there she was, glaring at her. Mabel was only seven years older than her niece, but Monica suspected she was seen as a rival for her Uncle's affections. When she was younger, he had always been more interested than Aunt Mabel in what she'd been getting up to.

"I am so sorry!" Aunt Mabel announced. She was having to go to an urgent engagement, one, unfortunately, that couldn't possibly be postponed.

Monica was delighted!

"It would have been lovely to get to know you again, my dear niece," she added. Monica suspiciously took this to be a sarcastic comment. The farewell peck on each cheek from her aunt also felt grudged.

Uncle Syd was a great man. Not a blood relative, but so much friendlier towards her than his wife, and that made Monica feel ever so slightly guilty because what she was about to tell him would be downright lies. But surely it wouldn't matter if it was to his benefit? She'd tried to convince herself about that. The more important thing was that it could benefit her and Harold in the long run – they hoped!

"I am getting married," she told him, the first person to know other than Harold.

"Lovely, Monica," he said, genuinely pleased. "When's the big day?"

"Oh, could be years away, the rate Harold goes. I've known him for six years. Taken him all that time to work up courage to ask!"

"So, is that what you wanted to talk about?"

"There is something else," she said. "I think I am psychic! I seem to imagine what the future could be and it happens. A simple example is with horse racing. I remembered you liked that, and, as a game I started choosing horses."

"Better not tell your Aunt Mabel that I was an influence," he smiled.

"...And each time they've been winning!"

"Good for you – but probably just luck," he said. "Have you put it to use? A fly bet, for example?"

"Oh no..." she said, piously. "I couldn't do that, not in Woldenham, everyone would know, and anyway, I meant to say that, Harold, he is the minister. He wouldn't be pleased..."

"And...?" he was interested.

"Well... I remembered that you used to tell me you liked a flutter."

"Still do!" he said, "But getting it right more often would be nice."

Monica was feeling more confident now.

"And I remember you saying that it felt great to beat the bookmaker, and if you could do it more regularly, you might become one yourself."

"And...?"

"It was just an idea of course but, if I could guarantee winners, I reckoned that you..."

His eyes lit up immediately!

"I left a list with him," she told Harold when she returned.

"And you didn't mention Scuffo, or my travels?"

"Of course not. That's our secret..."

The Horse Racing Almanac for 1959 had been well used. It had been a hard task for her, memorising so many horses names, never mind which races they competed in and when and where they were happening, but even if she hadn't left a perfectly correct list, it should be pretty impressive for Uncle Syd – after the races were run.

And it was. Five weeks later, she received a letter, from Uncle Syd.

'Been making use of some of my contacts, since I saw

you. Impressed with the results of the races you left. Made a few bob on bets myself, thanks to you, so I owe you. As you suggested I've been looking at the possibility of setting up a bookmaking business once the legislation is sorted out. I even have a slogan. 'For the Best Bet – Syd's Your Man'. I haven't mentioned any of this to your aunt, and I presume your Harold doesn't know either. Thought it could become a secret business deal between you and me if it goes ahead, that is, if you are able to continue foreseeing winners. Anything for the 4.30, Saturday, at Aintree?'

22 CITY LIFE

A pretence at normality had to go on for Harold. He put in an appearance at the occasional church social and, now and again, showed up at the various small Church groups run by the ladies of the village – those dedicated do-gooders who churned away collectively at a variety of mundane self-inflicted duties for the community. He didn't want them to think he'd abandoned them totally, but his double life as Scuffo was of much greater interest, and quite exhausting.

Monica was still recording and experimenting with different ideas but, landing in Codgestone Library, in the correct year – and having intended it, was obviously pure luck, because subsequent visits had been totally random. All Harold knew for certain, was that the pain from jamming his fingers in the kitchen drawer had been the current trigger.

...So, where was he now?

The noise!

Scuffo was at the bottom of an empty, giant metal container, suffering the continuous growl of passing traffic at its worst during the peak period. He didn't choose to be there. He'd no idea where he'd landed this time, and though there was no top on the container, all he could see was the sky, and the face of an adjacent building, and that gave no clues. He wanted out. He'd tried leaping to grab the edge, but the sides were too high and the surface too smooth for him to scramble up and escape. If he'd still been Harold he could at least have sat and twiddled his thumbs, but, being Scuffo, he was prowling around in frustration. He could do that only for so long, because it got boring. It was too noisy to have a snooze – but he was going to try...

BANG!

Oh my goodness, what was that?!

BANG! BANG! BANG!

Large lumps of masonry were raining down. With his dodgy back, craning his neck to look up, in order to perform panicky avoidance, was not the easiest thing to do – but it was essential for survival!

BANG!

Not masonry this time – a plank of wood. Salvation! Hallelujah! It had dropped in at an angle and stuck. An emergency exit! Up he went at the double, leaping the remaining gap, and grabbing the edge.

Now he could see what was going on. He was in a large skip, sitting at the side of the road, outside a shop that was being refitted. Two men were preparing a ramp for a wheelbarrow, but the third was throwing scrap in by hand.

"You nearly killed me!" yelled Harold angrily, and really loudly, in competition with the traffic noise, but all the men heard was, *MIAOW!*

"A ruddy cat's been in there," said the one standing doing the throwing, and then with a wicked grin, shouted to the other two, "Watch me hit it!" and threw the lump of masonry in his hand. The aim was terrible. Scuffo was ready to dodge, but he didn't have to. It sailed passed.

Crash!

It was Scuffo's turn for a wicked grin, as he jumped down and sauntered off along the road, leaving an embarrassed cat-hater to explain to the motorist why he'd thrown a half-brick through his windscreen...

The road alongside was very busy, masses of cars and buses, most of the cars with only a driver, stopping and starting for no apparent reason, and sounding horns every so often.

So, this is what a modern city was like!

Surprisingly, one person seemed to sail along the road, weaving in and out of the traffic, having little problem in all the chaos. It was a fellow on a push-bike. It had a large pannier bag that said, 'Pizza4U'. *What language was that,* Harold wondered, *and... What's a Pizza?*

It must have been a busy shopping street at some time, but not now. Empty stores, still with signs in the windows telling of all the wonderful bargains that were in the closing down sales! Rubbish had accumulated in these doorways, at least it looked like rubbish – until it moved, and Harold realised that people were sleeping there – and not through choice, he guessed. He came to others who were awake but sitting, gazing blankly into space. *This couldn't be what the future was for the country – surely!* In Woldenham, an odd tramp appeared and went round the doors and was given food. That was an exception. This? It was like a lost tribe of outcasts living in these doorways.

Scuffo nudged up to an old man, who reached out a bony hand and patted his head. Harold felt quite sad. He would have liked to help – but what could a cat do? *Miaow...*

He carried on along the pavement, feeling downhearted. *What a sad state of affairs.* It was not a surprise to see many charity shops with names of good causes, full of assorted goods and still trading, but why weren't the charities helping those poor souls in the shop doorways?

The notice in the newsagent's window was asking for contributions of food. 'Help feed the hungry of the city. Donate at the Food Bank.' *A food bank?* As he walked along, he could see many buildings that looked as if they'd once been banks, but precious few still operating. Back home, at least Codgestone had a 'Savings Bank' and a 'Royal'? He wondered where people obtained money now, *but then again, maybe money wasn't used...*

How far forward in time had he travelled? He'd no idea yet.

Then he saw the queue for a hole-in-the-wall machine, dispensing cash merrily on request. So money was still in use. Scuffo sat and watched. He never seen that before. *What a system, and what a machine with an endless supply! All it needed was a magic plastic card. Why didn't the doorway sleepers have one?*

Outside a chemist there was a fancy sign with impressive neon lighting. It changed the display every few moments. It showed him the outside temperature, it showed him a smiley face, then the day, then the smiley face again, and then... *Ah, yes* – what he was looking for! It told him the date! He had reached the year 2016. That made Harold think!

Gosh, I'm eighty-eight! If I'm still alive... And the smiley face was showing again, then the temperature, then the... Wonder who winds that up every day?

He continued along the street.

His eyes lit up when he came to a betting shop. It was only one of many that he'd padded passed, but what made this one special was the name.

'BETter with SYD' said the big sign above the door, and it looked like lots of activity was going on inside. The sound of a commentary for a race could be heard easily at the entrance, and the activity he could see through the door surprised him – and it wasn't even 10.00am yet! He didn't enter, but he read a poster in the window.

'Have you visited SYD's CASINO?' it asked. '*Blackjack, Roulette, Poker, and all your favourite slot machines are there for your enjoyment. Have a meal in the luxury bar restaurant. Bring lots of money. You won't find a BETter establishment!*'

What a boost it would be to Uncle Syd's confidence if he were to be told that his success was assured. No chance of telling him, of course, but at least it would please Monica to know. A Casino too!

Wonder if he ever does make it to the States?

Scuffo reached a café. 'No animals permitted except Guide Dogs' it said but, as a couple left, Scuffo skipped in through the self-closing door. Although busy, with most of the tables occupied, it was remarkably still and silent, heads down, everyone gazing intently at the device being held in hand. The only sound was the hiss of a piece of equipment behind the serving counter, and one person placing plastic cups under the nozzle.

The smell of coffee was dominant. Now, that surprised and delighted Harold. He could breathe deeply and appreciate the aroma – without choking! *Why? No smoke!*

Go into any café or restaurant back home in Codgestone and the smell! *Yugh!* A cigarette would be in every hand – except his. Harold being a non-smoker, hated leaving those places with his clothes reeking.

This was so different...

A large display showed a menu that astounded

Harold. All sorts of food was available, and how many different types of coffee can anyone drink? Open twenty-four hours! Back home in Codgestone, you'd be lucky to get a tea and a simple bacon roll in their cafes, and only if you were there at the right time!

No-one seemed to notice a cat wandering freely, probably because each person was so focused on the object in their hands. Harold was fascinated watching how both thumbs were constantly active, and soon realised that that was how they were changing the screen. Even the person on the other side of the counter was looking at her little screen, except when she, one-handedly with the other, lifted coffee cups and cakes. All attention was on the mobiles, but what had him baffled, was where the information they were looking at came from.

Not one person was reading a newspaper, or a book. *How odd!* Then he noticed the faces of all the males. Everyone had a beard. At home, only elderly gents had beards, usually due to laziness, or a visit to the barber being overdue.

Another thing, all the men that were in there – they were bald!

"Alopecia, I think it's called," he told Monica when he returned. "Looked like a major problem. An epidemic, I guess... Either that, or they'd all shaved their heads – but how likely is that?"

It was in the café that Scuffo's demise occurred.

Curiosity had been too strong for Harold. He'd been desperate to see what they were all looking at on their little screens. It also occurred to him that if he could get a hold of one of these mobiles, he could take it back, like he'd managed with the Racing Almanacs. *These things were just toys for adults, weren't they? Probably fairly cheap for someone to replace, if he 'borrowed' one.*

Scuffo prowled around, still without being noticed, looking for an opportunity to grab one, but that didn't appear likely. As individuals prepared to leave the café, the first thing they did was pocket their mobile. His chance eventually came when one male needed a toilet break. He was with pals, and left his mobile lying safely on the table, beside his partly drunk coffee. Scuffo leapt up onto his vacated seat and sat a moment, expecting to be chased, but no, the pals were so intent on viewing their own screens. He reached out a paw and touched the mobile's face, and the screen lit up, and what had that fellow been watching?

Two cats playing with a ball!

Scuffo felt immediately comfortable. He'd made the thing work, and it was a video starring two little catty friends... How nice! *Miaow...!*

The two guys on either side immediately looked at their pal's screen, then at each other, and smiled.

"Oh no, not again! Cats! Pete's becoming a little bit strange these days!" said one.

"It's an obsession. What a loser...!" said the other, despairingly, and then noticed – it wasn't Pete operating the phone...

"What the...!" was the yell, as Scuffo swiped at the mobile and tried to grab it in his jaws, but failed. The coffee in the part-full plastic cup went splashing over the table, and the phone went flying through the air to land on the floor, near the plant pot with the plastic rubber plant, in the corner of the café, unbroken, and still showing fluffy cats playing together...

Suddenly, all mobiles were forgotten. The two pals had knocked over their chairs in springing up to rescue the phone, and all attention was on the action at the corner of the café.

A fight!

Scuffo had jumped down, like a shot, and tried again to grab the slim mobile, but couldn't manage to scoop it up. As he tried once more, he didn't see the assistant rush over with the empty frying pan in her hand, nor did he see that she was about to swing it in his direction...

CLUNK! Whoooosh...! TINKLE!

The last thing Harold heard, before leaving 2016, was Pete's wailing.

"Look what you've done to my phone, you silly bitch!"

23 WHAT A GAY WAY...

It was a day out for Monica and Harold. The sun was shining brightly, it was warm, the bus had been on time, and they'd been walking briskly for half-an-hour, smiling and happy to be together. Their relationship was still under wraps, so a visit to the woods on the far side of Codgestone appeared to be far enough away from home to ensure they would be safe from contact with anyone who'd recognise them, and, so far, so good, but it's amazing how wrongly a simple stroll in woodland can go, especially if you are Harold Scuffington.

Trying to pretend to Monica that he was fit and youthful was really silly. Basically, he was showing off, and should never have climbed into the tree, and though, if he'd stepped onto the stronger branches, they would have been tough enough to support his weight, Harold didn't. He stepped on a weak one! Also, everyone knows that falling out of a tree is the reserve of youngsters, everyone except Harold, because that's what he did.

"Ahhh!" he yelled!

Monica spun round to see the body dropping, but just before hitting the ground...

Whoosh...!

Harold vanished!

There was music coming from the shed at the bottom of the garden. The voice was clear enough for the words from a portable radio to be heard in the surrounding gardens.

"Jive talkin', you're tellin' me lies... Jive talkin', you're wearin' disguise..."

Out of the shed danced a female.

"Jive talkin', so misunderstood, yea."

She carried a placard in one hand, and a paintbrush in the other.

"Jive talkin', you're really no good..."

Scuffo just sat gazing. Harold had no idea where he was, or what time period it was. The girl... No, she was old enough to be called a woman, could be nearing fifty, Harold decided, but still capable of wiggling her hips very nicely. Hmmm, yes... She was carrying a placard that she placed carefully on the side of the shed, then danced back inside.

"Jive talkin'..."

A very catchy tune, he thought, a bit different from Doris Day and Perry Como, and Monica would think it great to dance to! Wonder if she could wiggle her hips like that...?

He was curious. What did the placard say? When she'd carried it out, he couldn't see it, and it was sitting with the message hidden. Scuffo went slinking cautiously down the path towards the open door.

"Any more red paint, Charlie?" came from another

female, inside.

"There's a tin on the shelf, Jo, already been opened," Charlie shouted back, over the music.

"Is Belle bringing more hardboard? We've almost used it all."

"She said she would." She straightened up, another slogan completed. "Where did you put the hammer?"

Scuffo was peeping into the shed. It was large, almost like a workshop with benches either side and pots of paint and brushes dotted about. Harold still couldn't see what was on the boards.

"Hi all!" a new voice called out. "Only me."

"Hi Belle. You're late!"

"Yes, sorry. Had to help that idiot of a husband pack his case. Can't expect a man to be able to do something as complicated as that, especially my husband."

"Don't know why you stay with him?" commented Charlie.

"He pays all the bills, and he's away from home a lot too, so I can have total freedom to do what I really like."

"Even sex?" Jo asked jokingly.

"Certainly, but not with him, that died a death a long time ago."

"And he still doesn't know about us?" asked Charlie.

"If he's guessed he's never said," answered Belle. "But important matters, what's still to be done? Oh, hello you." She'd looked down and found a ginger cat with a short tail at her feet. Without any hesitation she picked it up. "You are a lovely little fellow. I wouldn't mind you as a pet, and your name is...? Scuffo!"

Scuffo was delighted to be cuddled, and Harold was delighted to be able to see what was on the placards lying drying. She sat him on the bench.

'Gay is good!' 'It's my body!' 'Equal rights for women.' 'We'll dress how we want!'

He would never have guessed that! *Are they modern suffragettes?*

Belle had been and collected hardboard from her car.

Gay? Does that mean what I think it does?

'Against our will!' 'Women's Rights Now!'

"You could nail them onto the poles, Belle. They're in the corner," said Charlie.

Belle put Scuffo back on the floor. Harold noted that what seemed to be a dislike for men didn't appear to extend to a male cat. *Are they all... whatdoyoucallthems? It used to be lesbians, but that sign says 'Gay'. But, as I'm not able to talk I don't suppose it matters. Wonder what Monica would think about this? Bet she would never say 'lesbians' out loud!*

Jo's and Charlie's haircuts were quite manly, whereas Belle's was not. They were all wearing denim overalls with bibs. To Harold they were very attractive women, no matter the clothing, or the haircuts.

It didn't take long for the placards to be joined to the poles.

"What time tomorrow?" Belle asked.

"Trafalgar Square at 2.00 pm," said Jo.

"Oh, that'll be an early start then. All in my car?" said Belle.

"A couple of good speakers to be there, one's an MP who's just come out, I've heard."

"Let's get this finished off then. Another two placards, and then its coffee time," announced Charlie.

Surprisingly, Scuffo was still awake. Normally, he would have found a soft cushion and dozed off at the earliest opportunity, but regular attention from each of the girls was keeping him on the move. It was Belle currently, with the strand of wool. Just dangling that in front of Scuffo's nose was sufficient to maintain his active attention.

Some serious politics were being talked over, and Harold was interested.

He hadn't realised how badly treated women had been through the ages. Each of the three females had plenty to contribute, but with Scuffo's constant leaping, Harold was having difficulty concentrating on what was being said.

As well as a really sore head from jarring leaps, a guilty conscience was developing, but how could he absorb what was being discussed – because it was interesting – when all Scuffo did was leap at a silly bit of wool that was snatched away every single time...?

Maybe he hadn't experienced too much of the grumbles back in Woldenham, because there probably were very few females in the village who knew anything different to the life their mothers and grandmothers had led and accepted their lot with resignation. Had he been ignoring what had been happening around him? *Were there problems, but hidden, and on his own patch?*

Harold was all for what they were demanding. It seemed perfectly sensible arguments that were being made, and up to a point he was beginning to feel extremely guilty on behalf of the male gender, but it became a little repetitive, and slightly boring.

Let's go to sleep, was the message he was trying to convey to Scuffo, but Scuffo, who would normally be eager to do just that, wasn't listening.

Grab the wool! Missed! Try again... Nearly got it. Try again... Ahhh! Missed...

Eventually, Scuffo too got fed up and went behind the settee for the snooze.

Harold was convinced that Belle never even noticed the departure, because her outstretched arm continued to dangle and shake that length of wool.

It was the squeals and laughter that wakened Scuffo. *What a noise they were making on the settee. Behaving like young giggly schoolgirls. What were they doing at all...?* He could have peeped round and found out but no, he went back to sleep.

It must have been a particularly loud shriek, or squeal, that did it. He was awake, well awake! The noise had moved. There was still lots of giggling, but no longer coming from the settee.

Scuffo stretched himself, padded round to the front of the settee. As expected, no-one. What there was, though, was clothing. One, two, three sets of overalls... They were strewn across the floor creating a trail that continued with assorted ladies underwear and guided him to another room.

The squealing had stopped and been replaced by various other sounds that he found hard to reconcile... They were coming from a bed. *Oh no,* he thought, *not another bed scenario! I've been over, under, and in a bed – what's left?*

He went into the room, but could see little from floor level, *so what does a cat do to remedy that? Jumps onto a chair to look.*

Three naked bodies, and they were...!
Gulp!

Harold couldn't understand why he didn't revert back to his own body and to his own time just then, because that had been a real shock to his system. It was bad enough a long time ago when he'd seen that photo in 'The Sun'. This had been three times worse!

He wasn't used to seeing life, quite so, well, in the raw...

Does Monica look like that?

Scuffo was still in the future, and in the house. It was morning. Charlie, Belle, and Jo, were also there but to Harold's relief, they were fully clothed again. None of them would be there for much longer. Everyone was in a rush to have a quick breakfast before the long drive south.

The selected placards were loaded, some drinks and snacks prepared, and they were ready to go – when Belle remembered the cat.

"Scuffo! We can't go without Scuffo!" she cried.

"But she's not your cat," said Jo.

"I think she wants to go with us," said Charlie.

Miaow...! Scuffo said indignantly! *I'm a fella! Can't you tell the difference?*

"See, Jo, I told you. She does..."

So Scuffo was bundled in beside three happy, giggling lesbians who were going to put the world to rights, and off they went.

"Should we make a name for ourselves – get on TV – go topless?" asked Jo.

"What a great idea!" Charlie followed up enthusiastically.

"No!" said Belle, almost driving onto the pavement "I've looked in the mirror..."

Harold was inclined to agree, still suffering from last night's surprise, *none of them should be doing any more exposing!* Anyway, it wasn't the sort of day to be exposing bare flesh if it could be avoided for, when they arrived, it was cold and damp and, overall, a miserable late morning.

"Whoopidoo!" said Belle, when she eventually found a parking place that was not going to cost the earth, "And, hello London!" But they were a long way from the start of the march.

There was indecision about whether to carry the cat, or let it walk. They expected him to probably run off, so Scuffo would be carried. Actually, he would have followed them dutifully, because he wouldn't have minded a leg stretch after his long sleep in the car, and anyway, he liked the company of the three females, and they obviously liked him.

They'd been walking for about twenty minutes towards the assembly area when the rain started. It then worsened.

"I had an old umbrella in the car," said Belle. "Wish I'd brought it."

Being carried in Belle's arms meant Scuffo was the driest of them all when they eventually came across a newsagent who was making his fortune selling lightweight plastic ponchos to the many who'd come unprepared. Four sheets of plastic, with a hole in the middle, were bought and put on top of already uncomfortably damp clothing, and it did help. Scuffo was being carried again, underneath Belle's poncho, and though he was warm and dry and could see out, the feeling of claustrophobia was never far from Harold's mind... The fourth poncho was covering the placards that Charlie had been carrying. She wasn't too sure that the correct type of paint had been used. She hadn't thought it might rain. Jo had the bag of pamphlets and the snacks.

It had stopped raining when they reached the assembly point, so they could remove the ponchos. To rest her arms, Belle had cautiously let Scuffo down onto the pavement, ready to catch him again if he tried to dash away, but she needn't have worried. Scuffo was pleased to be moving, and content to wander around the three girls, stopping at each in turn, rubbing himself against their legs. They seemed to like that. He certainly did.

There was a good turnout, according to Charlie, who knew about these things. More people than she'd expected.

To Harold, this was a novel experience, his first chance to be part of a protest. Earlier in the year back home, he'd read in his Guardian, about the CND March that had taken place in London. It had been a huge gathering, similar to the previous year, and a really effective demo.

If he'd lived nearer, he might have joined in because it was for a good cause – Ban the Bomb! "Isn't it sad," he'd heard Belle say last night, "that we still have wars and have to pray that they only use conventional weapons. Heaven help us all if they ever resort to a nuclear solution."

So, here they were sixteen years later, and the bomb still hadn't been banned.

Oh dear!

How Harold wished last night that he could have had his say too. Still, he'd picked up a lot of useful knowledge from them. He wasn't just playing with a strand of wool, you know!

"Come on," said Jo. "They're about to move off. Let's get going."

The march began.

Scuffo was pleased to be lifted by Belle again. Being carried on her shoulders meant less chance of being accidently trampled on. Unfortunately, they hadn't gone far, walking at a snail's pace, when the rain restarted. Poncho's on again!

Belle let Scuffo sit on her shoulders, on top of the poncho. It left her arms free to carry the banner and to hand out leaflets. It did mean Scuffo getting wet, but he enjoyed the fresh air, and for Harold, no claustrophobia...

Unfortunately for Belle, occasionally in holding his balance Scuffo's claws caused leaks in the plastic coat, but she just grinned. She thought of the cat as being her very jaggy, warm – but wet, scarf!

It rained for the rest of the march, but the trio chanted slogans all the way and distributed leaflets with smiles that remained bright and cheery. To bystanders, they appeared totally unfazed by the weather. It would have been better though if the water paints they'd used for the posters had lasted a while longer, more people might have appreciated their messages.

It wasn't all sweetness and light though. Harold was surprised at some of the verbal abuse that came their way, and equally surprised that the girls didn't show their annoyance. *Oh, well... other than using Mr Churchill's famous victory-V sign in return, while still grinning!*

The march appeared to be successful. It was large but not an enormous gathering, and the marchers were a mixture of male and female. It was good natured and well behaved, plus there was a great deal of jocularity, and plenty noise. Thankfully, at the culmination, the rain had eased, and the trio were bolstered by some very stirring speeches from the platform.

However, a little bit of their enthusiasm had gone by the time they reached the sanctuary of a café.

"Three cappuccino's, please," was the request.

What the heck is that, thought Harold...

The trio brightened up when the TV news appeared on the café's large screen, and guess who was starring! The three smiling girls! One with a cat on her shoulders. Unfortunately, when the camera panned along the notices they carried, each had almost washed clean...

"I didn't think it would be so wet," said Charlie.

"Well, I am glad we came. We have to fight for what's right!" said Jo.

"And, what the heck!' said Belle. "It's been fun." She gave Scuffo an extra cuddle. Scuffo liked Belle, and Belle liked Scuffo, so it seems a shame that parting would be inevitable.

Earlier, when they'd come to enter the café, a window cleaner was washing some upstairs windows and his ladder straddled the pavement.

"Careful," Belle had shouted to Jo, as she sidestepped onto the busy road to avoid going under it.

Charlie hesitated. Under the ladder, or brave the traffic?

"Bad luck, remember," said Belle, nodding towards the ladder, and Charlie stepped onto the road, and beyond, safely.

Belle bent to lift Scuffo, who'd been walking beside her, but he'd carried straight on – under the ladder. Belle, shook her head, stepped onto the road and returned to the pavement.

Into the café went all four.

Later, when they left, the window cleaner had made progress and moved further along the road – in the direction they were going, so they had to go through the same procedure, cautiously stepping onto the busy road again, as were other pedestrians. Scuffo was the only one who went under the ladder, gaining two red crosses for bad luck – and one full bucket of dirty water, spilled, accidentally, on his head!

He vanished with a *whoosh*...

They were all mystified. The window cleaner had scrambled back down the ladder to apologise to whoever had suffered and was pleased to find nobody soaked. "Only a cat," he was told. That was a relief.

"Where's he gone?" asked a crestfallen Belle.

He'd been in the future for two full days, but it was as if time stood still in his absence, and Monica hadn't moved from the spot where he'd vanished from.

Whoosh... he was back and dropping from the tree.

Fortunately, landing on a deep pile of dead leaves in a hollow, in an upright position, feet first – before falling over, had somehow prevented serious injury. It was a soft landing, but as he stood up shakily, Monica panicked.

"Why are leaves sticking to your head? What have you done to yourself? Your head! It's bleeding!" she cried out.

Harold panicked too – until he realised that his head had been soaked! It was dirty water! Of course, he had to explain... and to recount everything that had happened.

"Is that what... *lesbians* do...? And you were... watching?"

"No, I wasn't," Harold protested, wishing that he'd omitted that bit of the story.

"And what year was it that these..." Monica hesitated. It seemed wrong to say the word out loud, it wasn't one she was in the habit of using. "...*lesbians* went on their march."

"I saw a calendar in the café." said Harold. "It showed 1975. They were fighting for the rights of all women, not just Gay persons and I think they'll succeed, at least I hope they do. They deserve to."

They'd impressed him in the short time he'd known them.

"I've never met anyone in Woldenham, who is a... One of these. Have you, Harold?"

Harold shrugged his shoulders and shook his head. He couldn't be certain.

"Harold! You're not Gay, are you?" she asked. "It just that sometimes, you are..." but she didn't finish the sentence.

Harold, was just... Harold!

"Harold, we've been invited out. Uncle Syd wrote me a letter. He says it would be nice to meet my future husband."

Harold looked blank.

"That's you, remember!"

Harold smiled.

"He said, as there aren't many family relatives around, that it would be nice for you to visit their house and meet him and Aunt Mabel."

"Oh..." he didn't sound enthusiastic. "He doesn't know, that I... does he?" and his eyebrows rose with the question. "You know... about you being a pretend clairvoyant? Or me being a cat?"

"Of course not, silly!" Monica was more worried about Aunt Mabel. It had been rather frosty many months ago. *Would anything have changed? Would there still be no love lost?*

Getting there was not easy. Two buses, and then a long walk from the nearest bus stop. At last, they arrived. On the way, Harold had been hoping at the end of this evening on getting a lift home from Uncle Syd. Seemed unlikely though. Monica thought he drove a sport's car, with only two seats!

Harold recognised the manor. He had been here as Scuffo, in rather different circumstances, about forty years in the future, and, on that occasion, the present occupants had recently departed this earth. He had been impressed by the house then, and he was again. It was not yet as grand as it becomes, but still a fantastic home. Probably originally the residence of a wealthy local dignitary, a local Lord, Harold would have guessed. Scaffolding at the side of the building indicated expansion was currently in hand.

But their view was from the wrong side of an imposing wrought iron gate, because it was closed!

"There's a padlock on it," said Harold, and, beyond the gate, before them stretched a long driveway. Both very good reasons in Harold's head for not continuing! He was thinking of having to walk all that way back again later in the evening. He was about to suggest that they should just go back home now, when a figure appeared, hurrying down the path to meet them. It was Uncle Syd.

"Meant to unlock this earlier," he said, "but fell asleep in the chair. It happens at my age, unfortunately. You must be the Reverend Harold Scuffington! Monica's beau! Pleased to meet you."

He's only in his mid-forties, Harold guessed, *but he's portraying himself as an old geezer. Why? To do with having a younger wife maybe? Given up trying to keep pace?*

They went inside. It was tastefully decorated, and the furnishings seemed just right for the style of house. Money had not been spared here. Must have a very successful business, so far, plus new money coming from the race winnings.

"Your Aunt will be back shortly," said Uncle Syd. "Had to collect some additional food. So, sit down, both of you. Make yourselves comfortable and tell me a little about how you met."

"Not much to tell," Monica started to say.

"How rude of me," Syd interrupted. "I should have offered you something to drink. What will you have? Whisky, sherry, vodka, or is there something else?"

"I'll have a small sherry, please," said Monica.

"Just a cup of tea for me, please," requested Harold.

"Oh!" Uncle Syd had been taken by surprise. "Tea? I...

uhmm... Mabel usually looks after that sort of stuff. Oh dear..."

"I could make it," suggested Monica. "The kitchen still in the same place?"

Uncle Syd was grateful, but Harold was not.

I should just have asked for whisky. I would have liked a whisky, but it would have given the wrong impression. Don't go Monica! Oh no... Now I am going to be left alone with your uncle. Going to get the third degree now!

The sound of a distant door closing interrupted his panic.

"That'll be Mabel now. She's been looking forward to meeting you, Harold."

Voices in the kitchen could be heard. Harold listened, hoping that there wouldn't be any ill feeling between the two women, because Monica was sure her aunt still disliked her. The voices came closer. Sounded like pleasant chatter.

"Like your house, Aunt Mabel. Makes mine seem like a matchbox."

Aunt Mabel laughed.

"It's much too big for us really, but your uncle likes it, and it's his money."

There was something familiar about that voice. He'd heard it before, fairly recently, but where? Was it in the village, or the town? He couldn't put a face to it, until...

Aunt Mabel appeared at the doorway and he realised with a shock he knew her! Sixteen years younger than the last time he saw her and, being younger, even prettier.

This was Belle! Mabel was one of the three lesbians!

24 GETTING TO KNOW YOU

Four people sat around the large dining table, all feeling slightly awkward in the way that first meetings can be, and though Mabel had done a wonderful job and spent most of the day preparing a meal that should have tasted delicious, not one of the four had appreciated it fully. Each had something else going on in their head, while they struggled to maintain casual, light-hearted conversation.

Syd was being cautious because he was afraid that he might let it slip that Monica was supplying him with betting certs; Monica was still unsure how her aunt truly felt about her, and also felt guilty because she was lying to Uncle Syd about where the information for him was coming from; and the hostess, she was wishing herself far away and thinking that she could be having much more fun with Charlie and Jo.

For Harold it was even worse. Every time he looked at Aunt Mabel, he saw the vision of her, naked, in the company of another two naked bodies, all with that slightly excessive podginess that comes with age, writhing about on a bed and indulging in... In what...? An overly-friendly group relationship, for want of a better description! His dog-collar felt as if it was choking him, and every so often he had to wipe drops of perspiration from his upper lip and brow.

"More wine, Monica?" asked Uncle Syd.

"Oh, yes please," she said, with what Harold considered to be too much enthusiasm.

"More water, Harold?"

"Yes, please," he replied, with even more enthusiasm than Monica. He needed to be cooled, what with the combination of the visions – and the food!

"What is this called?" asked Harold, gulping down some more water.

"It's a curry, Harold. Have you not had one before? Chicken madras it's called, a recipe I got from my friend, Charles, and it's all the rage in London, you know. Don't you like it?"

"Of course..." he replied immediately, breathing flames as he said it – he didn't really, but it did feel like that! "Yes, yes, it's lovely," he lied. "But... very hot! Could I have more water, please?"

Uncle Syd filled his glass again and turned to Monica.

"More wine, Monica?"

"Yesh, pleashe, Uncle Shyd."

Harold had been pleased that there was a pudding – fresh strawberries with homemade ice-cream, two portions, because Monica wasn't wanting hers, and it helped cool him a little. He was very glad that he'd refused the whisky!

Aunt Mabel had cleared the dishes and was in the kitchen.

The others were now sitting in the lounge. Nothing as common as a front room, like it was at home, but admittedly this was far more sumptuous. Monica had sunk into the large settee, and had immediately dropped off to sleep, leaving Harold to hold the fort.

"Wake up, Monica," called Uncle Syd, but to no response. "You are not sozzled already are you? I was hoping you would read the tea-leaves, or something. Do a bit of fortune telling. Tell us all about the future... Oh, I shouldn't have said that. You're not supposed to know," he said hurriedly, glancing at Harold.

Harold was sitting opposite, wondering how to reply, when Aunt Mabel wheeled in a trolley with freshly brewed tea, and cups and saucers, and cakes.

"We don't eat like this every evening," said Uncle Syd. "Beans on toast, very often, or cheese sandwiches."

"What rubbish!" said Aunt Mabel.

"How would you know what I eat? You're always out with your men friends – Charles or Joseph, and who knows how many others, several times a week!"

Harold didn't know where to look. Charles or Joseph? The vision had appeared again, and they definitely weren't naked men! Does Uncle Syd really not know?

"At least when I'm away I get a decent meals in the hotel!" exclaimed Syd. "I'd have died off by now if I was waiting for you to serve me proper food."

It must be the effect of the wine. Uncle Syd had been keeping both himself, and Monica, topped up all during the meal. Harold and Aunt Mabel had stuck to water.

Moments later, Syd dozed off too. Bang goes any chance of a lift home thought Harold.

"Have we met at some time, Harold?" asked Aunt Mabel, giving him a hard stare. "I have the impression that you know me better than I know you."

Harold gulped and supressed the vision.

"I think you can blame your niece for all my knowledge." He felt his face colouring. "Monica said so many wonderful things about you."

"Oh, that is a surprise. I always thought that she disliked me – her naughty aunt..."

Naughty Aunt... The vision appeared again! Control yourself Harold!

"Don't know where you could have got that idea," he said with a forced smile.

"That's nice to hear," she said, and stood up at the trolley. "Now, would you like tea, or would you rather have that whisky?"

Harold was glad that he'd chosen tea, because if he'd gone for whisky, Aunt Mabel would have done the same.

They'd had a very interesting, sober conversation about almost every subject under the sun, it seemed. They felt as if they knew each other very well, and Harold was now seeing her simply as Aunt Mabel.

But he wasn't stupid with the chat. No mention was made of Syd's betting, or Monica's clairvoyant pretence, nor of Belle, Charlie, or Jo.

There was a happy end result. Harold liked Mabel, and Mabel liked Harold – and Mabel remained sober enough to drive them home and, thankfully, her vehicle was a four-seater.

Monica was still slightly under the weather when they arrived at her home. Harold had a door key. Aunt Mabel acted like a kind mother and helped Monica into her bed, then took Harold home. Being gentlemanly, he invited her in for a cup of tea, but she behaved like a lady and made the excuse of it being late and having to get back to put Syd to bed. They thanked each other for an enjoyable evening, and she left.

Harold's head hit the pillow and it returned – the vision of the three naked females! He got up, went back downstairs, took out the Guardian and folded it open at the cryptic crossword, grabbed a pencil, and gave that some thought. That got rid of the vision – but then kept him awake for the rest of the night!

Mabel drove back home with the strange sensation still continuing of some connection with her niece's fiancé. She had definitely never met him before. She dismissed the thoughts of him looking similar to someone else, but wondered what he would think if he knew who her men friends, Charles and Joseph, really were...

"Monica was much nicer than I remember her," she said to her husband, next morning at breakfast, as she poured his tea, and buttered another slice of toast for him, as usual.

"I didn't say anything out of turn last night, did I," he asked, feeling slightly guilty for some reason he couldn't pinpoint. "I had a drink or two, I remember, but I must have dozed off at some point."

"No. Nothing out of the ordinary," she replied with a smile.

She'd let herself in, a short while ago, and gone straight to Harold's kitchen and put the kettle on to make tea. Harold had been very well-behaved last night and hadn't let her down, and deserved a little 'thank you', so the teapot was now filled and brewing nicely. In a few more minutes the boiled eggs would be ready for breakfast, and the toaster was about to supply hot fresh toast. She felt good this morning and had wanted it to be a nice surprise. *In a moment she would go upstairs and waken him with a kiss, if he wasn't up already. It would brighten his day to have his breakfast prepared for him.*

That had been the plan and it was progressing nicely. *Last night had been very pleasant. The sherry was excellent, and the wine! Must be really expensive stuff that Uncle Syd buys, because she'd hardly any after effect.*

Being wakened at 9.00am by Monica giving him a shake and a little peck on his cheek, should have been a delightful experience for Harold. However, him having at long last managed to get to asleep only half an hour previously, took a little of the shine from it.

"Go away," he grunted, and turned over, pulling the bedsheets over his head.

Why was he so grumpy? That wasn't the way it was supposed to happen! So, she left him and went back downstairs. Another half hour is what he needs, she decided.

Yesterday's Guardian, with the crossword only half done, lay on the table beside his favourite chair. Monica lifted the paper, sat down and had a look at the clues he'd failed to solve, thought for a few moments then filled in one clue. Moments later, another. When she'd completed it and glanced at the clock, she was surprised how easily the half hour had passed.

She went back upstairs, knocked gently on his bedroom door, opened it slowly when she received no reply, to find Harold flat on his back with mouth wide open, snoring, and very obviously in a deep sleep.

"It was going to be such a beautiful day..." she said to herself and closed the door again.

25 IT HAD TO HAPPEN

It had been a surprise for Monica to find that Harold now knew Aunt Mabel better than she did. It was her relative after all, but what Harold had failed to tell Monica was where his greater knowledge came from – that he'd already met her aunt in the future, learned a lot about her when she hadn't been wearing fancy clothes, in fact, when she hadn't been wearing any!

Tonight's meeting had been at Harold's suggestion. "It'd give you a chance to catch up", he'd said. So, she'd been going to invite her aunt and uncle for a meal to her place, but she'd not been confident about that. With them living in a grand mansion and being filthy rich, she felt that they would not be impressed having to come round to her humble abode. Her house wasn't large, nor was it full of fancy furnishings, well... except for the new radiogram! "Use my place then," suggested Harold. "I don't mind you cooking a meal there," and that was the other problem. Harold was easily pleased – but cooking for four?

"I can't make them suffer my cooking? It could ruin a developing relationship! Aunt Mabel produced a delicious meal."

"You can do it!" said Harold reassuringly, but she wasn't so sure...

What to have? Fish Pie. I can't go wrong with that, she decided.

It was lucky for Uncle Syd and Aunt Mabel, and Monica herself, not to have been landed with the portion containing the fish bone. That had to be Harold's misfortune, and hence the choking fit. He'd left the room and was coughing and spluttering when Monica came through to join him in the kitchen, and immediately came to his rescue.

Well... Slapping him on the back had been the natural thing to do, but it was not the first time that Monica had been unaware of her own strength. Admittedly it had been unintended, but... That first powerful blow from her triggered the change.

Whoosh!

Yet again, Harold was gone.

Surprisingly, Scuffo didn't actually go anywhere, other than in time. He was still in his own home kitchen, but now alone. There was sobbing coming from the front room.

"Goodness! It's Monica! She's in trouble!" Harold immediately thought, and shouted, *Miaow....*

The cat padded quickly towards the crying, but it was Aunt Mabel. She was sitting on the settee sobbing her heart out, while Monica attempted to cajole her into stopping, but it looked to Harold that Aunt Mabel considered that she was entitled to wail and therefore determined to get full value.

"And he said he wouldn't be returning!" Her whole body shook with each sob.

"Calm down, Auntie," said Monica, and put her arm round her shoulders.

"Call me, Belle, please, Monica," she managed to say through the sobs. "It's all out in the open now! He knows."

"Knows what?" said Monica innocently.

"Knows that I am gay. I was going to tell you, but it all happened so quickly! I thought maybe that you'd already guessed, and that is why you disliked me."

Monica's mouth dropped open. *Gay? The aunt that she had gradually got to know so well, and now liked so much, she was... a lesbian!*

Harold was in a state of shock himself but for a different reason. Scuffo was looking up at two women who had aged considerably, two women who'd been young only moments before. *Which year was he in, and what had happened to the two of them? Why the tears?*

"He said he was going because of Margaret Thatcher, but I know that's not true."

"But I can understand that," said Monica, thinking frantically for the correct thing to say to an aunt, who'd confessed to being a lesbian, and whose husband had now left her to go to America. "I can't stand that woman either. He'd rather have Ronald Reagan then? I would too!"

"What if he cuts off my allowance? How will I manage? What if he decides to sell the house? What'll I do?" She'd stopped sobbing to say that, then started again.

Monica had no answers, only questions. "What is he going to do there? Has he already gone?" she asked.

Neither female had noticed the cat standing looking and listening intently. Harold was fascinated by this. Firstly, that he'd arrived at the same place in a different time, which hadn't happened before, and he was wondering what Uncle Syd would be doing in America... He would have loved to be involved in the conversation. He could think of lots of questions.

"What's happening about the betting shops?" asked Monica.

"They are doing great and that's another of the reasons that he's gone. He's got a manager to look after them, but I had to drag that information out of him. He never did tell me how he'd succeeded. Said he was always able to choose winners, but how could anyone be successful all the time? There's always been something suspicious about that."

At least Aunt Mabel had stopped crying.

She sounded more annoyed with her husband now. "Part of a syndicate, he told me, and they are about to open a casino in Las Vegas. Las Vegas? It'll cost him a fortune to do that! He's going to lose all his money and... And it's hundreds of miles away! He'll never be home again!" and the tears began again.

Miaow...

Both women looked down at the cat gazing up at them. "Scuffo. You've come to comfort me," said Aunt Mabel. "At least I know that someone loves me. Come up here, my little darling."

At least she'd stopped the massive sobs, but Scuffo, now in Aunt Mabel's arms, could feel the tears. They were dropping on him.

"Do you know I've always been meaning to ask, Monica, where Scuffo came from? I fleetingly met a lovely little cat with the same name a long time ago, and he had a stubby tail, just like you, Scuffo!" Mabel nuzzled his head and dried her face at the same time. "Must have been ten years ago, but he vanished that day. That was in London..."

A date! That was a clue! Ten years ago was back in 1975, when there were three of them and... He managed, with difficulty, to stop himself visualising that scene yet again!

"Where he came from? I think you'd have to ask Harold about that," Monica said.

"You are so lucky having a lovely pet like this, Monica. If you ever want rid of him, I'd take him like a shot. When I die, Scuffo," and Scuffo was nuzzled again, "I'll be leaving you lots of money in my will. I promise. Oh, unless my dear husband stops supporting me..." and the tears began once more.

"Surely, Uncle Syd would never do that," said Monica, but without confidence.

What's this about me being Monica's pet? What is she on about? Harold was puzzled. *It's only ever Scuffo, or me, one or the other surely? Or... Oh-oh! Is it possible that I don't return as Harold at some point? Goodness... I wonder if that could happen. I hope not... Wait! I was still there in 2002! Or has the future changed?*

"I am sure he'll come back," said Monica, and Harold hoped that she was talking about him.

Miaow...

Aunt Mabel was still crying... The doorbell sounding helped stop her tears.

"He's forgotten the key again," said Monica, and went to the door.

Maybe that's Uncle Syd coming back after all. At the moment, that's the only thing to stop her tears, thought Harold. But it wasn't Uncle Syd.

Into the room came a slightly overweight Harold.

"Evening Monica, sorry I'm late. Oh hello, Aunt Mabel... and how are you tonight Scuffo, old pal?"

"What the...?" exclaimed Harold. *Miaow...*

"I'll get you some food, Scuffo. We're late tonight."

The bowl was filled from a bag marked cat food, taken from the cupboard, as if it was a regular routine?

"Were you expecting me?" Harold was puzzled. *Miaow...?*

"Into your basket after you've eaten that," said plump Harold. "You have been crying, Aunt Mabel? What's wrong? Can I help?"

Monica wished her husband hadn't asked, because that restarted the sobbing, then between sobs she and Scuffo heard the whole story all over again. As Aunt Mabel talked, she was pacing the floor, agitated, her tear-filled eyes seeing very little. Monica was waiting on her tripping on the carpet and prepared herself to catch her.

Scuffo finished the cat food. It tasted surprisingly good. *Now for the usual snooze.* Into the basket, he'd been told, *but who needs a basket? I'll go where I want. The settee's for me.*

Aunt Mabel was still stumbling back and forward, non-stop, talking and crying, as Scuffo got settled. He was ready to shut out the sobbing and drop off to sleep, and that's when Aunt Mabel stopped, exhausted, in front of him. She was still for a moment, then swayed, then flopped down onto the settee – on top of Scuffo!

The yell of warning from plump Harold and Monica, and the wail that Scuffo let out, covered up the *Whoosh...*

Aunt Mabel leapt back to her feet in shock, and looked behind her... Nothing!

Of course, the wine that Uncle Syd had brought could have contributed to Monica almost falling over, but mainly it was Harold's fault, vanishing in the middle of a second backslap.

As she'd swung her arm again, he'd suddenly gone, and she'd overbalanced. She'd avoided a tumble by grabbing the kitchen chair. Incredibly, when she'd straightened up, there Harold was, back again, almost if he'd not been away.

"Are you all right in there," Uncle Syd shouted from the dining table, hearing the chair clatter.

"Yes," Monica shouted back automatically, as she blinked a couple of times, and straightened up and tried to stay calm. "It's Harold, being silly!" as if he could help it.

Harold gave another cough, and the fishbone dislodged. He was thankful to remove it from his mouth, and gave Monica a sickly grin as he followed her back to the other room.

"Sorry about that," he said to the other two, who had not let his little choking problem stop them enjoying the remainder of Monica's fish pie. Harold was relieved it was all gone – danger removed. A fishbone in the throat was not pleasant.

"Pudding!" was declared by Monica as Harold cleared away the empty plates.

"Where were you this time," she whispered to him in the kitchen.

"Here," he told her.

"You couldn't have been!"

"I was."

"But, you vanished!"

"I know."

"Then where were you?"

"Shhh! I'll tell you later..." But as he lifted the hot dish, he burned his fingers. *"Oh, no!"* he cried in a panic. *"It'll happen again!"*

But it didn't, he was still there and, luckily, didn't drop the pudding. That would have been even more trouble, because it had taken a lot of Monica's basic cooking skills to achieve that apple crumble.

"Has something happened?" called Uncle Syd, then, "Ah... that smells good," as the crumble was carried in by Monica, holding it sensibly, using a dish towel.

Eating the pudding for Harold was extremely difficult, and not because of Monica's cooking prowess. It was because of his knowledge, for, sitting opposite were the two people that would be dramatically affected by what he'd just learned. He mustn't say anything about Syd eventually leaving her.

Whether the future could be changed, by knowing what it was to be, was a big question that Monica and Harold had discussed many times recently, but nothing had occurred that convinced them either way.

"Wine?" asked Harold, who was drinking water again, as was Mabel. The glasses for Monica and Syd were again topped up. "Ever thought of emigrating?" said Harold, and it was out of his mouth before he could stop himself. He was relieved when it was picked up as a subject of general conversation.

"Oh, no," said Aunt Mabel immediately. "I'd have to leave behind some special friends. I couldn't cope with that. Anyway, where would I go?"

Harold noticed the quick look that Uncle Syd gave his wife at the mention of special friends.

"Yes, some things in this life are very important," she added.

"I must admit that I have thought of emigration," said Syd, "but there's a lot of work to be done here first. I seem to be having some success with the gee-gees these days, and I am waiting confirmation of the licences. Any day now I'll learn what I can do."

"So, where would you go, if you did emigrate?" asked Monica.

Harold wished he hadn't brought up the topic. There was a danger that it could expose what he and Monica already knew about them.

"Probably America. Las Vegas appeals to me. It's big-time gambling there, you know," Syd replied.

"But it would be terrible to die there, wouldn't it?" said Monica.

Harold almost choked again, this time on a mouthful of pudding. He was glad of no follow-up on the comment.

"Syd refuses to tell me how he manages to pick so many winners," said his wife, giving a sideways glance at her husband. "Says it's luck and skill, but I don't believe him. What do you think Harold?"

"Maybe there is a good fairy out there?" he replied.

"Who knows with that sort of thing?"

Uncle Syd smiled smugly – he knew!

Monica looked the other way – because, of course, she knew too!

"As long as you keep the money rolling in, Syd, I'll be happy," said Mabel.

Harold felt uncomfortable, because he knew her happiness was not guaranteed forever. Knowing so much felt an enormous burden sometimes.

"Strange though, how some people seem to know more about the future than others..." said Monica in an airy-fairy way.

"Some people are born with the gift," said Uncle Syd, with a knowing wink in the direction of Monica. That wink was seen by his wife. It reminded her of a previous suspicion of something going on between Syd and her niece. Maybe she had been correct...

"Lovely meal, Monica," said Uncle Syd. "Now who'd like a drop of whisky? I have a bottle in the car I'll bring in."

"Oh yes," said Monica, then looked at Harold with a naughty grin. "Isn't it a pity that you are teetotal, Harold?"

Harold found it hard to smile back. *That's exactly what he could have done with right now!* He now knew of Syd and Mabel's break-up, but Monica could not be told, so that would have to be kept to himself, and that could be difficult. *Yes, a whisky would have been nice!*

26 GOT THE BLUES...

Harold was feeling sorry for himself, the way that only a male can when suffering a man-cold! He'd retired to bed with a hot-water bottle, and he was cuddling it. He'd tried imagining that it was Monica he was holding close, but that didn't work.

She'd visited earlier and fed him a hot drink, but wouldn't approach any closer than necessary in case he infected her, so, he was feeling unloved, as well as really, really ill...

The bottle of Aspirins was sitting on the bedside table, unopened. She'd left a glass of water too, on the off-chance that for once in his life he'd try some medication, but she knew that it would be a waste of time.

"You'd rather suffer, wouldn't you," she'd said disparagingly.

His red nose and streaming eyes said it all, as she abandoned him, and now his throat was feeling sore. The only thing that he could think that could possibly make him feel worse, would be turning into Scuffo – with a cold.

"Wonder if, in the future, a cure will be discovered for the common cold," he asked the empty bedroom in a choked voice, then realised that he'd talked out loud.

Been doing it for years and never given it a thought. "But, what does it matter if I do?" he asked out loud again. "Nobody cares how much I am suffering..."

It had been a long time since he'd experienced being Scuffo, but the feeling was always there, that it could happen again, at any time, and probably when he least expected it. He certainly didn't want it to happen just now. He'd changed into Scuffo during sleep quite a few times, so he would have to stay awake, just in case, because he felt drained today. Couldn't possibly cope.

Today's Guardian lay unopened. Monica brought it along with the rhubarb tarts.

"Being so ill, you wouldn't want a tart today, would you?" she'd shouted up from downstairs, where he could hear her preparing cups and saucers. "...No?"

He was going to shout back, "Of course. I do!" because he was looking forward to that tart, but he was prudent, and didn't reply, because he would lose all chances of sympathy.

"Ok if I eat it then?" she continued, and after no response. "...Yes?"

He could tell what she was up to. She was trying to catch him out, prove that he wasn't as ill as he claimed. Women did that sort of thing, he'd once read. So he remained stoically silent.

"Right then, Harold. Thanks!"

At least he could look forward to a nice hot cup of tea, he'd told himself but, what she'd brought upstairs and handed him, was some horrid concoction that she'd found in her woman's magazine, a recipe she'd prepared specially for him. It was hot, but it tasted vile. Annoyingly, she'd remained in the room, at a distance, and wouldn't leave him be until he'd drunk every last drop.

And what had brought on this terrible illness? Harold was convinced it was the shock that caused it. The shock of Monica suggesting that they should buy a ring, an engagement ring, to make it clear to all the village that they were officially a couple. That had been unsettling for him – being rushed! Getting to know each other had been a slow process, mainly because of him, he realised, but they'd only met six years ago. It didn't seem all that long...

"I must stay awake," he announced to the room but, without realising it, he had been slowly slipping down the pillows, into his normal sleeping position.

"I must stay a..."

He almost managed to repeat it.

It was one of the female BBC technicians who discovered the sleeping cat. It shouldn't be there. How did it get in?

Scuffo opened up one eye, saw the figure in front of him but couldn't be bothered.

Miaow... and went back to sleep.

"Get the janitor," she was told. "It mustn't be left loose to run around."

"It's a dozy looking cat," said the technician. "Doesn't

look as if it's all that eager to run anywhere. Looks sorry for itself."

"Some animals are to be used for tomorrow's programme, but they shouldn't be here yet." The telephone beside the assistant producer rang. "Blue Peter Studio. Liz speaking. How can I help you?"

Scuffo had opened one eye again – the other felt sort of sticky, and viewed the bustling activity going on around him. *Where had he landed this time, and when?* Somehow, Harold cared even less than normal for this chance to visit the future, the effect of him being seriously ill. He was in a large room, a very large room, occupied by several people. On the floor were, what looked to him like large projectors, or cameras, and hanging from the roof, a multitude of all sorts of lights. Bunches of coloured balloons floated everywhere. Must be a theatre, he concluded.

I like the shape of that, though, a sailing ship logo, repeated about the room. Ah, yes! He remembered now. The name! 'Blue Peter', a television programme for children. It was in last week's Guardian. He'd never actually seen the programme. Is this a TV studio?

On the floor, in front of the large ship logo, an interview was being set up for future use. It was an informal setting, with the interviewer and interviewee to sit on brightly coloured cushions. Lighting was finalised and camera positions set.

"Tell them we're ready for them now. We haven't got

much time to get it recorded, so no fooling around, please."

Scuffo successfully opened his other eye and became interested. He'd moved position. He could view all around, without being seen.

In came the two participants, the young professional interviewer, and the other, a boy, or is it a girl? Must still be at Primary School. Both looked fresh and alert and ready to go. They took up their respective positions on the cushions and practised a few smiles.

"Are you ready?" asked the floor manager. Two heads nodded confidently. "Blue Peter Interview, 18 August 2017, take 1. Three, two, one," he signalled, and they were off.

Scuffo's eyes opened wide. Had he heard right? 2017! Wow! It started back in... It's lasted a long, long time...

"So, Conrad, welcome, and as everyone already knows you so well, we'll go straight on with a few personal questions. You have been playing tennis since you were very young? Yes?"

"I was five when I first hit a ball, Andrew, and I have to admit, with all modesty that, from that very first shot, I was good. Everyone, who was there that day who saw me, remembers that as a very special moment in their life."

The floor manager looked away. The two on the cushion wouldn't see the odd expression on his face. *What an over-confident, cocky, young blighter this is!*

"Your dad is a multi-millionaire and a major manufacturer of high-quality tennis racquets. He also sponsors international tennis competitions. That must have helped a lot."

"Yes, I have to admit, Andrew, it is nice. It gives me total privacy. I don't have to mix with ordinary people. I heard that you play, Andrew. I'd be been happy to ask Dad to let you come along and have a game with me, if you wish – you seem a nice chap. As long as you don't bring any rough friends."

"That is very kind of you, Conrad."

POP!

"You don't think having a father who is a multi-millionaire is the only reason for your success, do you?"

POP!

"Of course not, but it does mean that I deal with only the best people. My personal fitness experts are world class, the PR team has been carefully selected, Security around me is the best, and my tennis shoes are perfection... Yes, all of that has helped me become the young idol that everybody loves."

POP!

"Cut!" yelled the producer from upstairs. "What is going on down there? The balloons! Why are they bursting?"

There was silence as everyone on the floor looked around, but could see nothing untoward, because Scuffo had wisely slipped behind a large loudspeaker.

The janitor hadn't appeared and Harold had forgotten about his cold. He realised that he wasn't in a theatre. It was definitely a television studio, and he was hearing what was being said, but not liking it. What an obnoxious little upstart? Disrupting that conversation seemed essential! Anyway, why have balloons if you can't burst them?

"We can't use all of that," came over the loudspeaker. "Start again, please, and try some more, Andrew. We'll edit it all later."

The floor manager was annoyed. Bad enough having to listen to this snotty little brat. Was the heat affecting the balloons today? "Ready? Once more. Blue Peter Interview, 18 August 2017, take 2." He signalled to proceed again. "Three, two, one..."

"Conrad, as we were saying, you found fame early, but for a tennis player, isn't having your hair in ringlets unusual? Difficult to maintain?"

"Well, Andrew, as you know, not only am I a brilliant tennis player, I am also a fashion icon. You have looked at my Facebook page, haven't you?"

"So, is this a new head fashion that you are starting for eleven-year-olds?"

"It is indeed. Dad's hairdresser visits daily so he can keep my head in tip-top condition."

"He visits every day?"

"Of course. Don't you have a daily hairdressing appointment, Andrew? No... Of course you don't. I can see that."

The floor manager had to stifle a giggle. He knew that Andrew was a little vain himself. He did have a daily hairdressing appointment. This was one-upmanship at a professional level, and the young upstart was winning.

"Err... Conrad. I... Uhmm... I..."

POP!

"Cut!"

Andrew wasn't complaining. He'd been made to look foolish, but he wouldn't let that happen on the next take.

But Scuffo had been spotted. The technician had seen the last balloon being burst and was on her way over. It seemed wise to move, but he stopped for a moment. The television cameras had swung around, and there he was, displayed on the overhead screens, so he made sure they were catching him at a good angle. But the female was close!

Miaow...

"Come to me, my little friend," the technician begged, knowing that she would be getting the blame for this. "Let me help you. We don't want you getting hurt." She seemed nice and Scuffo was tempted, but he leapt away just as she reached out.

Miaow!

"Don't be so bloody awkward," she said angrily, swinging her hand at him but missing.

Oh, oh! True colours coming out now, Harold thought, and Scuffo leapt onto the scenery at a higher level.

The electrician came over, with a long pole. Scuffo changed position again, but that person was going to be able to hit him. In all the excitement he'd forgotten about feeling unwell. Suddenly, it came back. *Oh dear... Might as well give up,* he decided, but that pole was on its way to hit him and a natural reaction took over. He had to spring sideways, as the pole passed – and got too close to an overhead lamp. It was hot!

MIAOW!!!

Instinctively as he started to fall, he knew that it was all over. He was going home...

But, that's not what happened. He was about to hit the floor and...

Whoosh...!

Good grief. It had never been like this before! He'd become Harold! But he was still in the TV studio, and it was still 2017!

Wonderful, he suddenly thought. *I am human, the same as everyone else. I can tell them that I am from the past – just visiting, and I can learn things by talking to them all. They'll be pleased to meet me. This could make me famous!* But they were all standing, frozen, looking at him strangely.

"Where the bloody-hell did you come from, mate?" said the female. The language came as a bit of a shock to Harold's system. He was quite disappointed in her. He'd thought she was a nice young lady, but before he could tell her, there was a shout from the floor manager.

"Never mind him just now. Get that damn cat!"

Round the back of the scenery they went, leaving Harold standing, feeling both foolish, and very unwell once more.

"Can't find it!" was the yell.

"Oh, for goodness sake," and the floor manager, getting irate, joined the other two.

Harold could have told him that they couldn't possibly find the cat – because it no longer existed, but they didn't ask.

"You! How did you get in here? Have you a pass? Who let this yobbo in? How am I expected to do my work properly if the world's against me?" moaned the floor manager.

At last, the rant stopped. It was Harold's turn to speak... So he did.

He took a deep breath, and said...

Miaow...!

27 THE BLUES CAN'T LAST

Monica had a key, and let herself into Harold's domain, hoping no-one would see her. He needed to be cared for, and like a dedicated fiancé, she was the one to do it, but the engagement was not yet public knowledge and she didn't want the wrong type of rumours to be spreading. Harold would not like it.

He would still be upstairs in bed. She knew he'd be glad to see her and what she had for him. It was in her bag. Another dose of her special mixture concocted a few hours ago, and only requiring a quick reheat. It would have been a shame to disappoint him, she'd decided, because he'd liked it so much earlier.

Out came the pan. The magic mixture, reheated, was transferred to a mug, and upstairs she went with it. *Hmmmm... Smells good. Wouldn't mind some myself,* she thought.

When she opened the door, she wouldn't have been surprised to find him fully recovered, sitting up in bed and reading the Guardian, because deep down she thought he was play-acting, being a big softie. But...

No? He wasn't even in the bed. Instead, lying on the pillow was Scuffo, snoring happily away. At least, it looked like Scuffo. Although she couldn't see the tag to check, she let the cat sleep on.

Harold wasn't downstairs, that was certain, so he must be in the toilet, she decided but, when she checked, the toilet door was lying open, and so was the door to the spare bedroom. Where was he? She returned to the bedroom. The cat was still asleep, but had turned over and now she could see the nametag, and it was Scuffo – but why was he here?

"Oh dear!" She had a sudden thought. *If Scuffo's here – but Harold isn't, has he been away again? And could he have…? Wasn't there a time when he returned unintentionally as the cat? The time when I drank a little too much of the… and woke up, and…*

"What did he do when that happened? How did he change? Oh my, I can't remember." She was talking aloud, but it was a mumble that didn't appear to bother the cat.

Suddenly, it came to her! The possible trigger for *Cat* to *Harold*!

"Harold thought it was a shock to the system. So, that's what we need. A shock to the system!"

Prepared to jump away quickly if she was wrong, because she was about to disturb a cat that might react fiercely, she tiptoed over to the bed, and bent down towards Scuffo.

"BOO!" she shouted in his ear as loud as she could, startling herself with her own ferocity, and stepped back quickly – and it worked!

The cat twisted in mid-air, fighting an imaginary

attacker, then *Whoooooosh!*

Scuffo vanished and there was Harold, on top of the bedclothes, with a red, runny nose, and a painful expression on his face... holding his ears!

"Am I glad you had the presence of mind to take action," said Harold later. He was actually feeling better, but refusing to acknowledge that it could have been Monica's magic mix that worked wonders. "It would have been dreadful if you hadn't. For the rest of your life you might have been stuck with a cat rather than me! That would have been terrible for you."

"Oh. I don't know..." she replied. Disturbingly, Harold wasn't sure if she was joking.

He'd already explained about being in a television studio, the Blue Peter one, and how incredibly far forward in time that had been. Monica was impressed.

"But it was humiliating," he said. "Me... standing there and all I could say was 'Miaow...' The floor manager was going off his head."

"How did you manage to get passed our security?" he asked me, rather aggressively.

'*Miaow... Miaow...*' I replied.

"Would you stop fooling around and talk properly!" He wasn't a happy man. "Please, I am not in the mood for nonsense!"

"Can't see where that cat went to," called the female technician. "It's not round the back."

"You'd better find that creature – quickly, young lady, I warn you! You are going to have to work doubly hard tomorrow to make up for this fiasco!"

"Is that fellow always so bad tempered, Andrew?" asked Conrad, in a loud voice, lying back, relaxed on the large cushion. "Why not sack him? Have him replaced!"

Andrew didn't even acknowledge that the boy had spoken. He knew better, but the floor manager had heard him loud and clear.

"You!" said the floor manager, swinging round and pointing at the boy. "Conrad, or whatever your stupid name is!" and he mimicked the boy's whiny voice. "Daddy's little pet... You can just keep your egocentric little trap shut!"

Conrad's cheeks were burning! People didn't say these sort of things, not to him.

"When I tell my father that you..."

"Andrew, get this selfish little prat out of here! Get him off my floor, now! Before I..."

"Of course, Richard. With pleasure..." A smiling Andrew quickly ushered Conrad through the exit.

"Now," and the floor manager had turned back to me. "I'll ask you one more time. What are you doing here and how did you get in – and, did you bring in that ruddy cat? You are not from Channel 4 are you – trying a bit of sabotage? Well, are you going to answer me?"

'Miaow... miaow...'

"Keep the cameras on them – and keep recording,"

instructed the producer. "This could be useful."

That's when two burly blokes in security uniforms appeared, unhappy to have been called to eject a cat! But they brightened up when they saw that they had to deal with me. They grabbed me, one on each arm and hoisted me through the corridors to the main entrance. When they pushed me into the revolving doors, I banged my head, and next thing, I am back here – but I'd changed to Scuffo again!"

Harold had to stop talking and make a grab for his handkerchief. "If I was miaowing with his voice, I wonder... was he speaking with mine?" he said, and cleared his nose noisily.

Monica could have kicked herself. "I didn't talk to him..." That would have been a novelty, she thought, to hear a cat grumble in a pitiful way, about a man-cold!

"Don't know why it all went wrong," said Harold, "...but I do suspect your medicine!"

Aunt Mabel was not happy. Uncle Syd was spending more time at home these days, too much time in fact, and restricting her normal daytime activities. He was getting in the way of her visiting her two 'special' friends, and they were missing her affections. She was certainly missing theirs. She was aggrieved because she did not consider that she had reached an age where her love-life should be restricted like this, certainly not by her older husband hanging around at home.

No, life could be so unfair!

Having offices in two parts of the country normally meant Syd travelling back and forward regularly. He'd been doing it for years, spending one week each month to work at the distant office. That pattern had been perfect for Monica's 'playing away', but then there had been 'the crisis'. Syd had been apologetic, telling her that his routine would have to change, at least for a spell. He would be having to spend more time away. It would be alternate weeks at the other office.

Mabel had feigned disappointment, but inside was overjoyed. All the more time for her thing – having fun! But recently, in the last four weeks, her husband's attitude to life had taken a strange turn.

Syd was walking about with an unusual expression on his face. Annoyingly, it looked to her like a smile of satisfaction! Now, that was not like Syd, and he was rarely going to the distant office, where Mabel had understood his problems to be. Most of his time was being taken up at Codgestone, and that meant him living at home – all the time!

Then Muriel began to suspect that he had something going on with that blonde, Sylvia, in the Codgestone office, the one that was always flirting with someone, and often someone else's husband. The more she thought about it, the more likely it seemed, and though she considered it perfectly natural for her to be having it off with her two friends, it was not acceptable for her older husband to behave that way! *So,* she decided, *I'll catch him at it! I'll visit the office.*

"Morning Sylvia," she said, having walked straight in.

"Oh, good morning, Mrs Stepton," said Sylvia, with a surprised look on her face.

Sylvia had been typing away merrily, on her own, with a lot of paperwork ready for filing sitting on the desk. Syd's office was empty. Now, that was a disappointment for Mabel.

"It's nice to see you. You are not in here very often," said Sylvia. "Were you hoping to speak to Mr Stepton?"

"Yes, indeed," said Mabel, but really she'd been hoping to find her husband, and Sylvia, in a compromising position. "Where is he?"

"He was in earlier, but left a little while ago," said Sylvia. "He said he would be away for a while. Would you like a cup of coffee?"

Why is she being nice to me? This brazen hussy is canoodling with my husband!

"No!" was snapped out rather abruptly, then softened with, "...thank you."

"He didn't say where he was going. Sorry... Was he expecting you?" asked Sylvia. "I don't see anything in the diary."

"No. It was to be a surprise, so don't tell him I was here."

"Don't worry about that, Mrs Stepton. I can keep secrets..."

273

I'll bet you can, thought Mabel.

"But it really is nice to see you again. Your husband is a lovely man. You are a lucky woman."

Mabel left the office slightly deflated. It hadn't turned out as she'd hoped, but, then again, what had she expected? If they'd been up to any nonsense, surely the door would have been locked! *That Sylvia is a bit of a stunner though... I can see why he's having the affair.*

When her husband arrived home that evening, he was actually grinning. He even gave her a peck on the cheek when he came into the kitchen. That hadn't happened for a long time – a very long time! *Something's made him very happy. Mabel had one guess... Sylvia!*

"Had a good day then?" she asked.

"Absolutely brilliant!" he replied.

"At the office?" she asked.

"All day... Of course. Where else would I be?"

Now that was a lie. If he can lie about that he can lie about her! "How's Sylvia?"

"Very good. Very, very good at what she does..."

I'll catch you tomorrow, you rogue, Mabel decided.

Having her own car was useful, especially for following a recalcitrant husband. Next morning, when he left at eight, she was not far behind, but he didn't drive in the direction of Codgestone. She tailed him for over an hour and began to think that maybe he was going to the other office today. Just as she was about to give up and go back home, he swung into the racetrack car park. *I didn't know he liked horse racing again!*

She turned the car around and went back home. She thought afterwards, couldn't have been with that blonde anyway – he was well passed trying to cope with anything physical! Well... certainly with her. It had been a long time since... A long, long time...

Syd was happy because he was consistently using Monica's winners.

"I couldn't give a toss about the business!" he declared to Monica one day at one of their secret meetings. "This is the life for me. Never once have you been wrong. You will be getting your share, don't worry, because it's all due to you and your premonitions. We are going to make a fortune."

Monica blushed. To Syd this looked like modesty, but in truth, it was the embarrassment of her doing something that was totally wrong.

Using the Racing Almanacs that Scuffo brought back had worked beautifully. Syd was regularly betting on winners, increasing the stake each time as he gained more and more confidence in her selections.

The one thing that made Monica feel better about the whole thing was that she wasn't the only one on the fiddle. Admittedly God wasn't on her side, but it had to be the next best thing... The Reverend Harold Scuffington of Woldenham Parish Church. He was totally complicit, and giving her all the encouragement she needed.

28 IT'S ODDS ON...

Monica had never worked at a paid job. Looking after an ailing mother for many years had been her lot. Occasionally, she thought back to the opportunity she'd had when she left school to become a Tax Officer and has a little pang of regret. She could visualise taxpayers, queueing up to give their excuses for not paying their dues, and her sitting there in judgement, giving the thumbs-up sign for some, who'd leave smiling happily, and thumbs-down for the others, who would immediately be carted off to jail. It probably wasn't the way the tax system actually worked, but her way would have been anything but boring!

Her father had been a tax inspector, and came home every night from Codgestone, cursing the job. It eventually drove him to an early grave. A heart attack at fifty-two years old. Thankfully for Monica and her mum, Mr Winter had been a prudent man with his family finances and left them comfortably off.

Mrs Winter, Monica's ailing mother had outlasted her husband by two years, dying just as the new vicar, the Reverend Harold Scuffington arrived at Woldenham. Her funeral had been one of the first duties that the new preacher had to deal with, and, at the funeral, it was the first time that Monica had fancied someone, the Vicar, but she didn't say anything to him, and he appeared not to notice her in that way at all. It took some time to grab his attention. He was that kind of person... Dead slow. Things had changed, and as the years progressed she'd become more necessary as his support. To her regret, in those early years, it was only for church affairs. He'd failed so see any of the signals she sent out.

After losing her mum, she'd considered looking for a job, but not too seriously. Various office jobs had been applied for, but when she had the opportunity for the interview, she'd lost all enthusiasm. Looking after her mother at home, then being housekeeper for her father, had made her less enthusiastic for office jobs. She could manage, she told herself. She had enough money. Voluntary work would be her thing. Slowly she'd become a little closer to her vicar, and a little more essential to him.

The big breakthrough, she thought, had come just after the Christmas 'Do' in 1958, but that was now two years ago! Visiting the future, and being a cat, had been taking up a lot of his attention. He was different person when that happened!

Monica was living in her own house, coping with life, but with rarely any spare cash for luxuries, though she had been rash and bought the new radiogram. That was an exception. She would definitely never have dreamt of throwing her money away on betting, until today...

There would be no visit to see Harold today, and no rhubarb tarts either. She was going out. A day at the races was not something she'd ever craved, or even been interested in, but today, that was where she was destined, and it would be Uncle Syd's treat. He'd insisted that she was entitled to benefit from his good fortune.

It had been name after name she'd supplied to him, and all of them winners, so far. He couldn't understand why she had been so generous to him and been willing to supply him with names guaranteed to be first past the post for specific races, and yet to be unwilling to place a bet on a horse herself. He was convinced that she hadn't needed to involve him, but he wasn't complaining!

Today, he was determined to encourage her and demonstrate how easy the process was. That way they would both benefit.

What to wear was Monica's current problem. She'd tried on the blue, striped dress, but that had been too... blue – and striped! Then the red one, and that hadn't suited any shoes that she owned. So, it would have to be the navy one, the plain simple navy one. Anyway, who is going to be bothering about me?

A horn sounded. He'd arrived, so out she trotted. High heels were not her thing normally, so she had to be careful not to twist an ankle walking down the path, especially as she could see that nosey cow across the road peeping through the curtains. Another different fellow again, she'd be thinking, but, my goodness this one looks old! It was so obvious to Monica the way that woman's mind would work. Ah well, she sighed to herself, that's my reputation going farther downhill...

It is incredible that Monica was able to rise this morning and be ready on time. Uncle Syd had taken her by surprise when, yesterday, he'd offered to take her to see the horse racing. She spent most of the night trying to cram names of horses into her head, so that she would be able to respond correctly when they arrived there. It's only what he'd expect if she was a clairvoyant, to be able to conjure up a winner or two.

Uncle Syd stood with the door of his little sports car held open for her, and assisted her get in. How could he, at his age, manage to drop into the low bucket seats with such ease, while she had struggled in a most unladylike manner, especially knowing that nothing was being missed by the eyes across the road? One thing was certain in Monica's mind though – Harold would die to own a car like this!

Uncle Syd started the engine. It gave a satisfying growl, and they were off. Monica couldn't stop herself. She waved to her over-friendly neighbour, and saw the curtain give a surprised shake.

"My, you do look lovely this morning," said Uncle Syd. "Is that a new dress? It's just right for a day like this. And your hair... Been to the hairdresser?"

Oh, oh! Behave yourself, Uncle. She gave him a sideways glance and smiled. You sound as though you are flirting...

"Glad your Aunt Mabel doesn't know about us. Don't know what she'd think, but it's quite exciting doing something like this, isn't it."

Monica was sure of what Aunt Mabel would think!

"Harold would have loved to have come along," said Monica, "And he would love this car."

"Harold doesn't know about this, does he?" His head had swung round in surprise. The car had veered towards the centre of the road, but was immediately corrected as the horn from the car approaching blasted out. "...About our little liaison?"

"Oh no," she lied. "Of course not."

"Because if we are delayed, I thought we could always get a room at the hotel next to the racecourse."

The fact that she stared straight ahead at that comment, reminded him that he was her uncle, even though not a blood relation, and he shouldn't be making these sorts of suggestive comments. Anyway, she was even younger than Mabel. Today was to say thank you and help her.

But, Monica hadn't heard what he'd said! What with the noise of being in an open-topped car travelling at speed with the wind blowing her hair everywhere, and the panic that she was beginning to feel at getting confused by the similarities of horse names, and which races were which, she had more than enough to distract her!

They'd arrived, safely, and Monica was relieved to find her uncle was now behaving like a real gentleman, because getting out of the car by her own efforts would have been almost impossible...

It was an unusual experience for her to be part of this sort of jostling crowd, with the noise of laughter and the shouting of spectators and bookmakers, and people jostling in all directions, many that she suspected had already had a few drinks. Over the heads, sometimes, she could just about glimpse horses.

Why is everyone taller than me?

Uncle Syd guided her to the bar. It was slightly less frenetic in there.

"What'll you have, Monica dear?" he asked.

"Hmm..." she hesitated. "Oh, what the heck," she said, "I'll have a sherry." She wasn't likely to meet anyone from Woldenham here, so no-one could carry stories back to the village. Anyway, what's a sherry these days? Harold approves and Uncle Syd won't mention it to anyone. Relax...

Drinks in hand, over to a table at the window they went and Monica was able to view the activity without being part of it. She found that easier, and Uncle Syd began to explain all about betting.

"Don't worry about doing it yourself," he said, part way through the technicalities, "Because I'll show you the ropes down there. How'd you like another?"

It was obvious to him that she was struggling to understand what he'd been saying, but there was no rush. There would be plenty chances to earn a bob or two as the day progressed.

Monica had been desperately trying to follow the detail, but lack of sleep and the worry about remembering names, was hampering her little brain.

"I shouldn't," she said, "but alright then."

Uncle Syd had only left a moment, when the voice behind her said, "Well, fancy meeting you here!"

Oh, no! Elsa Middleton, the church organist. Quick, ground... Swallow me!

"Well, well, well... You are the last one I'd expect to have seen here. This is someone from the village, Charles. Charles is my very, very special friend," said Elsa, by way of introduction. The tall good looking chap beside her smiled a greeting.

"All on your own then?" Elsa asked, just as Uncle Syd returned from the bar. "Oh," she continued without taking a breath, "And this will be your boyfriend then. Hello, I am Elsa," and she held out her hand.

This could ruin the day, thought Monica.

"Hmm... I like you," said Elsa, as Syd put the drinks on the table, and shook her hand. "I like mature men," she added.

Charles, her special friend and younger than Elsa, shared a strange look with Monica.

"No, I am Monica's uncle," said Syd.

"Hmm…" said Elsa, slyly. "Yes… If you say so…"

A little of the drink that Elsa was holding spilled, as Charles grabbed her arm and led her away. "Nice meeting you," he said, as they departed.

Monica was grateful to have that second sherry.

"The church organist," Monica whispered to her uncle, and took a large mouthful of her drink.

"She's had a few," was all he said about Elsa. "Now to more important matters. What do you foresee for the one-thirty?"

Monica's head was beginning to feel hazy. Two glasses of sherry, lack of sleep, struggling to remember the names of stupid horses, the surprise presence of Elsa…

She closed her eyes, tightly.

"Are you all right? Oh sorry. Didn't think. You are in a trance. I'll be quiet," said Uncle Syd.

The one-thirty… What was it again? Pink something? Pink Prancer? Or was it Dancer? Yes, it was Pink Dancer!

"I've got it!" She opened her eyes and Uncle Syd had pencil and notebook at the ready. "Pink Dancer."

"Odds for that are 5/l. Right, there's a tenner. Put that on. I'll go with you."

"A tenner," she exclaimed. "That's an awful lot of money, Uncle Syd. What if it loses?"

"You've never been wrong up to now."

She wasn't. The ten pound note she'd held in her

hand such a short time ago, and that she'd reluctantly handed over to the bookie, had now turned into a massive fortune to her mind, and she saw it being used for a very good cause. Another couple of wins like that and they could afford to get married – and have a honeymoon in Scarborough! Harold would be over the moon!

"That was so easy," she said excitedly. "I thought that it would have been more complicated to place a bet. Look at all this money!"

"Let's go back upstairs," said Uncle Syd, feeling good himself. She was getting some compensation for this magical power she possessed. "Another sherry?"

"And why not? I'll pay," she said, and with a flourish she handed him a ten-pound note.

The euphoria could not last forever, and in Monica's case, it was until her glass had been drained, and Uncle Syd said, "But we haven't finished yet..."

He proceeded to tell her that he was becoming ridiculously rich, due to her great advice, and that he'd made it work, each time, by re-using the money he'd won. He had lost not a penny, and it was now her turn to go through the same procedure, but on her own. He would stand and watch, and all the money would be hers, but first – the winner of the one-thirty!

Oh dear... thought Monica, hazily.

She closed her eyes. Her world was spinning... Grand Duchess? Peer Pressure? Corn Plaster? Wonky Donkey?

Sampan? What was the blooming name? Which page was it on last night? Was she at the same racetrack? Harold, help me...!

"Ping Pong!" she said suddenly. "That's it. Ping Pong!" She gave a silly little giggle. She'd done it. She'd remembered the winner of the one-thirty!

Uncle Syd had gone quite pale. It wasn't illness – it was shock. That horse was running at 100/1! A guaranteed loser, or else a fantastic win.

"Are you... sure, Monica?" He'd asked that tentatively, because he'd expected her to feel very sensitive about her premonitions.

"Oh yes," she said. "But I am putting a fiver back in my purse – for the celebrations afterwards!"

29 NOBODY'S PERFECT.

"Oh Harold, I had such big ideas about what I was going to do with the money. We could have been married right away, if it had been the correct horse."

Harold's eyebrows shot up at that comment. No, no... That's maybe not a good idea. Mustn't rush things!

"I was useless," she said mournfully. "I should never have gone. How could I possibly have remembered their names, and all the other details? Especially after drinking a sherry... or two! In future it will be by phone or letter only. That is if Uncle Syd still wants to take a chance with our information. I'd hate him to start losing money. I don't want to ever visit a racecourse again. Do you know I never once was close to a horse! And I closed my eyes during the races."

Of course, Monica's chosen horse, the one that Uncle Syd thought could be a likely loser the moment she'd said it, had done as expected – lost, as did her following two attempts. So, it was lucky that Monica had retained a fiver for later, because that is all she went home with.

"Never mind," Uncle Syd had said kindly, and patted her hand. "The day is not over yet. We'll see if I can do any better. Another sherry?"

Afterwards, he had been philosophical, and had tried to cheer her up, by saying, "I didn't think you could possibly be right every time..." but that didn't make her feel the slightest bit better.

"...And meeting Elsa Middleton too!" added Monica. However, on her way round to visit Harold this morning, she'd bumped into that very same female.

Monica couldn't have been more delighted to realise that the obnoxious organist remembered nothing about their meeting. All she went on about, was how she had met the most wonderful young man at the races yesterday, and that it was love! "You ought to go there some time. It can be fun," Monica was informed. "You never know what you'll pick up," she added. "Oh... and that stupid Collie dog of mine! She wee'd on my good carpet, this morning."

At home, Syd was being given a severe grilling by his inquisitive wife.

Mabel had 'just popped in' to the Codgestone office, early on the previous day, to find her husband missing again, and Sylvia sitting knitting and reading a detective novel at the same time, with a hot cup of coffee within easy reach. Very obviously enjoying her own company.

"You on holiday again?" Mabel had said sarcastically, although she was someone who had to push herself to do something truly productive and would never in her life have dreamt of doing anything as complicated as multi-tasking. "He's out?"

Sylvia didn't have the chance to respond, as Mabel

slammed the door on her way out.

"You weren't in the office today, Syd. So, where were you?" she demanded.

Mabel checking his whereabouts was not something he was pleased about, and it was becoming an obsession for her. If he'd been checking up on her activities, she would have objected strongly, because he reckoned that she'd a lot more to hide. She wanted her freedom to get up to her kind of mischief and he didn't want to know. Unfortunately, she wasn't giving up on him.

"Where?" she demanded.

He decided to come clean. Somehow, she'd get to know anyway.

"I was at the races."

"Oh no!" she said. "Not the horses again. You know what happened the last time. How much did you lose?"

"The good news is – I didn't lose. Thanks to Monica."

"What has Monica got to do with it?" she asked suspiciously.

She'd been correct. Involved with another woman! Worse still, it was her very attractive niece!

"What were you up to with her?" she demanded, but she didn't expect him to answer. If he did, she was sure that it would certainly not be the truth.

"She was just being very nice to me."

"What? She's half your age, you dirty devil!"

"Not much younger than you... Anyway, what makes you think...?"

And so it went on... but she didn't break him. He kept the 'special arrangement' secret.

Mabel didn't need to know everything. Maybe he should start tantalising her, feed her a little tit-bit more, but then decided he couldn't be bothered. It would be simpler going off to work, so he left Mabel standing fuming.

Uncle Syd had truly not been surprised at the racetrack by Monica's failure to get every winner. He was simply amazed at her getting so many correct almost all the time, so he was certainly not giving up on his niece.

That she was clairvoyant had not been communicated to anyone else, as far as he knew, and that is the way he would prefer it to stay, for she was helping him build up a tidy little fortune, a fortune that he intended to use in the future in a very profitable manner. He would make it up to her, sometime... That's what a Will is for, isn't it? I must change a few things soon, be a generous uncle.

It was unlikely that Monica would continue helping him like this forever, so he'd been practising choosing the winners himself, before they were passed on to him by his niece. Not perfect by any means but he was getting very good at it, even though he said so himself. If he was going to join the betting world, he would have to stand on his own feet at some point, and that would mean being able to continue selecting the best results, but on his own. His achievements after Monica's failure, that day when he'd taken her to the track, had resulted in one winner, and one loser. He'd pointed that out to her at the time and got a glimmer of a smile.

Uncle Syd had big ideas. Initially his target was to open his own betting shop. He couldn't do that yet, but it would be possible very soon. The change in the law would have a dramatic effect shortly. He was certain of that and wanted to be in at the ground floor and make his mark.

He had always worked within the framework of the law, with occasional fudging regarding business tax, of course, but nothing that others weren't doing, therefore, there shouldn't be any question about a licence, but he had ambition that went well beyond being a simple bookmaker.

He wanted a share in a casino. It was highly unlikely to be in the UK though. Las Vegas was the place for that. If I can keep stacking up the dosh with guaranteed winners, my chance will come, he told himself, but that will need real money!

He'd come in to the office today. Had to show face now and again, and it was good to see Sylvia. Nice girl Sylvia... Maybe one day...

"Got a date tonight, Sylvia?"

Sylvia smiled and nodded. Lucky guy, he thought. Nice legs...

The phone rang. It was Monica.

"Do you still want me to try to guess some winners?" she asked, with the Horse Racing Almanac for 1960 open in front of her.

"Oh, yes please. I was hoping you'd phone," said Uncle Syd with a smile, taking his pen from his pocket. "I'm ready!"

Harold was jittery. His tummy felt a bit odd. Was something about to happen?

"Buuurrrp...! Oh, pardon me," he said, hoping that the person at the other end of the phone hadn't heard his rude noise. Uncle Syd probably hadn't because Monica was actually talking at that moment.

When would Uncle Syd twig that Monica was not clairvoyant? It was the question they'd been asking themselves. It was bound to happen at some point. He was a smart chap even though he was getting on a bit, and what would be his reaction if he does?

"Relax," Monica said, as she replaced the phone. "He is eager to continue and he doesn't seem bothered about the other day. Said, he has plans... and that he'll look after me."

"Buuurrrp...! Oh, I do beg your pardon, again," he said. "I don't know what's wrong with me today. It almost as if..."

And his tummy gave a rumble, and...

Miaow...

"What did you say, Harold? For a moment I thought it was..."

Miaow... came out again.

"Harold! Are you all right?" Monica was beginning to panic. "Oh dear! Harold! You've got whiskers!"

Miaoooow...!

Now, the bottom half of his body was fading away.

"Harold! What's happening to you?!" But, Monica was now talking to herself...

27 TIME TO GO?

Outside, Times Square was crowded. Inside, the bar was too.

It was five minutes to midnight, almost the start of the new millennium, when predictions had it that computers were about to reach the limit of their programmes and fail, and that airplanes would fall from the sky because of that, and that time would either stand still or go backwards, no-one could say anything for certain. In other words, when it happened, the world was destined to go pear-shaped!

Scuffo was sitting on the sill of a high window of the bar, looking out at the heaving mass of bodies outside. Harold was simply thankful that all bits of his and Scuffo's bodies had eventually transferred properly! Though, why he'd arrived here, in the middle of New York, was a mystery. As someone who'd never thought of going abroad, even on holiday, this was an enormous leap, but he was not going to let it overawe him. He was quite content to sit, recover and let everyone else get excited about the once-in-a-lifetime event that was about to happen.

He'd reached the year 2000. Harold found it hard to contemplate that he could possibly survive till this date. If he did, he would have exceeded the promised three score years and ten. Leaping forward forty years should have given him a thrill, but it didn't. Now, if Monica had been with him...

The rear wall of the bar was dominated by a large TV, with sound unheard, and sub-titles that no-one in the bar was looking at. It was a laughing, drinking, happy mob that tonight made up this congregation, and one that didn't care a fig about a cat who'd been a minister only moments ago, looking out of a window.

Harold was exhausted and would have appreciated a snooze, but Scuffo was in control. He was happily soaking up the atmosphere as the traditional countdown began. Thousands of voices synchronised, and all eyes concentrated on the gigantic colour-changing ball, high in the sky, as it began its descent...

... Seven... six... five... four...three... two...

Then WOW...!!! The world erupted into a mass of tickertape descending, lights flashing, fireworks shooting into the night sky and exploding, and everyone hugging and kissing and dancing, and cheering even louder than before! It went on and on...

For a minister of the church, who liked to know the entry of any New Year, every year, from the comfort of his own bed, this was too much. The noise inside the bar was painfully loud. How he'd loved to have owned one of these magical remote-control things, and perhaps he could have made the world a quieter place – especially now. Harold was appreciative when Scuffo curled up where he was on the windowsill, and went to sleep. That made the noise go away.

When he awoke, the bar was a lot quieter. It was still noisy and still full of merry makers, but with the euphoria greatly reduced. The crowds were still milling about in the street outside and it looked as if there would be partying going on for a long time yet. The world had not spun off its axis after all. The TV at the bar was regurgitating events from around the globe, and it looked as if everyone, everywhere in the world had gone just as crazy as the crowds outside in Times Square.

Every so often, there was a break in the pictures of fireworks and cheering crowds. Adverts, and other news events had their turn, but no-one in the bar was interested in the TV, and that included Harold, until something caught his eye.

Breaking news! Shooting of prime suspect in Casino Trial!

Guns! Typical of America, thought Harold, *only happy when they are shooting each other. Thank goodness we don't have that sort of behaviour in Woldenham!* But it had grabbed his attention.

Footage has been obtained by CNN, of the shooting that occurred, two days ago, outside Las Vegas County Court where the prime suspect in the highly-publicised Vegas Casino Fraud case was shot as he descended the courthouse stairs. He had just been released, and it is thought that the perpetrator was a hired assassin, who escaped in the crowd. The victim has since died in hospital. His bodyguard was seriously wounded.

The report went on to give details of the case and showed photos of the various people involved. *They looked a right bunch of rogues! Good riddance if one of them has been bumped off,* thought Harold. Who'd miss any of them? Then suddenly, there appeared a large photo of the victim's face, and the name – and it became personal!

WHAT! Oh No, it's...

Whoooosh!

In a noisy, happy bar, off Times Square, the beers continued to be poured, and nobody noticed that a cat had vanished...

What a dilemma! How should he break the news to her? It's a long way into the future, does she even need to know? But it's an awfully long time to keep a secret!

"Monica, did your Uncle Syd ever say he might go to America?"

"He did, once, in your house. Don't you remember? Why do you ask?"

"Do you think he is making a lot of money with his betting?"

"Yes, I think so. Why?"

"And, that when he makes enough, he'll emigrate?"

"What? Harold what are you rambling on about this

time?"

"To the United States?"

"I suppose that could be a possibility..."

"And leave Aunt Mabel behind?"

Hmmm... Monica mused, *and maybe it would serve Aunt Mabel right, after all her nonsense, carrying on with other men...* thoughts that Monica knew herself to be most uncharitable, especially now that she was Aunt Mabel's favourite niece!

"And would he make a lot of money if he went to the States, do you think?"

"How the heck would I know? I am not a real clairvoyant, remember? Ok... What haven't you told me?"

Obviously, what had been broadcast about the Casino Fraud was tiny by comparison with the Millennium Celebrations, but it had been enough to inform Harold of the fate of Monica's Uncle Syd.

Mr Syd Stepton, an ex UK citizen, who had been a surprisingly fit and active eighty-five year old, until he was shot, had become the head of the syndicate that operated one of the larger Casinos on the Las Vegas Strip.

He'd been accused by other members of the syndicate of fraud, and was accordingly charged, but being found innocent at his trial was probably not supposed to be the outcome. The enemies he'd made over the years had taken action, and killed him, but it appeared that he was truly innocent and had been made a scapegoat.

"Oh dear. Not a nice way to go." Monica took it remarkably calmly, thought Harold and, thankfully, she didn't ask about her aunt.

"He will have been well insured," Harold said by way of consolation, hoping that Monica would still figure in the will. It wouldn't happen for forty years, but in Harold's head, it was as if Uncle Syd was already dead.

"I wish you hadn't told me this, Harold. How can I speak to him and keep passing winners to him, without letting it slip that I know that one day he'll be shot?" said Monica.

"Try to forget it," Harold suggested. "Anyway, I think he'd dismiss it. He knows you don't get it right every time..."

Monica frowned.

After his visit to New York, Harold decided he'd had enough. There were some things that he didn't want to know about the future, and many he could certainly do without, but also, if the visits stopped, he should experience less pain. Each time he transferred, he was suffering more and more. Time seemed to be going too quickly too. He'd love it to stop.

Harold had often asked himself if there could be a limit to the numbers of times a cat could recover from a death sentence and he was convinced it should be no more than nine. By his reckoning, Scuffo had died many more times than that! Is that why he was feeling the strain? His body ached more with each return, and, recently, his brain had become fuzzier. Could Scuffo's excessive deaths be the cause?

What he would settle for, he decided, was a simple humdrum normal life, maybe even to possess a nice friendly cat, rather than being one. A nice pet, like Scuffo, would be perfect, provided he didn't have to share a life with him any longer.

Yes... if only!

It was obvious that Scuffo didn't care a jot. He was still as lively as a kitten!

But it was all about to end.

Harold was not aware of that, nor how it would happen, and he would not be made aware of the summons either. He would never know, because it wasn't for him. Some things are not meant for humans to know, but Scuffo's outrageous behaviour had not passed unobserved by the world's highest feline authority. That's why the stripy ginger cat had been summoned. Scuffo was about to face the music!

HIS WORSHIPFUL CATSNIPPER – The Supreme Cat, would be seeing him shortly...

28 WAS IT REALLY A CATASTROPHE?

Dear Reader, we are nearing the end of our story. The dénouement – to use a flowery term!

For Harold's life, we have jumped forward fifty-eight years.

For us it is NOW, and time to look back over the intervening period.

Some people are unwise to the fact that their lives are totally controlled by a cat, and very few, who are appreciative of that, are willing to admit it.

Many unenlightened individuals see that little furry shape as a pet, a pet that demands no more than their constant attention. These persons continually pander to the antics of a sweet little ball of fluff, often creating images put on show for 'likes' on Facebook, on Instagram, and You Tube, images to reach the eyes of the world through multi-million viewings, which inevitably generate a vast collective, "*Aaaaahhh....*"

For these weak-willed persons, a cat can supply the ultimate in satisfaction!

Whereas, we, the enlightened ones, see that as a problem.

Scuffo can be held up as an example of that excessive cat power. We are aware of the advantage he took of an, obviously, easily malleable human being, The Reverend Harold Scuffington, a minister of the church and a man for whom a little excitement was always more than enough.

Fortunately for the world, when a problem like this is recognised, there is a powerful authority springs into action, and back in 1961 controls were invoked, and the troublesome cat, Scuffo, received THE SUMMONS.

Thanks to the Freedom of Information Act, we have obtained an Extract from the Catastrophe Record for that year which describes what took place in the Grand Hall when he appeared...

"Call, Cat No. 469gg532lkv333lmyx!" was the instruction. That identification call was repeated and echoed around the enormous hall, until a small ginger cat with a rather short tail appeared in front of the official's desk.

"Are you Cat No. 469gg532lkv333lmyx, commonly known as Scuffo?" asked the official.

"Yes," answered Scuffo meekly.

"Escort him to His Catsnipper," was the instruction passed to the assistant official.

The large doors were opened wide, and, with the assistant official leading, Scuffo, carefully keeping in step, followed on the long walk towards the far end of the chamber. The Judge, The Right Honourable

Worshipful Catsnipper sat, high above, in the judgement seat.

Scuffo had never been here before. He'd heard about it, but never thought that he'd ever be summoned to attend, because he knew that only rogue cats were brought here!

"This is case number three for today, Your Catsnipper," said the assistant official deferentially. "Cat No. 469gg532lkv333lmyx, commonly known as Scuffo."

As the assistant official stepped back, Scuffo sat down on his hunkers and looked up at the high figure.

"Stand up straight!" the assistant official immediately hissed at him, and he was on his paws again like a shot.

It was painful on his neck, having to stand like this looking so far upwards, but he did as instructed. He'd heard tales of those who disobeyed in here...

There was a long silence, with the only interruption being the rustle of the pages of the Cat Report as they were turned over by the Supreme Cat.

"Hmmmm..." came from up on high, a threatening sound!

Oh... thought Scuffo.

"So many occasions... Good gracious!" the voice continued. "This is serious. Very serious..."

Scuffo glanced around. *Should he try and make a run for it?* The fierce look from the assistant official behind him, and the size of him was sufficient deterrent.

"Now look here," boomed out from on high. "You

have been having a really good time, young man, and, you should know, that that is not satisfactory behaviour. How many lives is a cat supposed to have?"

The face of the Supreme Cat peered over the edge and stared down at Scuffo.

"Nine, I think, sir," mumbled Scuffo, fearfully, feeling the pain in his neck getting worse.

"What? What did you say? Speak up Cat No. 469gg532lkv333lmyx, or you'll just make matters worse!"

"Nine, your Worshipful Catsnipper!" shouted out Scuffo.

"And how many have you used?"

"Don't know, Your Catsnipper. I forgot to count..."

"You forgot to...!"

It sounded as if the Supreme Cat was about to suffer apoplexy!

"And there is the little matter of the gent you paired with! The Reverend Harold Scuffington. Every transformation done with him – the same person! It is totally forbidden to stay and transfer more than once with the same human! It says on your record sheet that you are an intelligent cat. I am not so sure... You must know that it has to be with a different person every time."

A lot of harrumphing noise of displeasure came from way on high.

"Now tell me – **why?**"

That question was thrown at him in a most ferocious

manner. Scuffo stood trembling!

"Because..." He took a deep breath and tried to remember the rule book, "If the person remembers it happening, they should think it to be only a dream. If they don't and tell someone as if it was real, being laughed at will make them feel foolish, and afterwards, they will pretend to themselves that it didn't happen. We can then carry on as normal with someone different."

"Exactly... And what do we have in your case?"

"The human believes passionately that everything that happened was true – and so does his lady friend, and they both know that I am in control."

"And if they tell others this could lead to ruination. How can anyone trust us, and give us total freedom, if they find out that we are controlling them? There could be human rebellion. We could all finish up in the soup, or curry! Be dismissed as no longer essential pets!"

"I am truly sorry, Worshipful Catsnipper," grovelled Scuffo.

"And so you should be. As for your sentence, your power of transformation is being removed from you forthwith."

A gasp of dismay came from Scuffo.

"On top of that, I sentence you to become an ordinary house cat, and to live with the Reverend Harold Scuffington, and any other person who may reside with him, and, you must suffer them, until they both shall die."

"But I could be ancient by then, Your Worshipful

Catsnipper..."

"Tough!" was the unsympathetic response from high.

All of the foregoing happened fifty-seven years ago, and, at the time, it was a harsh sentence for Scuffo, but he took it on the chin. He has now reached the fine old age of sixty years.

Annually, The Guinness Book of Records calls with a question for Harold, "Your cat, Scuffo? Is it still alive?" The call is taken by him on his smartphone – provided he has not dozed off again and the battery is not flat, and "Yes..." is the always the answer.

So, Scuffo survives. What about Harold and Monica?

Eventually it had to happen – Harold proposed properly, and Monica accepted graciously, and they have been happily married for fifty-five years, but now, at the grand old age of ninety, Harold doesn't do a lot. Sitting on his favourite chair is where he can be found most of the time. He still buys The Guardian, but then uses his little smartphone to check their facts with all the different websites on the internet. The smartphone rarely leaves his hands, except to be charged for him.

He isn't nearly as plump as he was. When he realised his size, he joined the gym in Codgestone and followed a controlled programme of exercise for the older person, and that was beneficial. Of course, ending the habit of the daily treat of a rhubarb tart, probably contributed more.

Monica, being a few years younger, has been keeping her shape thanks to the home exercise bike. The Smart TV, that helps her pass time when she is cycling nowhere, assists in making her non-journeys feel shorter, and she likes being able to change channels whenever she shouts at it.

She also has a little unit that gives her voice control of other electronics. They supply her with endless amusement, but Harold gets a little irritated, when he is trying to read his Guardian at night, to hear, "Siri! Lights on! Siri! Lights off! Siri! Lights on... Siri!"

Their finances? When Uncle Syd's life ended, not only had he been well insured, very well indeed, he had amassed a tidy little fortune! He'd appreciated the help he received from Monica, the clairvoyant who was rarely wrong, but his own sixth sense and cunning had progressively ensured that he could manage very well without the jiggery-pokery!

He remained eternally grateful to his niece. However, after he died there was a bit of an argument about his will. He'd previously told his lawyer that he had changed it, Monica, was to be a major beneficiary. Unfortunately for her, after he was shot, it looked like he hadn't tied up the details properly because the only legitimate will that could be traced, was the original.

All his fortune went to Mabel!

A bit disappointing for Monica and Harold to receive nothing, especially after Uncle Syd's promise, "...To see

Monica all right". But life wasn't so bad though.

Belle, as they now were instructed to call Aunt Mabel, was very kind to them for the rest of her life, and she loved visiting the vicarage. It gave her the chance to see her favourite cat, and, if Monica and Harold went on holiday, she took pleasure in caring for Scuffo at the manor.

Belle passed away in 2002 while visiting her friends Charlie and Jo. Running a half-marathon to support a Gay Charity event, aged 78, had been pushing it a bit. Being a few years younger, her special friends, Charlie and Jo, survived but only for a few more years, because they then shortened their own lives by regularly having wild parties, splashing out the money that Belle left for them in her will.

After Belle's death, the panic about another will, with Harold and Monica already having spent a fortune in anticipation, was short lived. Monica was still the main beneficiary when it was all sorted between the solicitors in London and New York. Belle had added her two pals, and Scuffo, to the newer one. Her pals received ten thousand pounds each, and the promise, made many years before to Scuffo, was fulfilled, so Harold and Monica, as his carers, received another ten thousand for cat food.

In short, Harold and Monica have been enjoying an extremely comfortable retirement.

Along the way, Harold swithered on writing his

memoirs. Scuffo panicked and immediately became an extremely annoying pet. Every time the pen was lifted, Scuffo appeared and created a distraction, and if anything of Harold's scribblings reached the stage of being on paper, mysteriously the pieces of paper were later found shredded, or had vanished altogether. Eventually Harold gave up, and Scuffo heaved a sigh of relief. Exposure to the world could have led to another Cat Court visit, and an even worse sentence!

Scuffo often longs for the old days, and being still fit and well, he would like to have some more fun and adventure using Harold again but, by losing his power of transfer in '61, he can't. Anyway, it wouldn't work – because Harold's lost his get-up-and-go.

His punishment could have been much worse and he knows it. It was an odd sentence. Unusually, it was decreed by the Cat Court that he remain in a fit condition and become a beloved member of Harold and Monica's family for the rest of a greatly extended life. A life, incidentally, which intrigued many a university professor. Scuffo knew that one day when he went to Cat Heaven, his furry frame would be in great demand for research. "How did he do it?" they will be asking... but he knows that they will never find out.

If only he and Harold could have talked again, cat-to-man, they could have reminisced and he could have taken the uncertainty away for the poor fellow. It would also have eased his cat conscience to explain to Harold that it was all over, but he can't, and sometimes – but only sometimes, Scuffo regrets using Harold as he did.

He may have lost the power of transfer, but he still has the instinct to read the mind of the Reverend Harold. Oh yes... Scuffo sits there, curled up, trying to look wise – if he's not snoozing, watching his master growing older while he stays young, and every single day he feels guiltier, and sorrier for the old fellow – Harold's thoughts are so obvious!

When will it happen again?
  When...?
    Oh when...?

mac black

and for the kids...